"You were the only reason I was able to keep going,"

Ryan said.

Lacey's breath caught. He'd never said anything like that before. "Me?"

"You helped me remember…why it was worth it. I was sure it was the right thing. I knew it every time I came home to you. But now…"

"But now?" she prompted gently.

He looked at her. She'd never seen this Ryan before, never seen his dark eyes look so uncertain. "Now I…I'm afraid I'm going to lose myself." He rose to his feet, turned his back to her and walked to the mantelpiece, leaning against it. She could tell by the rigid lines of his body that he regretted what he'd betrayed. Even now, he still couldn't share those deep parts of himself.

"Why did you come here, Ryan?"

Everything hinged on his answer.

Dear Reader,

We've got six great books for you this month, and three of them are part of miniseries you've grown to love. Dallas Schulze continues A FAMILY CIRCLE with *Addie and the Renegade.* Dallas is known to readers worldwide as an author whose mastery of emotion is unparalleled, and this book will only enhance her well-deserved reputation. For Cole Walker, love seems like an impossibility—until he's stranded with Addie Smith, and suddenly… Well, maybe I'd better let you read for yourself. In *Leader of the Pack,* Justine Davis keeps us located on TRINITY STREET WEST. You met Ryan Buckhart in *Lover Under Cover;* now meet Lacey Buckhart, the one woman—the one wife!—he's never been able to forget. Then finish off Laura Parker's ROGUES' GALLERY with *Found: One Marriage.* Amnesia, exes who still share a love they've never been able to equal anywhere else…this one has it all.

Of course, our other three books are equally special. Nikki Benjamin's *The Lady and Alex Payton* is the follow-up to *The Wedding Venture,* and it features a kidnapped almost-bride. Barbara Faith brings you *Long-Lost Wife?* For Annabel the past is a mystery—and the appearance of a man claiming to be her husband doesn't make things any clearer, irresistible though he may be. Finally, try Beverly Bird's *The Marrying Kind.* Hero John Gunner thinks that's just the kind of man he's *not,* but meeting Tessa Hadley-Bryant proves to him just how wrong a man can be.

And be sure to come back next month for more of the best romantic reading around—here in Silhouette Intimate Moments.

Yours,

Leslie Wainger
Senior Editor and Editorial Coordinator

Please address questions and book requests to:
Silhouette Reader Service
U.S.: 3010 Walden Ave., P.O. Box 1325, Buffalo, NY 14269
Canadian: P.O. Box 609, Fort Erie, Ont. L2A 5X3

LEADER OF THE PACK

JUSTINE DAVIS

Silhouette®
INTIMATE™ MOMENTS®

Published by Silhouette Books
America's Publisher of Contemporary Romance

ISBN 0-373-07728-9

LEADER OF THE PACK

This edition published by arrangement with Harlequin Books S.A.

Printed in U.S.A.

Books by Justine Davis

Silhouette Intimate Moments

Hunter's Way #371
Loose Ends #391
Stevie's Chase #402
Suspicion's Gate #423
Cool Under Fire #444
Race Against Time #474
To Hold an Eagle #497
Target of Opportunity #506
One Last Chance #517
Wicked Secrets #555
Left at the Altar #596
Out of the Dark #638
The Morning Side of Dawn #674
**Lover Under Cover* #698
**Leader of the Pack* #728

*Trinity Street West

Silhouette Desire

Angel for Hire #680
Upon the Storm #712
Found Father #772
Private Reasons #833
Errant Angel #924

Silhouette Books

Silhouette Summer Sizzlers 1994
"The Raider"

JUSTINE DAVIS

lives in San Clemente, California. Her interests outside of writing are sailing, doing needlework, horseback riding and driving her restored 1967 Corvette roadster—top down, of course.

A policewoman, Justine says that years ago a young man she worked with encouraged her to try for a promotion to a position that was, at that time, occupied only by men. "I succeeded, became wrapped up in my new job, and that man moved away, never, I thought, to be heard from again. Ten years later he appeared out of the woods of Washington State, saying he'd never forgotten me and would I please marry him? With that history, how could I write anything but romance?"

Chapter 1

The wolf howled again.

Lacey sat up in bed, shoving her tangled hair off her forehead with an angry swipe of her hand.

"Damn you, Ryan Buckhart."

It came out as a whisper, husky with sleep, the first sleep she'd had in nearly three days.

The sound was, of course, only in her imagination. She was in the middle of Trinity West, the most civilized section of Marina Heights; wolves didn't howl here. The only ones that even lived here were the two-legged kind.

And, she thought wryly, there were certainly enough of those, but they weren't the type to announce their presence with a howl. They preferred to skulk in silence, taking their prey unaware.

And she was losing her mind. Sitting here in the dark, analyzing human predators. She knew why she was doing it, knew what she was trying to avoid thinking about.

She'd heard the howl of a wolf. Unmistakably. Here, in the middle of town. She knew what it meant. No matter how impossible, no matter how uncanny, she knew what it meant. What it had always meant.

Ryan was in trouble.

She swung her feet over the edge of the bed. She sat there for a moment, again pushing the stubborn fall of her hair out of her eyes. Then she stood and walked slowly over to the tall dresser that sat against the far wall of her bedroom. Twice she reached out her hand, then pulled it back. At last she completed the motion and lifted one of the small items that sat on the polished surface.

She cradled it in her hands, running a finger over the curved lines. She couldn't see it clearly in the dark, but she didn't need to. She could picture it in her mind all too clearly, this first thing her husband—ex-husband, she corrected herself somewhat vehemently—had ever carved for her. Carved with that huge, wicked-looking knife that seemed incapable of producing something so tiny, so delicate. As did the big man who wielded it so easily. A blue jay, tail up alertly, its head cocked to one side, a whimsical expression on its little face. A blue jay.

Because it's a bird as sassy as you are, and as blue as your eyes.

His words rang in her head as clearly as if he were standing right here and had spoken them now, and not five years ago.

She started to slam the small bird down on the dresser, then stayed her angry motion at the last second and set the carving down gently. Ryan was who he was. It wasn't his fault, just as it wasn't her fault, that she couldn't live with it. They just hadn't been meant to be. They'd been a poor match, held together only by a passion unlike anything she'd ever known. Fine in the dark sweetness of the night, but hell in the daylight of everyday life.

She was better off, she told herself as she padded quietly back to the big brass bed and sat once more on the edge of the mattress. And so was he. No more arguments, no more justifications. No more guilt for him, and for her no more nights spent weeping with fear.

But tonight she'd heard the wolf howl.

She lay down once more, curled up under the covers, searching for the warmth she'd built up before she'd been startled out of her much-needed sleep. She couldn't seem to find it. The bed had never seemed colder, more empty.

Or bigger. It had never been that way before. Ryan's big, warm body had made the bed seem small. It *was* small, for him, but he'd insisted he didn't mind; it just made for cozier sleeping, with her snuggled tight against him. And she certainly hadn't complained about that.

Sweet, painful memories began to stir, and she fought them down. Just as she fought the urge to reach for the phone. She grabbed her pillow with both hands, as if that could stop her. Then she turned her back on the nightstand that held the receiver she was trying so hard not to reach for. The minutes ticked away. Even when she knew she was going to lose, she still resisted. But at last she gave in and sat up once more. This time she turned on the bedside lamp.

She didn't bother calling Ryan's number; she knew there would be no answer except his deep, gruff voice on a machine, in the same way she knew why she'd heard the lone wolf howling. She dug into the nightstand drawer and came up with a small phone book. She flipped it open, read off a number and dialed. On the third ring, a sleepy male voice answered.

"Cruz? I'm sorry to bother you so late—"

"Lacey?" Abruptly, Detective Sergeant Cruz Gregerson no longer sounded sleepy.

"Yes. I'm sorry to disturb you," she began again, but he cut her off.

"What's wrong?"

She didn't dissemble; it had never been necessary with Cruz. "Do you know where he is?"

She knew she wasn't imagining his hesitation. "Not...exactly."

Foreboding rippled through her. She tried to suppress a shiver. "Is he... under?"

She thought she heard Cruz sigh. "Lacey..."

"He is, isn't he?"

"Yes," he said at last. "Way under."

"How long?"

"Nearly six months."

Her breath caught. "Where?"

"You know I can't tell you that."

"You have to, Cruz."

"Why?"

There was an edge in his voice that hadn't been there a moment ago. She could picture him, sitting up now, black hair tousled, bright blue eyes narrowed. Cruz had been there for both her and Ryan when their marriage had fallen apart, walking that fine line between two people he cared for who had been doing their best to tear each other apart.

She swallowed tightly, unable to speak, swamped for a moment by old, painful memories.

"It's one of your...premonitions, isn't it." He didn't say it like a question.

"You know?" Lacey steadied herself. "I know it sounds... crazy," she began.

"He told me about what happened when he got hit by that drunk driver. And the night of the fire. That you knew something was wrong."

She'd heard the wolf both nights. The accident had been the first time. She'd been awakened out of a deep sleep by a sound unlike anything she'd ever heard and had sat there trembling for a very long time, trying to lecture herself out of the inexplicable fear that seemed to be holding her paralyzed. She had almost convinced herself everything was all right when the phone had rung. It had been Cruz, telling her Ryan was in the hospital. It wasn't until later that she'd discovered the accident had happened almost at the very moment the howl had awakened her.

And the fire... She'd been dreaming, and in her dream she'd been suffocating, although she didn't know from what. And then she'd heard the howl...and the news that Ryan had nearly died of smoke inhalation after pulling three small children out of a house engulfed in flames.

Yes, she knew what the wolf's lonely cry meant.

"He's in trouble, Cruz."

"That," Cruz said dryly, "is a pretty safe bet at just about any given time."

She couldn't deny that. Ryan had the knack. "This isn't...generic trouble," she said. "I can't explain how I know, but it's... bad."

She—and Ryan, for that matter—only heard the wolf when the news was bad. Her fingers tightened around the receiver. She was skating around the truth because she didn't want to face it. She was a logical, practical woman, and there was no room in her life for the kind of quixotic nonsense this implied. It was Ryan's fault. He, with his mystical explanations, had planted these ridiculous ideas in her mind.

As he'd once planted his child in her womb.

She winced; finally running into a subject more painful than the one she was avoiding. Her mind recoiled, darting away from the darkness that never waned. And ran right into the truth she'd been avoiding: she heard the wolf only when Ryan was hurt.

"Lacey," Cruz said, "I honestly don't know exactly where he is. And I can't reach him until he checks in. You know he reports straight to Captain Mallery. I can ask Mallery to tell him to contact you, but you know how it is when you're that far under. You can't always pick up a phone and call."

Lacey glanced over at the top of her dresser, at the blue jay. Her fingers flexed again, this time as if she could feel every facet of the bird, every amazingly delicate line carved into the tiny piece of wood.

"Yes," she said, her voice stiff. "I know exactly how it is."

"Besides," Cruz said gently, "you know he won't call you. Not when he's in this deep. He won't take the chance."

She knew how that was, too. Ryan had always had very strong ideas about protecting her. When he was under, he never contacted her for fear that whoever he was investigating would somehow find out about her. She understood—or at least she tried to—but understanding had made the long periods of silence and aloneness no easier to live with.

But living with Ryan Buckhart had never been easy.

"It's the Pack, isn't it? He's working the Pack. From inside."

"Please, Lacey, don't ask. You know I can't answer."

Which was, she thought, an answer of sorts in itself. Her gut instinct had been right. Ryan was working the vicious adult gang that made teenage street gangs look like angels. She took a deep breath and at last voiced the words she'd been evading.

"He's hurt, Cruz."

There was a long, silent moment before she heard a soft, heartfelt "Damn."

"Yes."

"I'll do what I can."

"You'll let me know?"

"Of course. But don't—"

"Count on anything. I know. If there's anything I learned in two years of being married to him, it's that there are only two things you can count on with Ryan. One, if there's trouble, he's in it, and two, he'll never change."

"Lacey..."

"Never mind. I shouldn't have said that. It's old ground, and you've walked it with us before. Just do what you can, Cruz. Thank you."

She hung up the receiver with quiet care. With the same care she reached out and turned off the bedside lamp, then walked across the room to turn on the main overhead light. There would be no more sleep for her tonight. It felt like a flashback to all the sleepless nights she'd known before, when her imaginings were worse than any reality Ryan could have confronted her with—if he had deigned to confront her with reality at all, rather than try so hard to insulate her from the actuality he lived and worked with. The old memories had lost none of their power in the three years since their divorce; they merely came less often now.

She thought of all she could do. She could call every Trinity West officer whose number she still had, praying that one of them would know something Cruz hadn't and would tell her. She could call the hospital and every clinic in town, maybe even in neighboring Marina del Mar; it wasn't as if Ryan wasn't distinctive enough to be memorable. Women in particular never forgot him once they'd encountered him. An occurrence she could easily understand.

She supposed she could even try his pager number. She doubted if he'd had it changed; he knew she would never try to contact him. There was too much pain and too many tears between them now. She could—

She could, but she wouldn't, she thought with determination. Ryan Buckhart wasn't her problem anymore. Wasn't her concern. And if her heart and her stomach were having more trouble with that realization than her brain—tough.

Lacey went to her closet and pulled out her small carry-on suitcase. If she couldn't sleep, she might as well pack, she thought. She wasn't due at her parents' home in San Francisco until Saturday, but perhaps she would surprise them and come up a day early. Her mother would be glad.

Of course, her mother would be happiest if Lacey would move back to San Francisco permanently. Neither of her parents had been happy when she'd moved south. But they'd been worse than unhappy when she'd married Ryan, especially when she'd done it in the civil ceremony Ryan had preferred, with only the necessary witnesses, instead of the grand production her mother would have staged.

No, they'd had it in mind that she would marry a banker or a doctor, someone high up on the white-collar ladder. Certainly not a cop.

And certainly not a cop who looked like Ryan, Lacey added wryly as she pulled open a dresser drawer.

It was so ironic that the things about Ryan that made her pulse race—his chiseled features, his proud carriage, his size, his bronze skin, his raven black hair—were the very things that made her father go rigid-jawed and her mother wrinkle her nose in undisguised distaste. It wasn't the heritage obvious in his features and the bronze of his skin that disturbed her parents—that, she thought wryly, would be far too politically incorrect for the wealthy Bennetts—it was that touch of something untamed, that edge of wildness all the civilized trappings couldn't hide. For the Bennetts were, if nothing else, exceptionally civilized.

Searching the drawer for one of the soft cotton T-shirts she slept in now, her fingers encountered a swath of silken fabric. She yanked her hand back as if the cloth had been pure flame. A shiver rippled through her, and she fought the sudden weakness in her knees. But the feel of the silk coupled with the stirring memories of the man who had once stripped it from her with eager hands was overwhelming, and she had to grab the edge of the dresser to steady herself.

It was the wolf. That eerie howl had unsettled her, that was all.

She didn't know how long she stood there, her world seeming to whirl around her, before she made herself go on about the business of packing. She even managed to laugh at herself when she realized she was taking out clothes she hadn't worn in ages, the conservative, expensive, always-in-style classics her mother had taught her to buy. She wondered if children ever outgrew the influence of their parents. Even at thirty, she found herself haunted by the teachings of a lifetime.

But at least she'd had the good fortune to have loving parents, she added silently, as she folded a pair of tailored slacks and laid them in the suitcase; jeans were out of the question in her mother's house.

The thought of children and parents roused an old pain, and she dodged it with the ease of long practice, although she wasn't certain she liked where her thoughts ended up any better. Ryan had never had that good fortune. She'd tried once to explain to her mother that that was why he seemed uncomfortable around them; never having had parents, he didn't really know what function they filled in the lives of their children.

"Sometimes," she muttered to herself, "neither do I."

And her mother had already been so set in her response to Ryan that there had seemed little point in trying to persuade her. Lacey had learned early in life her mother could be more than stubborn when she wanted to be.

She supposed, she mused as she carefully folded the blazer that matched the slacks, she would be wearing these clothes again now that she'd been promoted to a level where the hotel uniform was no longer a necessity. At least she wouldn't have to go out and spend her entire first month's salary on a new wardrobe to look the part, she thought. She'd never been much of a shopper, not for clothes, anyway. She'd never fit the fashion industry's ideal of the American woman. She had curves, and too many of them, despite an active life that included running, biking and the occasional swim. And, of course, her weekly karate class, but she looked upon that as more a necessity than exercise.

She soon realized her relatively compact carry-on bag wasn't going to be enough for this trip. She'd forgotten the detailed requirements of a visit with the Bennetts. Dressing for dinner, entertaining, socializing, the theater, the opera...all required as much in the way of wardrobe as they did patience on her part. The fact that their only child found it all rather tedious didn't slow the Bennetts down one bit. She supposed they kept hoping she would at last see the light and come back to the life they wanted her to have, rather than insist on this foolishness of making her own way. Only the fact that the hotel industry was faintly respectable had saved her from even more pressure from them.

They only wanted the best for her, she thought as she removed the things she'd just packed and went to exchange the carryon for her bigger bag. It was just that they wanted to decide what that best was.

By the time the larger suitcase was neatly packed, the faint lightening of the sky told her dawn was nearing. The thought made her yawn, and she wondered if maybe, just maybe, she'd progressed to the point where she could go back to sleep. Even a couple of hours would help. She could—

The sound that cut off her thoughts came from the back of the house. She cocked her head, listening. The backyard? That is, the huge expanse of nearly wild greenery that was her idea of the perfect yard, but had made her always-the-cop husband think only of how easy it would be for someone to get close to the house without being seen? Had Mrs. Hutton's spaniel wandered in again and gotten tangled in the bougainvillea? Or had the sound been closer to the house?

Now that she thought about it, there had been a sort of wooden quality to the sound, whatever it had been. Could it have been as close as the back porch?

Reflexively her heart's pace sped up. She tried to consciously slow it; she didn't have to worry about this kind of thing anymore. A thump in the night was just that, not someone out for revenge, hunting down the cop who had arrested him, or someone who didn't like cops in general and had decided to harass this one. She wasn't part of that world anymore.

However, that didn't put her out of reach of your average burglar. Cautiously she made her way toward the back of the house, flipping on every light as she went. Ryan had told her it was the surest way to scare off a casual burglar—let him know he'd been heard. She hadn't asked what he meant by a casual burglar, because she hadn't really wanted to think about what a noncasual burglar was. Someone who had targeted a specific house for a specific reason. Or a specific person.

It's just a noise, she told herself again, but it didn't slow the hammering of her heart. She paused in the hallway to pick up the cellular phone Ryan had bought her when she'd begun working the night shift at the hotel, which ended at three in the morning. He'd wanted her to have it to call for help should she need it. She'd been touched by his concern but thought him a bit paranoid at the time, in those early days of their marriage. She'd soon learned he wasn't really paranoid, just much more aware of the ugly side of life.

She held the phone tightly as she walked the last few yards toward the back door. She supposed she was more reluctant than she should be to call the police; too many people at Trinity West had once been friends, and they would all recognize her name. But she kept her finger poised over the buttons for the police just in case this was something more than Mrs. Hutton's precious and spoiled Mitzi.

She stepped into the kitchen, holding her breath, staring at the back door, wishing she could see through the curtain that masked the small window. Was that really a shadow? And if it was, was it simply something she'd never noticed before? Some trick of the streetlight shining through the big juniper beside the porch? Maybe Ryan had had a point about letting the shrubbery grow so close to the house.

She reached for the light switch, trying to steady her hand.

Just call the police, her mind prodded. But the urge was followed almost immediately by the expected speculation. *"It's Buckhart's ex. She must be looking for an excuse to talk to him. Calling in every little noise and shadow."*

She knew cops well enough to know that they tended to band together when it came to persons beyond the pale. Like ex-wives.

She flipped on the light.

The bright, red-and-white kitchen was cheerful and welcomingly familiar. And not a thing was out of place. The shadow she thought she'd seen had vanished. Nor did she hear another sound from the porch outside the back door. She'd been hearing things, or Mitzi had found her way home, or the wind had died down, Lacey told herself gratefully. Everything was fine.

She turned the cellular phone off and flipped it closed. She reached for the light switch.

A horrific thud froze her in midmotion. Wood splintered. The back door swung open. Lacey barely bit back a scream of terror as she whirled around. The scream escaped as a large, dark shape hurtled into the room. She grabbed frantically at the phone, trying to open it again. The shape resolved itself into a man. A big, solid man who towered over her, although she wasn't short.

He grabbed her before she could dial and pried the phone out of her hand.

"Hello, Lacey."

She'd known, the minute she'd seen his size and the way he moved. It had been two years since she'd seen him, and that had been at a distance, but she'd known him in an instant.

"You finally learned to lock the back door."

"Yes, I did," she said, her voice rough with her lingering fear and a growing anger. "But it didn't help, did it?"

She pushed at him, her anger at being so frightened growing. She heard an odd hissing sound as he sucked in a breath. God knew where he'd been, she thought as she felt a sticky wetness on her fingers from the shirt under his heavy jacket. Probably rolling around in grease and oil and dirt with some scummy member of the Pack, she thought. She pulled back her hand, thinking it only figured he would show up—after three years without a word—like this, in the middle of the night, filthy, wanting . . . wanting God knows what.

Her breath lodged in her throat as she caught a glimpse of her fingers. It wasn't oil she'd felt. Or grease.

It was blood.

Chapter 2

He shouldn't have come here. He'd known it the minute he'd glimpsed the fear in Lacey's eyes. He wasn't even sure why he had, just that it was the only thing he'd been able to focus on in the dark of the night, when his side had begun to ache unbearably.

He didn't understand that, either. It shouldn't hurt this much. The bullet hadn't hit anything vital. It had merely plowed a deep, ugly furrow in the flesh of his side, just above his left hip. It was just a fraction too deep to be called merely a surface wound, and although he'd bled a lot, it was hardly going to kill him.

So why was he feeling so weak in the knees?

"God, Ryan. Sit down."

Her voice was soft, husky, just as he remembered it. Saying his name. Making him shiver. A sexy, morning voice, although Lacey had it all the time. He set the telephone he'd wrested from her down on the counter and turned to look at her.

Or tried to. Inexplicably, he staggered. She caught him,

with the strength that had always surprised him. She wasn't a small woman at five foot seven, but next to his solid, broad frame, she seemed almost fragile. Yet she was strong enough to prop him up until he managed to stumble to the kitchen table.

"Sit down," she repeated, sternly this time, reaching with one foot to pull out a chair.

He sat. He needed to, suddenly. He'd caught his first clear look at Lacey. He had touched her again, felt her arms around him. The sensation was overwhelming, more powerful than the bullet that had nearly taken him down.

It had been three years since he'd walked out of this house for the last time. He'd managed to avoid her during that entire period, and he'd convinced himself she wasn't—because nobody could be—as beautiful as he remembered.

He'd been wrong.

Oh, some might look at her and see only the pale, fair skin, unusual in this land of sun worshippers. Or see only average light brown hair, not the gleam of the sun when it lightened to nearly blond in the summer. Or they might see the upward tilt of her nose and think "cute" but not beautiful. Or, conditioned by thousands of photographs of women whose figures resembled the straightness of an arrow much more than the curve and recurve of a bow, they might think her soft. But to Ryan she was soft only where she should be. And tough, fit and resilient everywhere else. The perfect balance. To him, her curved figure had screamed female to his male, and he'd thought her the most beautiful woman on the planet.

Apparently, he thought as his heart thudded in his chest, he still did.

Or else he was in much worse shape than he knew, he thought, pressing his right hand over the gash that continued to bleed—and ache—despite his efforts. He'd been up all night, and he hadn't been sleeping much lately anyway, not with everything threatening to come apart around him. He felt as if he was moving through the thick fog that blanketed the coast in the early spring, making it impossible to move at any faster pace than a crawl.

But one thing did register. Lacey had been frightened, until she'd realized it was him. Then she'd been angry. Even worried, judging by her expression when she'd pulled her hand from his side to find it coated with his blood.

In the space of thirty seconds she'd been frightened, angry and worried. But not surprised. She hadn't shown a trace of surprise.

Before he could dwell on that fact, he realized that she had gone to the counter and again picked up the portable phone and turned it on.

"What are you doing?"

She lifted her head at the sharp inquiry. "What do you think I'm doing? You're hurt. Bleeding. I'm calling the paramedics."

"No."

"Ryan—"

"No. It's not that bad."

"Obviously, or you wouldn't have been able to take down the door. Have you ever heard of knocking?"

"I... it's late. I didn't want to scare you."

"So you broke down my door?"

He gave her a sheepish look. "I... I'm sorry. I wasn't thinking straight. I just... I was focused on getting in, and I..."

She grimaced as his words trailed off. He heard her let out a compressed breath. She set down the phone. "All right, then, we'll go to the hospital. I'll get my keys."

"No."

She stared at him silently. He could see her thoughts as clearly as if she'd written them out for him; her face had always been expressive. To him, at least. Finally she seemed to decide that he truly wasn't going to keel over dead in front of her eyes. She spoke softly.

"Still running alone, eh, Buckhart?"

Her use of his last name, the name he'd taken from the small rural town where he'd been found abandoned as a baby, told him all he needed to know about her mood. She used it only when she'd reached the breaking point with what she called his "lone-wolf attitude." Apparently she reached that point a lot more quickly these days. He tried to explain.

"It's minor, but it's a bullet wound, Lacey. Any doctor would have to report it. And that will bring on questions I can't answer right now."

"You're a cop. What questions are other cops going to ask that you can't answer?"

A sharp twinge from his side jabbed him into answering more sharply than he normally would have. "It's not them I'm worried about."

"Who else would be asking ques—" She broke off, her eyes narrowing. "The Pack. It's true, you're under with the Pack, aren't you."

It wasn't a question, so he didn't answer, just looked away. He doubted he could have convinced her that she was wrong, anyway. He never had been any good at lying to her. He'd tried it a couple of times, rationalizing by telling himself that he was doing it to protect her, but he'd quickly found he couldn't look into those wide blue eyes and tell anything but the truth. He'd quickly resorted to this same kind of silence. And she'd quickly learned to make guesses that were uncannily accurate.

"I'm not your concern anymore, Ryan. You don't have to protect me."

His head came up sharply, and he winced as the sudden movement tugged at his injury. She took a step forward, then stopped, as if her instinctive reaction had been to come to him. Did she really believe that? Did she really believe that just because some judge had declared they were no longer married, that that put an end to it? That cutting off the legal relationship ended his concern for her, his need to protect her? He was no obsessive ex-husband—he'd left her alone—but his feelings were another matter.

He looked at her for a long moment. She didn't look away. He remembered when he'd first met her. She'd been so wary that he'd found himself uncharacteristically wondering what she saw when she looked at him. He usually didn't care about such things, indeed, had looked upon the intimidation factor that seemed inherent in him as an advantage. But with Lacey he'd cared since the first moment he'd seen her.

"I've stayed away," he finally said quietly, "because that's what you wanted. But that doesn't mean I ever stopped . . . worrying about you."

If she'd caught his hesitation, she didn't react. "Please do," she said, her voice almost prim. "I've stopped worrying about you."

He would have believed her if not for one thing. "Have you?" he asked softly. "Then why weren't you surprised when I showed up here, Lacey? You were scared, and angry . . . but not surprised."

Color tinged her cheeks. For the first time she looked away.

"Because you knew," he said. "Just like you always know."

Her head snapped back. "Is that why you came here? To see if I'd heard that damn wolf howl again? Or did you come just to bleed all over my floor while you justify not asking for help?" she asked, gesturing at the tile floor, the floor they'd put in when they'd first moved into this house. Instinctively his gaze followed her movement, and he saw the trio of small red drops on one of the unglazed terra-cotta tiles.

He looked back at her face. "I am asking for help. From you."

"Wonderful," she muttered. "So I patch you up, and you go on your way, right back to whatever situation put you in this shape in the first place?"

"I'll do the patching. I just need . . . a place to do it. And to rest for a while. I can't go back to the Pack's warehouse, not now, when it's too obvious I'm vulnerable."

She'd heard rumors that, although their tentacles spread throughout Marina Heights, the Pack operated out of a warehouse on Steele Street. And she'd read speculation that they ran a legitimate shipping business as a front, which was why, she supposed, Ryan had gone undercover in the first place—to prove it was just that, a front for their various and widespread illegal activities. But no one had ever confirmed that, and she knew how drained he must be to have let that slip.

"Ryan Buckhart, admitting he's vulnerable?" she said in mock amazement.

"It's been . . . a tough few days."

"It always was, wasn't it? You'd come home from a case after not a single word for weeks, sleep for two days, then expect us to go on from there like you'd just been on some business trip or something."

"Lacey . . ."

She waved a hand at him. "Never mind. I know, this is pointless. And old news."

He wondered why it was still so close to the surface for her if it was such old news, but he realized this wasn't the time to point that out. In fact, now that he'd rested a little, now that he'd finally stopped moving, he was thinking much more clearly. And clearer thinking meant he was more convinced than ever that his first gut reaction had been right: he shouldn't have come here.

He shifted his feet and braced a hand on the back of the chair, preparing to get up.

"Going somewhere?"

He looked at her wearily. "I don't want to bleed on your precious floor anymore."

She paled, as if only now realizing how cold she'd sounded. "Damn you, Ryan Buckhart," she whispered.

The words sounded like a curse, an entreaty and a sigh of despair all at once.

"Yes," he said flatly. That really said it all, he supposed.

"Will you at least let me call somebody at Trinity West? They should know you're hurt."

"No." He didn't try to explain that they probably already knew by now. "They'll pull me. I can't let that happen. I'm too close. I've been on this for six months, the longest damn six months of my career, and I'm not going to let it go down the drain now."

"Then call Cruz. He'll help."

He shook his head. Lacey shook hers in turn, her eyes wide with disbelief, and tinged with a pain he didn't understand.

"You know he wouldn't give you away if you asked him not to," she insisted.

"Maybe."

"My God, Ryan, this is Cruz we're talking about. The guy who visited you in the hospital every day after the fire. The guy who pushed you all over town in that wheelchair after you got hit by that drunk, to keep you from going stir crazy. The guy who's been there for you, and for me, no matter what. And you still don't trust him?"

No matter what. She was right. Through pain, injury, despair and divorce, Cruz had been there. For both of them. Cruz had never taken sides; he had just walked that treacherous middle ground. He wanted to trust Cruz. He did trust Cruz. As much as he trusted anyone. It just wasn't enough for Lacey. He didn't trust anyone enough for Lacey. Except for her.

He had to assume Trinity West already knew he'd been hurt. Too many people had been there last night, people who had no idea who he was, people who would no doubt recount everything that had happened. Including the fact that the man they knew only as Ryan, Alarico's right hand, had been shot. That was instant grounds for being pulled off a case. If he called Cruz, Cruz would have to remind him of that. And tell the brass.

And if by some fluke they were unaware of the situation, calling Cruz would still put him right in the middle. Cruz would have to tell Captain Mallery, and Mallery would be wondering why Ryan hadn't just checked in normally. He didn't want the brass suspicious, if by some chance they didn't already know.

The bottom line was simple—they couldn't pull him if they couldn't find him.

"I don't want to put Cruz in that position," he said at last. And it was the truth; it just wasn't the whole truth.

For a long moment she just stood there and stared at him. She looked troubled. At last she sighed audibly. "I'll get the first aid kit."

Ryan sagged back in the chair, grateful he hadn't had to really test his strength and get up. Whatever the cause—his long string of virtually sleepless nights or loss of blood and shock from his injury—he could feel he was on the edge of collapse. That was, he supposed, what had truly driven him here. He'd known he was running out of functioning time, so he'd come to the one person he trusted completely, the one person around whom he dared risk relinquishing control.

Now that she'd decided to help, Lacey worked with brisk efficiency. He knew she had been trained as an emergency medical technician during her early days at the hotel, and things like basic first aid had changed little since then. She came back with the first aid kit she'd always kept well supplied and set it on the table beside him. She reached toward him, but he stopped her and moved to sit on the edge of the table, so that she could work sitting down, which put her nearly at eye level with his wound.

He sucked in a breath at the pain when she tugged at his shirt. She stopped, glancing at him, but he nodded sharply at her to go on. The fabric gave after a moment, telling him the groove plowed by the bullet from Alarico's gun was still seeping fresh blood. He wasn't surprised. He'd been moving since it had happened, and it hadn't had a chance to close up.

He felt her fingers at his waist, and then her sudden stillness. He guessed she'd felt the dampness that was nearly invisible on the black denim; he'd felt his own blood spreading the moment the impact had sent him to his knees. If he hadn't been trying to make sure he was the one who'd gotten hit and not an innocent civilian, he doubted if he even would have gone down, but his balance had been off, and he'd fallen right on the wound and blasted his own breath out of his lungs.

"Unbutton your jeans."

He blinked. "What?" Then he belatedly realized she simply couldn't get at the jagged furrow just above his waistband. "Oh."

He reached for the waist button and managed it, but when he got to the buttons of his fly he found his fingers strangely awkward. He fumbled for a few moments, then stopped.

"You'd better do it."

She looked at him sharply. He gave her a wry, lopsided grin that he was fairly certain was pretty feeble.

"As much as I'd love to imagine it's for some other reason, I don't have the energy to even pretend."

She looked away quickly, but she did as he asked. He'd meant what he said; he was getting closer to exhaustion by the second, but still, the sight of her fingers unbuttoning him sent a little jolt of need through him. Wishful thinking, he thought tiredly. Never again would Lacey's hands touch him as they once had, with eagerness, with longing, with love. He'd killed that feeling in her. Completely. He just hadn't quite figured out how to kill it in himself.

He winced as she began to examine the wound, probing with gentle fingers.

"I don't suppose you're going to tell me what happened," Lacey said, keeping her eyes on what she was doing rather than looking at his face.

"I got in the way," he said frankly. It was the truth, but, once more, not all of it; he wasn't about to tell her he'd done it intentionally. Or why.

"Clumsy of you."

Her jaw was tight, and he didn't know if it was because of the ugliness of the gash or his uninformative answer. Both, he guessed. He also guessed that she was just angry enough not to be gentle with the antiseptic, and he braced himself not to pull away. Or yelp. The yelp nearly won when she applied the sterile gauze liberally soaked with the cleansing, stinging liquid. She wasn't rough, just thorough, and he felt every motion, every touch. By the time she was finished, his head was feeling hazy, threatening to start in that kind of spiral spin that meant he was headed for the floor.

"You're going to have another charming scar to add to the collection."

He tried to concentrate on her words, looking down at her bent head as she taped a heavy bandage over the wound. Her hair had fallen forward in a smooth, sleek curve, hiding her face from him. His own hair was almost longer than hers now. She'd always liked it that way, had hated it when he'd gone back for a rotation in regular patrol and had needed to cut it short. He'd hated it, too, for many reasons, not the least of which was missing the way she played with it when it was long, constantly touching it, running it through her fingers, smoothing it back from his brow, stroking it as if she simply loved the feel of it.

The image of what that loving stroking had usually led to finished what the bullet had begun. The spin began, slowly, making him close his eyes.

"Lace... I think... I can't..."

He forgot what he'd been trying to say, forgot how to even form words. His head lolled back on his shoulders. He heard her say something, ask something, but he was only vaguely aware of trying to move, to respond. It seemed they both were moving, slowly, painfully. Her voice, soft, soothing and so preciously familiar, coaxed him up some stairs. Then he was lying down, in a soft, warm place that held the faint but still sweet scent he remembered so clearly, that vanilla fragrance that made him hungry in more ways than one. And then there was nothing but the vast, spinning darkness, and the knowledge that with Lacey he could rest at last.

He'd barely touched the soup she'd fixed. He'd managed a few swallows, but not nearly enough. And he was running a fever, as well—she didn't need a thermometer to interpret the dull red flush on his cheekbones beneath the bronze of his skin.

He'd slept for most of the day, waking only slightly when she'd gone in to check his bandage. She'd seen him hurt before—too often—but familiarity did nothing to diminish the unease she felt at seeing this man down and hurting. Ryan was so big, so strong, so powerful, that when he was ill or hurt it seemed worse somehow than with other men. And she knew him so well, well enough to see what others might miss, like the weariness in his eyes, the grayish tinge of his skin. Or the darkness beneath his eyes, a darkness that had little to do with his injury and everything to do with a man living on the edge every hour of every day for far too long.

And now, when she'd awakened him enough to try to get some nourishment into him, she'd been frightened by the feverish glaze in his dark eyes. She held the cup of barely touched soup and looked at him.

"Ryan, please, you need a doctor."

"I'll be fine."

"But you're feverish, and—"

"I just need to rest. I'm as much tired as anything else. I haven't slept much lately."

"Look, there's a clinic just a couple of miles away—"

"No."

"Damn you!" she exclaimed.

"You already did that," he said, closing his eyes.

She was rarely given to cursing, but this man seemed to bring out the worst in her. That he also brought out the best was a fact she didn't care to deal with right now.

"Why do you have to be so stubborn? An infection could be starting, you could—"

"No."

"Why? Why on earth are you being so obstinate about this?"

One eye opened. "It's my nature."

The old joke, which had been funny when they'd first met but had grown old and worn by the time they'd parted, failed to make her smile.

"I'm not your wife anymore. You don't have to keep me in the dark because you have some misguided idea about protecting me."

"You're better off—"

"Not knowing. You've sung me this song before. Too many times. And it's a bunch of bull, Ryan Buckhart." His eyes snapped open then, but she didn't stop. "You come charging in here, break down my door, scare me half to death—you owe me an explanation."

"I told you—"

"You got in the way. Right. You've never done a clumsy thing in your life, so don't expect me to believe that. If you got in the way, you did it on purpose."

His startled look told her all she needed to know about the truth of her stab in the dark.

"So who was it this time? A child? A little old lady?"

"A civilian," he confirmed grudgingly.

"Caught in the cross fire, I presume?"

"Something like that."

"What's so hard to explain about that? You were just being your usual heroic self." Her mouth twisted as she tried to restrain the bitterness that threatened to creep into her voice. "So why can't you simply go to a hospital?"

"You don't understand."

"Of course I don't, because you haven't explained. But you'll find I'm a lot tougher than I used to be."

"You were always tougher than you looked."

"I still am. So you might as well explain now."

"Lacey..."

She shook her head. "I'm not the same naive girl I was at twenty-five. I won't be placated or let you toss off some silly axiom about what I don't know can't hurt me."

His mouth twisted wryly. "You're more stubborn than you used to be, too."

"I took lessons from an expert." He had the grace to look a little abashed. "You need rest, but you're not getting it until you give me a darn good reason not to call some nice, strong paramedic to cart you out of here."

He let out a breath as his head lolled back on the pillow. As she looked at him, at the contrast of his dark, tough beauty against the delicate peach color of her sheets, Lacey felt a flutter in her middle that, despite its long absence, was all too familiar. It only worsened when she forced her gaze from his face and was confronted with the bare expanse of his chest, rousing memories of all the nights she'd spent with her cheek pillowed on that hot, solid flesh. She fought her response with all the determination she'd once used to try to push him completely out of her memory. Her effort was about as successful now as then.

But she managed to steady her voice and say with relative calm, "If you're too weak to answer me, then you're obviously too weak to fight me over calling for help."

His thick, dark lashes lifted. She saw something flicker in his eyes, something beneath the feverish sheen.

"You've changed, Lace."

She tried not to react to the nickname only he had ever used. "Yes," she agreed simply.

His lashes lowered, but she sensed he wasn't on the edge of sleep. Not anymore. She saw his chest rise and fall on a deep breath, saw the slightest wince cross his face. She waited for a moment, but when she saw him swallow heavily, as if his throat were tight, she spoke quietly.

"I have changed, Ryan. You can't put me off so easily anymore. I know you're working the Pack. And obviously something went wrong. At about three this morning."

His eyes snapped open. For a long moment that fierce, penetrating gaze was fastened on her. She didn't try to hide what she knew he was looking for.

"You *did* hear the wolf."

He looked oddly relieved, as if he were glad this last link between them remained unbroken. She didn't confirm it; she knew she didn't have to.

"Don't look so satisfied," she said. "I called Cruz."

He blinked. "What?"

"You heard me." Before he could misinterpret her action, she added sourly, "I thought he could use a head start looking for your body."

"What did you tell him?"

"I didn't have to tell him anything. He guessed. I didn't know you'd told him about my...premonitions, I gather you called them."

"It...was easier to explain that way. So, he knows?"

"He knows I had one. Nothing else."

"He didn't...already know? That something had gone wrong?"

"No."

Ryan took another deep breath, but more tentatively now, as if he were testing the point at which it began to really hurt.

"It may take them a while to put it together," he said rather absently, half under his breath.

When he didn't go on, she tried again. "What happened, Ryan? Why can't you go for help?"

He hesitated. She kept her eyes level, meeting his steady gaze. Then, grudgingly, he answered her second question.

"The Pack will already be in chaos. Alarico—the leader—got arrested last night."

"But...not by you?"

He shook his head. "It's a long story. But what matters is that I...I'm supposed to be the one to take over."

"The new leader?" Her eyes widened. "You accomplished that in six months?"

He looked startled that that was her first thought. "I told you, it's been the longest six months of my career."

"You're *supposed* to take over?"

"It's likely somebody will challenge that, somebody who's been with the Pack longer. It's...expected, part of the ritual, to make the new leader prove himself. And that somebody's going to be looking for me, to show me who's in charge."

"You mean to make sure you're not around to take over," she corrected coolly.

Ryan lifted one dark brow. "You *have* changed."

"Because I see what you never wanted me to know?"

"I only—"

She stopped him with a raised hand. "Never mind that now. You surely don't think they'd come after you in such a public place as a hospital?"

"No. That's street kid stuff."

"Then why can't you—"

"Because," he said, his voice suddenly gruff, "they may be reeling from Alarico's arrest, but they still have spies and lookouts everywhere. And I'm too damn recognizable."

"You are that," she said dryly, eyeing his bronze skin and long hair held back with a red bandanna. "Especially now. But won't the Pack already know you were hurt?"

He shook his head. "Alarico and I were alone when he went down. For all they know, I've just disappeared until the coast is clear. But if we go to a hospital, even a walk-in clinic, we could be seen. And whoever the challenger is going to be would know I was hurt. And find out about you."

She blinked. "Me? What do I have to do with it?"

"Everything," he muttered, at last lowering his gaze from her face. "If they figure out you mean something to me, you'll be in danger. They'll see you as a lever to use on me."

Lacey's breath caught in her throat. Twice she bit back the words that bubbled up within her, but the third time they escaped despite her desperate effort to stop them.

"I...mean something to you?"

He looked back at her then, his dark eyes fierce with an expression that made her shiver.

"When I said I loved you, Lacey, it wasn't conditional on whether you loved me back."

She had no answer for that. And this time, when he closed his eyes, she left him in peace.

Chapter 3

Vanilla.

Ryan took a tentative sniff. He hadn't done this in a long time, awakened thinking he smelled that sweet scent on his pillow. For a while it had seemed to be everywhere, the scent that meant only one thing to him: Lacey. It had taken months before the strange olfactory hallucination had faded.

He resisted opening his eyes, wanting to cling to the scent this time, if for no other reason than that it was so much more real than usual this morning. He nestled his head deeper into the pillow, trying not to wish for the impossible, that he would open his eyes and see Lacey's tousled, sandy-colored hair on the pillow beside him. At least he could go back to sleep and dream she was here.

But the fragrance seemed so close, so evocative, that he couldn't drift back into sleep. The sweet scent drew him inexorably into wakefulness. He opened his eyes.

An odd sensation flooded him, a combination of chill and heat. He stared at the rough-hewn beam above him, at the long-unseen but well-remembered pattern of knots and grain in the flat boards of the ceiling, thrown into stark contrast by the slant of morning light. The familiar sight, the familiar scent, both so welcoming, rocked him, and for an instant foolish hope rose inside him, hope that somehow the past three years had all been some crazy, ugly dream.

He took a deep breath. Pain darted up his left side. And the foolish hope vanished with the same speed. Memory rushed into the void, not the memory of the other night, of the confrontation that had left him injured, but of the nights spent in this bed, in this house. The sweetness, the love...and the pain. The arguments, the angry, bitter words. The hurt he'd done that could never be undone. Simply by being himself.

Bitterness, acrid and harsh, welled up inside him, and he fought it down. It was a constant battle, this fight against the festering residue of what had once been their love. Sometimes the only thing that got him through was the vivid reminder of the night he'd realized Lacey was truly through with him, the night she'd finally convinced him that she meant what she'd said, that she loved him but couldn't live with him. He'd vowed to himself that night that he would never let the bitterness win, because he never wanted to hate Lacey. For any reason. But this was too much, waking up to that sweet perfume, in this house, alone in the bed where they'd shared so much.

He moved suddenly, jerking himself upright, counting on the pain he knew the movement would bring to yank his thoughts out of this old, painful rut. It worked. The motion sent a sharp and furious jolt searing up his left side. He bit back the groan that leapt to his lips. He felt much better, but he obviously wasn't ready for any quick moves.

So he would move slowly. Or he would crawl. Whatever he had to do to get out of here. He never should have come here. Not only because it was far too painful a reminder of what he'd lost, but because he never should have taken the chance of endangering Lacey. He still didn't know why he'd done it, when the one unbreakable rule of his life had been to never let his work jeopardize her. He hadn't been hurt that badly—there was no excuse for running to her for help. He could have just holed up somewhere, could have just gone to ground until he had healed enough to function. It wouldn't have been that long, judging from the way the pain was even now beginning to ebb. A couple of days, maybe three, and he would be fine.

But he'd come here instead. And that made him angry. At himself. He rarely did anything on impulse, but he couldn't put coming here down to any other reason.

But then, the few times he'd acted on impulse in his life had all been connected to Lacey. From the day he'd met her, when he'd been a street cop and she had witnessed a purse snatching where an elderly woman had been hurt, he'd acted out of character around Lacey Bennett. She hadn't been particularly nervous, or even hesitant to testify. She'd been outraged at the attack on the frail woman, and more than willing to put the suspect where he belonged—behind bars.

Still, Ryan went against all his own rules—and skirted the edge of a few Trinity West rules, as well—and spent hours with her, carefully explaining the court procedure. He'd walked her through what would be expected of her while testifying. He'd wound up giving her a ride to and from court when she had to appear, even though it was his day off. He'd stayed with her until she was called, and they'd ended up talking all morning while waiting in the court anteroom. And when she'd had to walk through the courtroom under the angry gaze of the defendant, he'd walked close beside her, giving the belligerent punk a warning look that was unmistakable.

After the suspect had been convicted, mostly on the strength of Lacey's testimony, and the legitimate connection between them no longer existed, he'd done the most out-of-character thing yet—he'd asked her to go to dinner with him.

"You don't have to do that," she'd said. "I just did what everybody should do. The police can't do it all alone."

"Thank you," he'd answered rather gruffly. "But this has nothing to do with the case."

Her eyes had widened, and he'd known she was surprised, but the smile that had lit her face then had taken his breath away. They'd gone to dinner. They'd talked nearly until dawn. Three months later they'd been married.

And they'd moved into this small but friendly split-level house, which Lacey had quickly turned into more of a home than anything he'd ever known before. She had an eye for color, and he'd watched in amazement as she chose soft, muted colors for the living room walls to set off the rich jewel tones of the chairs, sofa and pillows, while she reversed the scheme in the bedroom, rich rust-colored walls setting off the soft peach of the furnishings and bedclothes. He'd had no idea what the colors were until she told him, or that so many shades of one color existed; he would have called it light orange and been done with it. But Lacey's eye was unerring, and the overall effect warm and welcoming.

Welcoming. Right, he thought. There was no welcome for him here in this house, not anymore. He was surprised she hadn't followed through on her threat last night and called somebody to cart him out of here. But she hadn't. She'd tended to him, bandaged him and put him in their—her, he amended bleakly—bed and let him stay.

Somewhat gingerly, he swung his legs over the side of the bed. The sheet tangled around his waist, and he winced as it rubbed over the bandaged wound. He pulled it free. And realized he was naked. She'd apparently undressed him, as well.

"Damn."

It came out low and harsh. Logic told him she'd had to; his clothes had no doubt been bloody, including his briefs. But his gut was reacting to the vivid image of her doing it, clenching fiercely at the thought of her hands on him intimately once again.

Obviously he was going to live, he thought dryly, as his body also responded to the image his mind was all too willing to provide. Or he'd been right when he'd teased Lacey about being the kind of woman who could arouse a dead man.

He smiled despite the pain and his unruly body. She'd always blushed when he said that. He knew she didn't see herself that way, although how anyone could fail to see the beauty in the bright blue of her eyes, the soft fullness of her mouth, the warm silk of her hair, the wholly feminine shape of her body, was beyond him. And even if they didn't see the beauty there, how could they not see the beauty of her spirit—that lively, bright, quick spirit that fairly glowed around her like an aura that was almost visible?

He'd sensed it that first day, that here was a living example of the old cliché about still waters. There were depths to Lacey Bennett that she kept well hidden. And while he was usually content to leave people like that alone, respecting that they had their secrets as he had his, he'd felt compelled to understand Lacey, to probe until he knew what lay behind the serene, composed surface she presented to the world.

And remembering the passionate, fiery woman he'd found—and then lost—only made his aching body tighten all the more. He stood quickly, again using physical pain to stave off the less tolerable memories. He swayed for a moment, feeling a little weak-kneed, and had to grab at the brass bedpost to steady himself. It held him easily, but that didn't really help much; he was suddenly swamped with the memory of the afternoon he'd spent fitting reinforcing braces to this very bed after a night when their fervent lovemaking had finally taken its toll on the frame.

"Why the hell did you come here?" he muttered to himself. "Are you a masochist, or just stupid?"

And this time the thought had little to do with anything but the fierce anguish that welled up inside him at the knowledge that he no longer had the right to be here. No longer had the right to be in Lacey's house, in her life. So he should get out. He just wasn't sure he could yet.

He drew himself up, ignoring the wobble in his legs as best he could. The best he could say about trying to move was that the effort made his arousal recede. He walked slowly but steadily to the master bathroom, which was tucked under the slope of the back roof of the house. He tugged the bandanna, which had slipped during his restless sleep, free from his hair. Then he shoved his hair back from his face and tied the red cloth around his forehead again.

He grabbed a towel that hung on the rack just inside the door and wrapped it around him, low on his hips, below the bandage she'd taped to his side. Not that there was an inch of him Lacey hadn't seen, touched and kissed, but he didn't really want to advertise that she still got to him as no other woman ever had. And it seemed anytime the pain wasn't driving all thoughts from his mind, that fact became more than apparent.

He glanced at the counter. That, at least, hadn't changed. Lacey was a tidy, organized woman...except for here. It was here that her natural orderliness seemed to explode into a profusion of brushes, combs, bottles and other items she never seemed to quite have time to put away. He'd teased her once about needing three different kinds of combs and brushes, but she'd merely demonstrated the uses of each as if explaining to a not-too-bright child. He'd finally surrendered in laughter, saying as long as she left him room for a comb of his own and a toothbrush, he didn't care if she had a dozen.

The cheerful, feminine clutter tugged at some deep, hidden part of him, some part that still felt raw and torn when he thought about her, of how happy they'd been here. He remembered how she'd laughed and told him that since she was feeling generous, he could have room for his razor, too.

They had ended up having to rush to get to work on time after they had wound up back in bed sharing far more than mere counter space.

The familiar shape of a graceful glass bottle caught his eye. That lovely perfume, the fragrance that he'd bought for her so often once she'd told him what it was. The scent that made him frequently declare vanilla as his favorite flavor, usually in public and in front of an embarrassed Lacey. He'd done it partly to see her blush, but more to see her eyes flash with the memories of the times he'd shown her exactly what he meant by tasting every luscious inch of her.

It was time, he thought ruefully, to get moving again, to nudge that distracting pain into existence again, or covering himself with this little towel was going to be a pointless exercise.

He turned and walked slowly across the room to the door, pausing there to rest for a moment, his mouth twisting at his own weakness. Then he walked along the short hallway and down the half flight of stairs into the living room, the relatively small room made both bright and cozy by Lacey's expert hand.

He'd known she would be there, and she was, curled up on the sofa beneath a dark green afghan, her head on the silly, bright yellow, fish-shaped pillow he'd once bought her as a joke when she'd said she wished they had time to have a pet. He wondered why she'd kept it. Perhaps she didn't even associate it with him anymore. Perhaps he was no more to her than a bad memory she could forget most of the time.

For a long time he stood there, watching her sleep. He stood there until his side was throbbing, reminding him explicitly that he wasn't quite up to par. At last he turned and made his way into the kitchen, hoping she still kept the aspirin in the same place.

He found the aspirin bottle and a glass, then nearly dropped both when Lacey's voice came at him from the doorway. He managed to stifle his groan as his instinctive quick turn yanked at torn flesh.

"What are you doing up?"

He took as deep a breath as he could manage without being obvious, and without tugging again at his injury. "Taking some aspirin."

"I can see that. But you shouldn't be out of bed. Why didn't you call me?"

"You were asleep," he said reasonably, nodding at her tousled hair and rumpled sweats nearly as bright a yellow as that silly fish.

"You didn't know that until you were already up and out here," she observed.

He didn't have an answer for that, so he didn't try to find one; she had the knack of doing that to him. For a long moment she just looked at him. He wasn't sure what she saw in his face, but she gave up the discussion.

"You're going to need something stronger than aspirin. I'll get you something." She turned and walked toward the kitchen doorway.

"Aspirin is fine."

She glanced back over her shoulder. "As stubborn as always, I see."

He didn't have an answer for that, either. But when she came back with a small brown bottle containing several white, single-scored tablets he recognized as acetaminophen with codeine, he looked at her sharply. Then he checked the date on the prescription. Nearly three months ago. He didn't know who Dr. Pierce was.

"What were these for?"

"Pain," she said succinctly.

"Lacey..." he said warningly.

"Just take one, will you? You need something. I know you're in pain. You're too pale, and your jaw is so tight, like it gets when you're hurting...."

Her voice trailed away as if she'd realized the implied intimacy of what she'd said. He let that slide, but not his question.

"What happened? Why the heavy-duty pills?"

She sighed. "I had some . . . surgery."

He stared at her, looking her up and down as if he would be able to see the scar. "What kind of surgery?"

"Nothing major. That's why almost all the pills are left. I only took one of them. Now, will you do the same and go back to bed?"

He didn't quite know how to tell her that he could no more get back in that bed than he could go out and run the hundred-yard dash right now. Or why.

Nor was he about to give up on his question.

"What kind of surgery?" he repeated. She gave him a sideways look. He read it instantly. "I know, it's none of my business anymore. Tell me anyway."

"Why?"

He leaned back against the kitchen counter and lowered his gaze from her face to the familiar pattern of the tiled floor. He had no answer for that, either. None that he could put into words, anyway. None that she would accept. She'd never been nasty about it, even in the beginning, right after she'd filed for divorce, when he'd had so much trouble letting go. She'd just gently reminded him that there was no connection between them any longer. Not in the eyes of the law or the world, anyway.

But nothing could ever change the fact that they'd once had something magical, even if they hadn't been able to hang on to it.

"How about because of the day we spent laying this damn floor?" he finally muttered.

He heard her move, but he didn't look up at her. He didn't want to see her face, didn't want to see the proof that the memory of that day didn't mean anything to her anymore. They'd spent nearly fourteen hours setting the unglazed tiles in place in a careful pattern, then, exhausted, cranky, sniping at each other and wearing nearly as much of the adhesive as they'd spread on the floor, they'd stumbled into the shower together with the idea of saving time and getting to bed for some much-needed sleep. What had followed was not sleep but one of the most passionate and unforgettable nights of their marriage. They'd made love in the shower, then against the bedroom door, and then, by way of mutual apology for losing their tempers with each other during the long day, had taken a blanket and adjourned to the kitchen to christen that new floor.

"It was a biopsy."

His head snapped up. "What?"

"I... found a lump."

"Oh, God."

His stomach knotted, instantly and ferociously. Sweat broke out on his skin as if he'd purposely tweaked his wound again.

"It turned out to be nothing. Just a cyst."

He saw in her eyes the echo of the days she'd lived in fear, the days of waiting to learn what she was facing. And the words broke from him involuntarily.

"Why the hell didn't you call me? Tell me?"

She drew back slightly, looking at him. After a moment she repeated that single, crushing word, made even more painful by the gentle way she said it. "Why?"

"Why? Because—" He broke off, knowing she didn't want to hear all his tangled reasons. He wasn't sure he wanted to hear them himself. "Never mind," he muttered.

She accepted his disclaimer quickly, as if grateful he was willing to let this particular conversation end there. "Take the pill and go back to bed."

He shook his head and set the bottle down on the counter beside him. "You know codeine knocks me out."

"That's the point."

"I have to get moving."

She frowned. "Moving?"

"Out of here. I never should have come."

"Oh, yes, the fabled Buckhart lone-wolf approach," she snapped. "Well, you did come here. So don't be an idiot now. You're hurt, and you need rest. Even you should be able to see that."

"I'll rest."

"Just not here?"

"No. You could be in danger."

"And I won't be if you leave?" She grimaced. "There's a hole in your logic. You're already here. If they know it, it's too late to change that. If they don't, then we'll both be better off if you stay put. If you move, you leave a trail. Isn't that what you always said?"

He blinked. She was using his own words to beat him. And it was working. She was right. If they—and his money was on the slightly crazed Carlos and whoever he could get to follow him—did know he was here, he couldn't leave her to face them by herself; there was no guarantee they would go after him and leave her alone. But he doubted they knew; they would have moved by now if they knew he was here and hurt. They wouldn't wait and give him time to recuperate.

And if they didn't know, they would both be safer if he did exactly as she said and stayed put.

"Tell me something, Lace," he said, his tone rueful. "Were you always this tough and I just never realized it?"

"You never wanted to believe it," she said. "You just wanted to protect me. You never bothered to ask if I needed it. Or wanted it. You did it as much for you as for me. More."

He leaned back against the counter, feeling abruptly as tired as if he hadn't slept at all. And the oblivion promised by the painkiller now seemed welcome.

"You're right," he said.

She raised one arched brow. "About leaving, or about you protecting me?"

He let out a weary breath. "Everything."

He traded the aspirin bottle for the smaller brown container, shook out one of the more powerful tablets, picked up his glass of water and took it. When he'd finished and looked at her again, she was studying him intently, forehead creased. He'd admitted she was right, so why was she looking so bothered? She'd never been one to be smug, but he would have expected at least satisfaction that she'd won. Unless, of course, she hadn't really wanted to win this round.

"It's early still," he said, glancing at the clock that read barely six. "Go to bed. I'll take the couch."

"You need—"

"I took the pill, Lacey. Don't push your luck."

"Fine," she said abruptly. "I'll take the bed, and you can try to fit on the couch. It's your back."

"Lacey..."

"Far be it from me to try and make you comfortable just because you've been shot."

"Thank you for... helping."

As an effort to defuse her anger, his words failed miserably.

"Oh, of course. Don't think a thing of it. Bleeding cops show up on my doorstep in the middle of the night all the time. And I'll tell you what. Just to make things easier, I'll close the bedroom door. That way you can sneak out and I won't hear a thing. You won't have to explain—"

"Lacey, stop."

To his surprise, she did. She just stood there for a long moment, looking at him. Then, without another word, she turned and walked out of the kitchen. A moment later he heard the bedroom door close. Not slam, just close quietly. As if she no longer cared enough to even be angry at him.

Once she was gone, he gradually became aware that his side was throbbing and a dull, pounding ache had settled in behind his eyes. In fact, without the distraction of Lacey's presence, he felt damn rotten.

Which pretty well defined the state of his entire miserable life.

Chapter 4

Had she really shared a house—this house—with this man for two years? Day after day, night after night?

Lacey dumped coffee into the coffeemaker's filter holder, trying to push away the image that had confronted her when she'd awakened late in the morning and walked sleepily out of her bedroom. She hadn't expected he would still be there at all. It would have been just like the Ryan she'd known to quietly decamp while she slept, certain in his stubborn mind that it was the only way to protect her.

So she hadn't been prepared. Not that anything would have prepared her for the sight of Ryan, naked except for the bandage taped to his side, sprawled facedown on the couch, the towel he'd worn pushed aside in his restless sleep.

There had been an odd, stunned moment when she'd just looked at him, when she'd thought almost dispassionately that he was still the most beautifully made man she'd ever seen. Every line of his body flowed into the next, every delineation of muscle seemed the perfect balance of power and leanness, every flat plane solid and strong. The black silken thickness of his long hair only emphasized the breadth of his shoulders, and its flow led her eye inevitably down the straight indentation of his spine to the taut curve of his buttocks, then to the rangy, powerful muscles of his legs.

And then memory had kicked to life, reminding her with stunning suddenness exactly what that body felt like pressed tightly against her own, or beneath her hands, her lips. Reminding her exactly what that body had done to hers, what it had taught her, with a gentle tenderness that had left her nearly as breathless as his touch. Lord, no wonder there had never been another man for her in the three years since their divorce. Who could ever measure up to Ryan Buckhart, in every sense of the word?

She dug fiercely into the can of coffee, scooping up an overflowing measure as she forced the vivid images out of her mind. Only when she realized she was making the coffee as Ryan liked it, strong enough to bend a spoon, did she stop herself, shaking her head in chagrin. She stood there for a moment, the scoop in her hand hovering over the mound of coffee. Then she sighed and left it that way, pushing the container into the coffeemaker and turning it on.

Oh, yes, you lived with him all those days, she thought wryly. Long enough to automatically change your habits the moment he shows up after three years. Of course, Ryan Buckhart never just showed up, he . . . arrived.

Had she somehow forgotten how big he really was, how he dominated a room simply by being in it? It wasn't just his size—not that two hundred pounds of muscle beautifully distributed over six feet two inches wasn't imposing enough. It wasn't just his eyes, those quick, dark eyes that seemed to see past every facade, every artifice. It wasn't just his features, the wide, masculine jaw, the high, distinct cheekbones, the bronze tint of his skin, that made him so striking. It wasn't even the fluid power with which he moved, although coupled with his size it made for an almost frightening package. It was all those things together, united by a fierce spirit that radiated from within him, that made women curious and men wary.

He had fascinated her from the first moment she'd seen him. He was so big, so powerful, yet he'd been so exquisitely gentle with that hurt, frightened old lady that it had nearly brought tears to her eyes. And he'd been so kind to Lacey herself, walking her through what could have been an intimidating experience of testifying in court, face-to-face with the young thief, who had glared threateningly at her until Ryan had silently but pointedly moved to walk beside her.

She suppressed a shiver. She'd tried so hard to forget. At first she'd tried to hang on to some of the good memories, but any thought of Ryan seemed to bring both good and bad flooding back. Perhaps if she hadn't loved him quite so much she might have been able to separate them more. But loving Ryan Buckhart had been an all-or-nothing proposition. Just like forgetting him had been. And she'd failed at both.

She was so lost in melancholy contemplation that the ringing of the telephone made her jump. She grabbed at the wall phone, hoping to catch it before a second ring woke Ryan. Not, she thought ruefully as she answered, that he ever slept through the phone ringing. He awoke instantly alert and annoyingly coherent, no matter what the hour.

"Lacey? You sound odd."

"Hello, Mother." God, she wasn't ready for this. She caught the receiver between her ear and shoulder, then reached for a cup and the coffeepot. "No, I'm . . . fine. Really."

"You're not ill?"

"No. I'm just a little tired."

The understatement of the decade, she added silently as she poured the literally black coffee into her cup. She took a sip of the dark, hot brew and winced at its strength. Ryan would gulp it down, she thought, and like it. She turned to the refrigerator for a liberal dose of milk to both cool and weaken the potent stuff.

"You work far too hard, dear."

"It's not that. I just . . . didn't sleep well."

Her mother's cool, almost prim voice warmed slightly with concern. "We'll take care of that when you get home," she said. "Dr. Michaelson will give you something."

Home. She hadn't lived there for ten years, yet her mother persisted in calling it that. "You know I hate pills, Mother. It was just a . . . restless night."

"You'll sleep better in your own bed," Constance Bennett declared, still speaking as if Lacey were a child away from home for the first time. "Now, Barton will pick you up at the airport tomorrow, so you—"

"Uh, Mother?" Lacey interrupted, setting her coffee cup down on the counter beside her. "There may be a little problem with that."

"Problem?"

"I . . . may not be able to leave as soon as I'd planned."

"Why ever not? They promised you this vacation, surely they aren't going to—"

"It's not that, Mother. Something's...come up here that I have to take care of."

"Can't it wait?"

"No. I'm already . . . in the middle of it."

"Whatever it is, surely it isn't important enough to interfere with your first trip home in ages," Constance insisted. "We're counting on you for the charity ball at the tennis club tomorrow night, and the Harcourts are expecting you at their party."

Lacey had, finally, learned to deal with her mother's imperious expectations. Ryan had done that, had taught her how to deal with Constance Bennett's sometimes unsubtle manipulations. She'd almost forgotten how hard it had once been for her, before she'd had Ryan's quiet, indomitable support behind her.

"They'll all survive without me, Mother, as they have for years. Besides, I didn't say I wasn't coming for the rest of my vacation, just that I might be... delayed."

There was a pause as her mother sniffed audibly. "Well, you've certainly become—"

"Independent?" Lacey interjected. "Yes, I have. It happens in the best of families, Mother, so don't fret."

Her mouth quirked as she shifted the receiver to her other ear. Too bad it had taken her thirty years and a divorce to get to this point.

Over her mother's protests, she said she would let them know when she knew for sure when she would arrive and determinedly ended the call. If her mother got the slightest inkling that the delay had anything to do with Ryan, she would be furious, Lacey thought. She reached for her coffee again.

"Don't stick around on my account."

She whirled at the familiar voice. The deep, sonorous sound of it always sent shivers down her spine. At times like this, when it was husky with sleep, it made her ridiculously weak in the knees. She gripped the counter behind her for balance, staring at him as he stood there in the doorway. A shaft of sunlight angled through the kitchen window, catching him as if he were standing in a spotlight. He seemed to glow, as if painted by that golden light, and Lacey had to tighten her grasp on the edge of the counter.

"Do you always have to do that?" Her voice was edgy, almost querulous, as she fought the impact he had on her. "Sneak up on me like that?"

He shrugged. "You were talking to your mother. I didn't figure you'd want her to know I was here."

She should be grateful for that, she supposed. The newly reestablished bonds with her parents were still fragile; she'd never quite been able to forget how cold they had turned when she had ignored their exhortations not to marry Ryan.

To their credit, she supposed, they had never once said, "I told you so" when, a good month after it was final, she'd at last told them that she'd divorced him. They'd acted as if they'd expected it—as she supposed they had—and had invited her home to visit. She'd declined, afraid they would want to celebrate while she was grieving for the loss of her marriage, but it had been the first tentative step toward mending their strained relationship.

"Don't change your plans," Ryan said.

Lacey fought for equilibrium, but it had always been hard for her, looking at him like this. He'd pulled on the jeans she'd laundered this morning and left beside the sofa; they would never be quite the same, but, unlike his shirt, they were dark enough to be wearable. He hadn't put the shirt on, though. The black jeans rode low on his narrow hips, baring a disconcerting stretch of his chest and ridged abdomen. The white of the bandage stood out starkly against the bronze of his skin. The long black fall of his hair was a rich counterpoint to the white and bronze, its satin sheen evident in the bright midday light despite its sleep-tousled state.

But he looked better. Still tired, but better. That frightening gray tinge was gone. The red bandanna around his forehead emphasized the heritage obvious in his face and gave him a rakish, reckless air, and she wondered if he'd adopted it simply to play a part, or because he liked it.

He shifted his weight to lean against the doorjamb. She wondered if it was as casual as he was making it seem, or if he needed the support.

"You should still be sleeping," she said. The few times she'd known him to take anything stronger than aspirin, he'd been out for the count. She'd always found it slightly amusing that his big, strong body reacted like a child's to almost any kind of serious medication.

As he usually did, he ignored her attempt at diversion. "Take your trip. I'm fine now. I'll be out of here as soon as this damn pill wears off. And after I fix that door I broke. I should have done that yesterday."

"You need to rest."

"I've been resting."

"Not enough. You lost a lot of blood, and—"

"Not that much. It looked—"

"If you say it looked worse than it was, I swear I'll clobber you, gunshot or not."

He blinked. Then, slowly, his mouth curved into a grin. "I think I believe you."

Lacey had to stifle a gasp. Ryan rarely grinned like that, and when he did, the effect was...staggering. She'd never forgotten that, although her memory seemed to have underestimated the potency of that slightly crooked curve of his mouth. She could feel the heat of the mug of coffee beside her hand; it was nothing compared to the heat this man could generate in her by simply grinning. With an effort she drew around her the shield of three years without him.

"Believe me," she recommended. "And I may do it anyway, if you don't go back to sleep."

"Lacey..."

"I mean it, Buckhart," she said.

He let out a long breath that sounded almost like a sigh. "If I do, will you go to San Francisco when you're supposed to?"

Lacey smothered a sigh of her own. "Bargaining now? You're that anxious to get me out of town?"

He straightened, as if she'd surprised him. Then he gave her a look that seemed oddly shy. "I...wasn't thinking about that. I meant you should go see your mother."

She blinked in turn, startled. "What?"

He lowered his gaze, not answering. Ryan had known what her mother thought about their marriage, about him, so this made no sense. She waited, but he still didn't look at her. Lacey's brows furrowed; she couldn't remember him ever avoiding her eyes like that.

Still without answering, he took a couple of steps into the kitchen, toward her. She tensed, then realized he was looking at the coffeepot.

"You sure you want to mix caffeine and codeine?"

His mouth twisted wryly. "You know it takes more than caffeine to clear my head when I take that stuff."

She reached for another cup from the cupboard and filled it for him without doctoring the powerful brew. He took it with a nod of thanks, crossed to the kitchen table, pulled out a chair and sat down. He moved a little carefully, but not gingerly, and she hoped that meant he really was feeling better. But that still didn't explain what he'd just meant.

"Ryan?" she finally asked, her voice soft.

He rested his arms on the oak table they'd spent a long weekend refinishing. He stared down into the cup in front of him. He ran a finger along the curved rim of the mug. And he still didn't look at her. But he didn't pretend not to understand.

"I. . . hated that I came between you," he said at last. "I knew once I was. . .gone, you'd patch things up. I don't want to mess them up again."

Lacey's breath caught in her throat. This was a Ryan she'd never seen before, never even known existed. The Ryan she'd lived with had been stoically cold in the face of her parents' disapproval. She'd thought that if he'd given it half a chance, if he'd let her parents see the gentle side of him that she knew, he could have won them over in time. But instead, the more displeased they became, the more he pulled back, and although he'd never said it, Lacey had known forcing him to deal with them would damage their marriage irretrievably.

But in the end it had all been for nothing; the marriage hadn't survived, anyway. She took a step toward him, then stopped. If he'd sensed her movement—as she knew he had; Ryan never missed a thing—he didn't look at her. He lifted the cup to his lips and took a swallow of the hot coffee that would have seared her mouth and jolted her with its strength; he never even blinked.

"You. . . never told me that," she said at last. "I thought you just hated her."

He gave her a sideways glance. "I never hated her. I didn't like her much. I know she's your mother, but it's hard to like somebody who looks at you like you're something she thinks should be in a cage."

Lacey brushed that aside. "I never blamed you for not liking her. She was horrible to you. But I never knew you felt that way. Like you'd...come between us."

He shrugged.

That simple movement, so familiar, so frequent with him, so infuriatingly ambiguous, sent anger arcing through Lacey with the same suddenness that fear had shot through her when he'd come crashing through the door.

"I suppose that would have been too much to tell me?" she snapped.

At last he met her gaze straight on, setting down the cup. "It wouldn't have made any difference."

Lacey let out a wordless sound of frustration. "Of course it would have!"

Ryan looked puzzled. "It wouldn't have changed anything. Your mother still would have hated me."

"Ryan Buckhart, I swear, for a smart man you can be as thick as that wood you carve. It would have changed how *I* felt."

"Why?"

He was genuinely perplexed. Lacey felt like kicking something. To be honest, she felt like kicking him. And if he hadn't been sitting there with that bandage reminding her why he was there, she just might have done it. Instead, she pulled out another chair and plopped down in it, not caring much that her testiness was obvious in the way she was moving. She wanted him to know how she felt.

"Why?" she repeated a little caustically. "Why, indeed? It was only my husband and my mother at each other's throats."

He turned his gaze back to the table, seemingly fascinated by the grain of the oak, running a long, strong finger along the variations in color as though he'd never seen them before, although she knew it had once been as familiar to him as the tiled pattern of the floor. Her mind veered away from the visions that thought conjured up, still too fresh in her mind after his reference to the day they'd laid that tile.

"If I'd known," he said slowly, "that it would matter to you..."

"You still wouldn't have told me," Lacey said wearily. "Ryan Buckhart runs alone. Nobody gets through those walls. Not even his wife."

His head came up swiftly. "What was I supposed to do? There'd already been enough damage done. Your parents practically disowned you, they never even called."

"You've got that backward, haven't you?"

His dark brows lowered. "What do you mean?"

"They didn't call," she noted, "because they knew their calls weren't welcome."

His eyes widened. "I never told them that. I swear, Lacey, I never would have..."

His words trailed away as she stared at him. "I know. *I* told them," she finally said.

For one of the few times since she'd known him, Ryan gaped at her. "You... what?"

"I told them not to bother calling until they were willing to accept the fact that I...loved you, and that you were their son-in-law."

He stared back at her in apparent shock. "You told them... that?"

She shook her head, puzzled. "I told you I was going to have it out with them."

He shook his head in turn. "And I told you not to! My God, Lacey, did you think I wanted to be the wedge that drove you and your parents apart?"

Her chin came up. "And did you think I wanted to watch you get so quiet for hours after she said those awful, hurtful things, disguised as concern for me?"

"You didn't have to do that. She never hurt me."

His denial was salt in a very old wound that was still surprisingly raw. Lacey leapt to her feet. "Of course not. *Nothing* ever hurts you, does it? How can anything hurt you when you never let anything—or anyone—close enough?"

He stood, slowly. Lacey saw him waver slightly, saw one big hand grasp the back of the chair. "Lacey," he began.

She cut him off. "Never mind. Just go sleep off the rest of that pill. Then go do whatever you have to do. Whatever solo heroics are calling your name. And leave me in peace."

She spun on her heel and fled from the room, not caring that "fled" was the right description for her rapid escape. She was beyond pride with Ryan Buckhart; it seemed as if she always had been. No one had ever stirred up her emotions like this man, and after three years without him she was beginning to think no one else ever would. What she didn't know was if that was something to regret or welcome.

Ryan's first reaction when he rolled over on his left side and woke himself up was surprise that it was getting dark, then surprise that he'd fallen asleep at all. He'd thought he would lie awake for hours despite the lingering effects of the painkiller, thinking about either the way he and Lacey had so quickly reverted to old, tired arguments . . . or the shock of learning that she had been the one to cut off contact with her parents. And why she'd done it—because she'd thought their cool aloofness and disdain were hurting him.

His mouth twisted wryly. How could they have hurt him, when he knew they were right? He wasn't good enough for Lacey, he never had been. She deserved that doctor or lawyer or CEO type they'd wanted for her. Somebody who could give her the things she should have. Somebody who would take care of her properly.

Somebody who was there when she needed him.

His mind recoiled from the old, painful memory. Once he hadn't been there for her, at the time when she'd needed him most, and the guilt would haunt him forever. That she'd never uttered a word of blame made no difference; he knew he'd killed her love, knew it by the way she had looked at him afterward, the way she had gradually withdrawn from him, the way she had cried when she'd thought he wouldn't see. It had chilled him. And at last it had frozen him. Although he'd forced himself to go home to her, as a sort of self-inflicted penance, he'd been unable to reach out to her in the face of that icy withdrawal. When she had finally told him that they couldn't go on, it had almost been a relief.

Except for the fact that he had still loved her more than he'd ever thought it possible for him to love anyone.

And if his reactions since coming here were any evidence, he still did.

He smothered a groan by burying his face in the silly yellow fish pillow. It, too, smelled of Lacey, that sweet, hunger-producing vanilla scent. He drew a deep breath, wondering if there was anything in his life that he wouldn't manage to ruin sooner or later.

Born under a dark cloud, you were, boy.

The old voice, the long-ago words, rang distantly in his mind, like the faint echo of a bell rung long ago. He didn't know who the man was whose voice spoke the words in his mind. He didn't even know if he was real or a figment of some childhood fantasy, some attempt to give himself a past beyond the years spent in the homes of strangers who were paid to house him.

"Give it a rest," he muttered to himself.

He'd thought himself long done with that kind of self-pity. It rarely bothered him anymore that he knew nothing of his past, nothing of who or where he came from except for what greeted him in the mirror every morning. He knew all he needed to know. There was one thing in his life he'd never failed. The job. He was a good cop, had always been a good cop. And as soon as he got this dope he'd foolishly let Lacey talk him into taking out of his system, he would go back to being just that. A good cop.

And alone.

He hadn't expected this, hadn't thought that just being under the same roof with her would be so...powerful. Would make him ache so much, in ways he hadn't known for three years. Would make him long for a kind of life he'd proven he wasn't cut out for. He wasn't husband material—Lacey had proven that to him. He would have cut his heart out for her, but that hadn't been enough. She'd wanted to look into his soul. And he knew his soul was much too dark a place for a woman like Lacey.

He was better off alone, and she was better off with somebody else. Anybody else. Even if the thought made him cringe inside. And it did. The thought of Lacey with another man tore at something deep inside him with the fierceness of a wolf's fangs. And it wasn't just the images of that phantom other man in their bed that tortured him, it was images of Lacey talking, smiling, laughing that silvery little laugh with him. Or simply being in the same house, under the same roof.

He'd never realized how precious those times were, times when he'd been busy doing some mundane task and had heard her moving around in another room, and he'd smiled to himself just knowing she was there. He'd never known how much he treasured those evenings alone, when she sat quietly reading while he worked on some new carving that had caught his fancy. He'd never had a relationship before where that was enough. With Lacey, it had been riches. And he'd never known it until he'd lost it.

Until he'd thrown it away.

Chapter 5

It was like a return to pleasanter days, Lacey thought as she sorted through her mail, picking out the items that had to be dealt with before she left. Sitting here in the cozy living room, the aroma of spaghetti sauce—the only thing for dinner she had on hand, since she'd been going to leave in the morning—wafting through the house, soft music playing, Ryan sitting on the floor, his long legs stretched out as he leaned back against the sofa near her legs, the blade of his big knife glinting in the light as it moved.

He'd said little when he'd come out of the bedroom clad only in his jeans and socks, other than to rather sheepishly swear he would never take anything stronger than aspirin again. But she knew, by the fact that he had brought out the knife and had dug out of his jacket pocket one of the small blocks of wood he always seemed to have handy, that he was feeling better. She also knew what else it meant; she'd realized long ago that carving was a release from the tension of his job, tension he seemed to refuse to let out any other way.

For a long time it was a scene out of the more peaceful

days of their marriage. Then she heard him take a deep breath, hold it for a moment, then let it out slowly. She wondered if it was a sigh, or if he was merely testing the soreness in his side.

His quick, precise movements with the knife slowed, then finally stopped. She looked up to see him staring into the cold, empty fireplace as if he were seeing it lit with dancing flames. They'd often had a fire in the winter. And more than once they had set one of their own on the floor in front of the hearth.

Her breath caught in her throat as a stabbing rush of heat flooded her at the vivid memories of those times, of Ryan making sweet, hot love to her until she lay in trembling exhaustion in his arms. No man had ever made her feel as he had, and until this moment she hadn't really realized that nothing had changed, that she still responded to him on that same instant, instinctive level, with the same passionate longing. Her mind might be certain he was utterly, totally wrong for her, but her heart and body had very different opinions.

"How did we lose this, Lacey?"

His voice, soft, oddly husky, as if he were remembering the same thing she was, sent a shiver through her, as if a draft had blown in over that empty, cold hearth. The heat her memories had stirred fought with it, and it was a long, silent moment before she could answer.

"We didn't lose it. It just wasn't enough. Or there wasn't enough of it."

He went very still, but he didn't look at her. "There were... times when we had weeks on end like this."

She couldn't deny it. There *had* been times like that. But even they had been—for her, at least—tainted. "And every night," she said quietly, "I'd sit here wondering how long it would last. Jumping every time the phone rang, dreading that it would be for you, calling you in on some piece of ugliness they thought only you could deal with."

"It's my job, Lacey. You know that. You knew it before you married me."

She gave a sigh that was half-groan at the old, familiar refrain. "Yes. And it's my fault, I suppose, that I didn't realize what that meant."

He stared into the barren fireplace, the knife utterly still now, the piece of wood hidden in his big hand. "I told you what it would be like."

"Yes, you did," Lacey said, knowing that, to be fair, she had to admit he had. He had told her at length what she'd be facing. "You told me all the unadorned details. But the emotions?"

"I told you it would be... hard."

"I know. But there was no way you could tell me what it would feel like watching you walk out that door, every time never knowing if you would come back."

"Everyone married to a cop goes through it."

A wry chuckle escaped her. "Some more than others."

He glanced at her over his shoulder. "What's that supposed to mean?"

"That I should have known what I was in for when I got all those sympathetic looks from the other wives."

He blinked. "What?"

Looking away, she set the stack of mail on the oak end table beside her. She tidied the stack as she said, "Oh, they never said why I was to be pitied more than the rest of them, but it didn't take long for me to figure out."

"They... pitied you? For being... married to me?"

The tightness in his voice made her look at him. When she saw his expression, realized what he was thinking, she explained.

"They pitied me for being married to the cop with the worst penchant for solo heroics. The one most likely to get himself killed. The man who would never share the biggest thing in his life with me." Then she added, softly, because she couldn't stand to see that look in his eyes, "But they envied me for being married to Ryan Buckhart."

He flushed, the wash of color only faintly visible beneath the bronze of his skin. Then he looked back at the fireplace, but not before Lacey saw a glint of relief tinged with shame in his eyes.

"I thought I understood," she went on. "But I didn't realize that with you it would be even worse than all the stories I'd heard."

"Worse?"

"Being a cop is bad enough, but the chances you take, the recklessness, the running alone...and you never thought about what it was doing to me."

With a swift movement Ryan shoved the knife back into its sheath, the small piece of wood out of sight in the pocket of the jacket on the floor beside him, then swiveled around to face her.

"Of course I did. I thought about it a lot."

"While you were doing it? Can you honestly say that when you went into that burning house, you were thinking about what it would do to me if you died there? I loved you, Ryan. Did you ever think about that before you pulled your solo heroics?"

Something flickered in his eyes for an instant before he shifted as if uncomfortable. "There was no time to think. There were kids in that house."

"And how about the time you agreed to go in first after that barricaded suspect?"

"I was the only one who knew him by sight."

"And the time you went up on that fifteen-story scaffold to talk to the man who wanted to jump?"

"Somebody had to, and I was the senior officer on the scene."

"I rest my case."

"Lacey, there was no time to think in any of those situations. Something had to be done."

"Yes, but why is it always you? Why not the fire fighters who are trained for that kind of rescue? Why not the SWAT team? Why not one of the negotiators trained in suicide prevention?"

"I told you—"

"There was no time. And there was apparently no time to think about me, or how I would feel when some chaplain in uniform showed up at the door to tell me you were finally dead, when you didn't have to be."

"But it didn't happen!"

"And you haven't changed." She looked pointedly at his bandaged side. "You're still taking crazy chances."

"This is different."

"It always is, Ryan." She shook her head sadly. "I loved you. But you kept that part of you, the job, that huge, major part of you, from me. You let me into your life, but you never really shared yourself. Never let me completely into your heart. If you had, you would have thought before you took those chances."

"I always thought of you."

"Do you think I want some Hollywood movie scene, where you die gallantly with my name on your lips? No, thank you. I may have been a fool over you, but I'm not a masochist."

He scrambled to his knees with a speed that belied his injury. "What did you want me to do? Let those people burn? Let that guy shoot up some innocent bystanders? Let the other guy jump?"

"I wanted you to do the one thing you've never been able to do. Admit that you don't always have to do it all yourself. That you're not the only one who can do the job."

"I've never said I was!"

"I can't believe you think nobody can do the job as well as you do. You've never been arrogant. So what is it?"

"I was the one who was there. I had to do it."

"Everyone admires heroes, Ryan, but it's pure hell living with one. And I was the one who was here, all those nights, alone and waiting, terrified that this would be the night when you wouldn't come home."

Something flared in his eyes for an instant, something dark and pained and grim. She recoiled from it, afraid to even admit she'd seen it.

"This is pointless," she said abruptly. "We've been over this again and again, and it never changes."

Ryan sat back on his heels. He let out a long, weary-sounding breath. "You're right," he said in a dull, flat voice she'd never heard from him before.

Sadness welled up inside her. "It seems we've always been destined to do nothing but hurt each other."

He shook his head then, tiredly. His big hands rested on his thighs, and he stared down at them. His broad shoulders slumped. It was a long time before he spoke.

"That's not true. When we were... together, you never hurt me. You were the only thing that kept me sane. The only reason I was able to keep going."

Lacey's breath caught. He'd never said anything like that before. "Me?"

"You helped me remember... why it was worth it. That it was you I was trying to make this little piece of the world better for. I was sure it was the right thing. I knew it every time I came home to you. But now..."

She stared at his lowered head, at the strong lines of his jaw and cheekbone, cast into stark relief by the thick, dark length of his hair as it fell forward, half-masking his face. This was a Ryan she'd never heard before.

"But now?" she prompted gently.

His head came up then. She'd never seen this Ryan before, either, never seen his dark eyes so uncertain. Not about his work. She'd never heard him sound like this about his job, and it bothered her. Bothered her in a way she didn't want to analyze.

"Now I..." He paused and tried again. "Now I'm not sure of anything anymore. Not even myself. Sometimes I... forget why I'm there. That I'm a cop at all. I'm afraid I'm going to lose myself, without you there to... remind me who I am."

He rose to his feet, turned his back to her and walked to the mantelpiece, leaning against it. She could tell by the rigid lines of his body that he regretted what he'd betrayed, even to her. Even now, he still couldn't share those deep parts of himself.

"Why did you come here, Ryan? Why didn't you go to Cruz, or Gage Butler, or any of the Trinity West cops?"

For a moment she thought he wasn't going to answer. She stared at his back and shoulders, her eyes instinctively following the lines and curves of muscle. She saw the flexing and knew in the instant before he did it that he would turn to face her. This time he didn't avoid her gaze.

"It was the only thing I could think of to do. You're the only person I really trust, Lacey."

She sighed. She supposed she should be moved by that trust, and she couldn't deny that she was, but she was disappointed, as well.

"You haven't really changed at all, have you? You still can't trust anyone, even your closest friends."

"I trust them," he protested.

"Sure," she said. "You trust Cruz to cover for you, and maybe to teach you street Spanish. You trust Gage to warn you when Robards is on the warpath. You trust them to help their brother cop. It's Ryan Buckhart you don't trust them to help."

"I do trust them. Especially Cruz. I just don't want to put anybody in the position of having to either tell the brass what happened or lie about it."

"You trust Cruz?"

"Of course."

"Is that why you never told him we'd separated? Why I had to tell him, a month after the fact?" He went very still. "Never mind," she said. "That's not the kind of thing Ryan Buckhart shares with anyone."

"What good would it have done? What good does it do to pour your guts out to someone when there's not a damn thing he can do about it?" His voice was tight again, as was every line of his body.

She'd opened her mouth to speak again when it hit her. "You're thinking of Yeager again, aren't you?" she asked.

He drew back the barest fraction, and she knew she was right. She'd always suspected that what had happened to Clay Yeager, the man who had pulled a troubled kid off the streets, who had turned Ryan from a life that would no doubt have been as criminal as it would have been short, was behind much of Ryan's wariness. Although he was only seven years older than Ryan, Yeager had become a mentor of sorts, never running out of time or patience with the younger—and somewhat wild—kid he'd rescued.

What had happened to Yeager had devastated Ryan, and the Ryan she knew would never have been able to deal with that. Except in the way he had, by withdrawing. If you don't care, you can't be hurt.

"Ryan, you can't compare the two. What happened to Clay Yeager was... beyond any comparison."

"Is it? Or is it the same thing? He trusted me, Lacey. But when it came to the crunch, when his life fell apart around him, I couldn't do a damn thing to help."

"So you use that as an excuse? To keep everybody at a distance?"

His jaw tightened. "You were right. This is pointless. We've been over this ground a thousand times."

She recognized a Buckhart shutdown when she saw one. She also knew there was no use trying to fight it. She stood. "I'll check on dinner."

She left him standing there, locked up inside himself, in that closed-off place she'd never been able to get him to open up, no matter how much she'd loved him.

It was strange, Ryan thought as she walked away from him and disappeared into the kitchen. He'd known she didn't love him anymore—he'd known it for three years now—but hearing it, hearing her speak of her love in the past tense, was somehow worse.

He thought he'd accepted it, but the hot, tight knot in his gut belied that. He clenched his teeth, silently ordering himself to get over it. He knew all the reasons, knew it was more than just his job that had killed her love for him. Knew that it was he himself, that it had been who he was and what he hadn't been able to share with her that had destroyed even Lacey's fierce love.

And, of course, the fact that she'd nearly died because of him.

His mind shied away from the memories violently, like a skittish horse from a coiled rattlesnake. For all his supposed courage, for all the recognition it had brought him in his work, he was a coward when it came to those images, when it came to the memory of all the desperate praying he'd done to gods he didn't even believe in.

But all his praying hadn't been enough to save their marriage.

He shoved his hair back with a despairing gesture. Maybe what he should have been praying for instead was the ability to do what she asked, to share those parts of him he'd never trusted anyone with. It was a simple enough thing, really. Yet nearly impossible for him to do. Even with Lacey, and he loved her more than he loved anything in his life. Even the job, although it seemed clear she didn't believe that. Maybe she never had.

And why would she? Why would she believe he loved her more than anything else?

The man who would never share the biggest thing in his life with me.

It was true. He'd never shared it with her, not really. He'd thought he was protecting her, had never thought it might seem to her that he was shutting her out.

He heard the sounds of dishes in the kitchen. For a moment he just stood there, staring at the doorway. Then he took two steps toward it before stopping.

His mouth twisted wryly. He was known for his nerve; he was six foot two and a solid two hundred pounds, yet here he was, brought to a standstill by one woman seventy pounds lighter and better than a half-foot shorter than he was. Of course, he knew better than anyone the surprising strength hidden in Lacey's soft, feminine shape. She'd been taking martial arts lessons for years, and was quick and strong and determined, three qualities that went a long way toward making up for what she might lack in sheer height and bulk.

And she lacked nothing in courage or spirit. And that, he'd found to his surprise, was what he'd missed most.

With a sharp shake of his head, he made himself move, heading for the kitchen. In a rush he rounded the stub wall that separated it from the living room. And collided head-on with Lacey.

She let out a startled exclamation. Reflexively—he knew it wasn't voluntary—she put a hand up to his chest to steady herself. But reflexive or not, the feel of her hand on the bare skin of his chest sent fire racing through him so swiftly that it was all he could do not to grab her and pull her hard against him, to show her that, if nothing else, this was still very alive between them.

The instant she had her balance back, she jerked her hand away, as if she'd been just as singed as he was.

"Remind me to find a shirt for you," she said, sounding a little strained.

He couldn't help smiling. He'd been right. This, at least, hadn't changed. "Bother you?"

Her eyes flicked up to his face. Two spots of faint color stained her cheeks, but she held his gaze. And her voice was shaky but strong when she answered him.

"Of course it bothers me to have you walking around half-dressed. I've never denied that you're the most beautiful man I've ever seen."

Ryan nearly gasped aloud at the impact of those simple, honest words. "Damn, Lace," he muttered.

"What good would it do to deny it? You already know you can turn my knees to water, and denying it would only make you want to prove it to me."

It was so close to his previous thought that he felt a twinge of guilt even though he hadn't acted on it. "Do you really think I would do that to you? When I know you don't... want me even touching you?"

Lacey let out a low, rueful chuckle that made him shiver. "Oh, I want, all right. I've always wanted you, and I probably always will. But I've learned with much pain that what we want isn't always good for us."

"Damn."

It was low, grated out from behind clenched teeth, and heartfelt. He should have known better than to try to tease her. She'd always been excruciatingly honest about this, disarmingly so. So honest that sometimes a mere look from her, in that way that made it so clear to him what she was thinking, sent him careening out of control.

"Dinner's ready," she said. And then she turned and walked back into the kitchen as composedly as if she hadn't just blasted the breath right out of him.

Was it really so distant to her now? So far away that she could acknowledge the desire that leapt between them and just walk away from it? When he wanted more than anything else to hold her once more, so tight and so close that she could never slip away from him again?

I've learned with much pain that what we want isn't always good for us.

God knew, he hadn't been much good for her. He'd done little but hurt her in the two years they'd been married. She had every right to feel the way she did.

With a smothered sigh he walked into the kitchen. To his surprise—and some embarrassment—his stomach growled rather loudly at the spicy scent of Lacey's spaghetti sauce; it had always been one of his favorite meals.

He saw the dishes and silverware stacked on the counter, and quietly went about setting the table. He found that that, too, was a painful task. The simple decision of whether to sit in his old seat, close at Lacey's right, or put the width of the table safely between them seemed monumental somehow. Would she think he was trying to act as if nothing had changed if he took his usual chair? Or would she think he was underscoring the difference by taking a different place? He should have left it for her to choose, but it was too late now.

And he was standing here like a fool, obsessing over what damn chair to sit in. He slapped the silverware down at his old place. If she didn't like it, she could just say so.

When she served up the steaming plates of pasta and sauce, then sat down without so much as a blink at where he was sitting, he felt even more of a fool. What did it matter to Lacey where he sat? He meant nothing to her anymore, beyond a nuisance she had to deal with before she could get on with her life.

They ate in silence for a while. His stomach calmed down with the arrival of the first food he'd had in far too long. But the quiet soon began to wear on him.

He'd always felt remarkably able to be quiet with Lacey, never feeling any compulsion to talk just to fill the time. Their silences had always been companionable. Until now. He felt the tension in him building as the minutes passed and she said nothing. Finally he broke.

"How are things at the hotel?"

She looked up from her plate. "Fine."

Well, that was productive, he thought, when she resumed eating after her monosyllabic answer. He tried again. "When did you start taking vacations?"

She gave him a sideways look this time. He waited, expecting some comment about the fact that during their entire marriage they'd never managed more than a weekend away. His work had always interfered, more than once forcing them to cancel plans at the last minute.

But after a moment she said only, "This is the first."

"Your mother will be glad to see you."

"Yes."

He tried to smile, although he didn't much feel like it. She wasn't making this easy. "Think the hotel will be able to run without their star concierge?"

"They already are."

He blinked. "What?"

She gave an offhand shrug of one shoulder, but something in her eyes told him she wasn't as blasé as she wanted to appear. "I'm not the concierge anymore."

He frowned; she'd loved her job. "You're not?"

She shook her head, that glint still in her eyes. Then, as if she wanted to but couldn't hold it back, she said, "I got promoted."

His brows lifted. "You did? You got the assistant VP job?"

"In Customer Relations," she confirmed. Then, with a slight crease of her forehead, she asked, "How did you know I'd even applied?"

"You always said you wanted to move upstairs."

"But how did you know it was that job?"

He grimaced, then gave in. "Cruz told me."

Lacey blinked. "How did *he* know?"

"He heard it somewhere."

"Somewhere? Where?"

"Lacey..."

"Where did he hear it?"

Ryan let out a compressed breath. "I don't know where he heard it. I didn't ask."

He didn't add that he'd been afraid to, for fear that whatever source Cruz seemed to have for information on Lacey might dry up.

"Has Cruz been checking up on me? For you?"

"God, Lacey, you make me sound like a stalker or something. I didn't ask him, he just mentioned it, okay? You're my...ex-wife, and I guess he thought I'd be interested."

She opened her mouth as if to speak, and Ryan braced himself for the sharp retort he sensed was coming. But she stopped before the first words came out and suddenly averted her eyes. He wondered what had stopped her, what thought had made her decide not to pursue the subject.

When she did finally speak, the complete change of subject caught him off guard.

"What happened to the civilian?"

He blinked. "What?"

"The one you got shot for."

"Oh. I... she got out okay."

There was a heartbeat's pause before Lacey said, "She?"

He nodded, wondering about that pause as he answered without really thinking about what he was saying. "She had somebody with her. A Marina del Mar cop."

Lacey looked startled. "Marina del Mar? Why? The Pack is out of their jurisdiction, isn't it? What was he doing there?"

"He had a personal interest."

Ryan didn't think his expression had betrayed anything, but Lacey had always been exceptionally adept at reading what he wasn't saying. It had been both a blessing and a curse for him, a blessing when he couldn't find the words and she understood anyway, and a curse when she knew he was closing himself off from her in that way he couldn't seem to help.

"Why do I get the feeling there was something personal for you in this, too?"

He felt it begin, that instinctive drawing back, the closing up that would keep her from knowing about the ugliness, as if that would keep her safe.

The man who would never share the biggest thing in his life with me.

"It was," he said suddenly. "Because it was my fault. I wasn't there to stop them."

"Stop who? The Pack?"

He nodded, wondering what had possessed him to let that out. It was bad enough that she knew he was working them, bad enough that he'd come to her at all.

"Stop them from what?"

He took a quick, long breath, looking for the determination he'd always used to keep this kind of thing from her. He couldn't seem to find it.

The man who would never share the biggest thing in his life with me.

He stared down at his empty plate. She wanted him to share the hideousness of his work? She wanted to know what he'd been at such pains to keep from her? Even this?

"Stop what, Ryan?" she asked softly.

It came out before he could stop it.

"An execution. Of a fourteen-year-old boy."

Chapter 6

"I'd been under for five months or so. Things were kind of quiet...but it had been tough getting in, and I was wound up. Too wound up. I told Alarico I had to go clean something up back home, and I bailed out for a few days."

Lacey sat still, her fingers curved around the handle of her earthenware coffee mug. She wasn't drinking it—a half-cup of Ryan-strength coffee was more than enough—but she needed something to hold on to. And she needed to remember to breathe; the shock of Ryan talking to her like this, telling her things he never would have told her before, had her holding her breath for fear he'd stop.

"When I came back four days later...it was too late. Alarico had found out Eddie Salazar was the one who'd talked to the police, who'd given them the info that let them hit a delivery boat down at the marina a couple of months before, in the biggest bust the locals had ever made."

Lacey's brows furrowed. "The one that was all over the news? With the boat full of drugs and the federal agents running all over?"

He nodded. "It was a real coup for the Marina del Mar detectives."

"And . . . it got that boy killed?"

"Murdered. Shot up with some local anesthetic and left next to a Dumpster like a sack of garbage."

Lacey shuddered. Fourteen years old. So young, and such an ugly way to die. Then something else struck her, something Ryan had said before.

"The Marina del Mar cop . . ." she began, stopping when he nodded.

"He was one of the detectives on that bust." And the one who had no doubt told the whole story of the other night to Trinity West, Ryan thought wearily, including the fact that the man known as Ryan had been shot during Alarico's arrest. "He was the one Eddie talked to."

"And that was his interest?"

"He took Eddie's murder very personally." An oddly wry smile curved Ryan's mouth. "He wouldn't back off. He nearly brought the whole thing down around my ears the other night."

"He's the one who arrested the Pack's leader?" At his nod, she asked, "He doesn't know you're a cop, too?"

"No. I'd heard of Romero before, but I'd never met him. I knew he was Chance Buckner's partner, though, so I knew he had to be good. He is."

There was no mistaking the admiration in his tone. "You sound impressed."

Ryan shrugged. "In his place, I would have done the same thing."

"If he's so good," she said sourly, "how did you end up shot?"

"He was going to have enough trouble getting himself out of that mess alive, let alone Caitlin."

"Caitlin?" She tried to sound merely curious, but something about the way Ryan had said the woman's name put an edge in her voice.

"Caitlin Murphy. She's a teacher, but she also runs a club for street kids called the Neutral Zone. She's an amazing woman."

"What was she doing in the line of fire?"

"Same thing Romero was. Looking for answers about Eddie's death. He was one of her kids from the club."

"She went poking around for answers about the Pack?" Lacey asked, astonished.

"That redhead has more nerve than sense," Ryan said. "She runs that place in the worst part of town and faces down anybody who tries to make trouble there. That club is safe ground. That's why she calls it the Neutral Zone, and that's about what it is, thanks to her."

That redhead?

Something stirred inside Lacey, something she hadn't felt in a very long time. It took her a moment of inner probing to recognize it. When she did, she nearly gasped aloud in dismay: she was jealous. Jealous of her ex-husband's obvious admiration for another woman.

"You... like her, don't you?"

He lifted one shoulder negligently. "I do. She's a gutsy lady."

"And... pretty?"

She hated herself for asking something so petty, but once it was out, she found herself waiting rather impatiently for an answer.

"Very," he said succinctly.

"Invite me to the wedding," she said snappishly, then wanted to bite her tongue. Apparently petty wasn't the least of what she could be, she thought.

Something flickered in Ryan's impossibly dark eyes. She didn't know what it was, but his tone matched it when, after a pause that was long enough to make her very uncomfortable, he said, "I think you'll have to talk to Romero about that. I get the feeling they're in pretty deep."

"You mean... involved? With each other?"

While it eased the unexpected, unwelcome jealousy, the idea didn't do much to alleviate her dismay at her own reaction. What did she have to be jealous about? She and Ryan weren't married anymore. She had no claim on him. So why was she reacting like this at just the thought that he might be attracted to another woman? She hadn't felt so mixed up in a long time. Three years, to be exact. Since she'd finally sent Ryan out of her life.

"Let's just say," he said, with a look that made her instantly wary, "that they look at each other like you and I used to."

His voice was low and husky, and every nerve in Lacey's body went on sudden alert.

"They look," Ryan said, still in that voice, "like they can't wait to get behind closed doors. Like they get hot the minute they see each other."

Color flooded her face at the blatant sensual reminder in his voice and words. It was followed by a burst of heated sensation and erotic memories that weakened her knees. How could he still do this to her, after all the days she'd spent crying over him? All the times he'd been a few minutes late and she'd dreaded the worst? All the times he'd clammed up on her, refusing to talk about what he was doing?

Anger welled up inside her, anger at herself, for letting him get to her like this.

"They look at each other like we did when we knew we weren't going to make it home," he added, his voice even huskier now. "When we had to have each other *now.*"

He could do it, she answered herself bitterly, because even then, even when she knew she was right, that she'd had to do what she'd done, that she was better off without him, she had still found herself reaching for him in the night. For that matter, sometimes she still did. And that fact made her even more furious.

"If that's all there is between them," she said, her anger at herself putting a razor edge on her words, "then I wish them luck. It was all we had, and it wasn't enough."

She'd thought Ryan would deny it, that he would get angry now, or turn cold—something, anything, that would stop that sexy, beguiling flow of honeyed words that were stoking the fire he alone had first kindled in her, a fire that she now had to ruefully admit had never really gone out. But instead he just looked at her. Looked at her in the same way he'd just been talking about.

"It really was that good, wasn't it?" he asked softly.

If she could have made a sound, she was sure it would have been a whimper. And that made her even angrier. She silently called herself every kind of fool she could think of, knowing it was all true.

And then Ryan nearly stopped her heart with his words.

"Even though you were scared at first, it was good, wasn't it?"

She went very still. "Scared?"

"Did you think I didn't know, Lace?"

A chill swept her. "Know... what?"

"What happened to you, all those years ago."

"I don't know what you're talking about." It came out sounding a little desperate despite her effort to control her voice.

"Lacey, Lacey... did you think I didn't notice how you tensed up any time I hugged you from behind? Any time I even came up on you from behind?"

She stared at him, wide-eyed. He couldn't know.

"And your karate. You don't practice with enthusiasm, you practice with resolve. Determination."

She leapt to her feet, her heart hammering, her breathing quick and deep. "No," she whispered.

"You brought it to bed with us, Lacey. It's why you could never stand to have me behind you. Why you tried, but could never... use your mouth on me. Isn't it?"

"Stop it!"

She whirled and ran out of the kitchen. He caught up with her just before she made it into the bedroom, where she could lock the door. He always had been able to move faster than any man his size had a right to. The axiom around Trinity West was that Ryan Buckhart needed only ten seconds to take anybody down.

He grabbed her shoulders gently but firmly and turned her around to face him. She was shaking. She could feel the little tremors rippling through her, and she couldn't seem to stop them no matter how hard she tried to steady herself.

"Lacey," Ryan whispered, a long-unheard but well-remembered tenderness in his voice, a tenderness she'd instinctively known was only for her.

"No," she protested again, trying to pull away. He was careful not to hurt her, but he wouldn't let her go. "You can't know. You can't."

"I've known for a long time, honey."

He pulled her to him. She tried to resist, but she was too shaky. And there was something elementally tempting about his solid strength and the fact that he was tacitly offering it to her when her own was so very tenuous. He would never take advantage of her momentary weakness. He never had. That wasn't Ryan's way.

And in that moment the lure of his warmth, his strength, his support, became irresistible. She let herself sag against him. His arms came around her, cradling her head against his broad chest. She could hear it again, feel it, that powerful, steady thud of his heartbeat.

This was all right—for now. For now she could take his comfort, knowing that it wasn't because she was weak, but because there were times when everybody needed this unquestioning, nonjudgmental support.

Ironic, she thought vaguely, even now feeling the tension ease, that while Ryan allowed this need in others, he never allowed it in himself. It always fell to him to be the strong one, the supporter. Never had he let even her comfort him. Never had he ever even admitted he might need it.

She let out a long breath. And managed to coherently repeat her implied question. "I never told you."

"I've worked too many assault cases not to recognize the signs," he said quietly.

"So this is... a guess?"

His arms tightened around her slightly. "It was at first. Then I did some checking."

She stiffened. "You checked... on me? On what happened?"

"I love you, Lacey. And I knew you were frightened. That somehow I was part of what was scaring you."

I love you, Lacey.

Not loved. Love. The words echoed in her head like an endless tape loop, for a moment blotting out all else. Then, slowly, the rest got through.

"You... used your badge, didn't you?" she asked, feeling a little numb.

"Yes," he admitted. "I read the Marina del Mar report. I know that probably makes you angry, but I had to know what I was dealing with. I was afraid I'd... lose you if I didn't."

And he'd lost her anyway. But not because of that. No one could have been more gentle than Ryan had been with her. And now she knew why.

"How... long have you known?"

She felt rather than heard him take a deep breath. Whatever the answer was, he didn't want to give it to her. She tilted her head back and looked up at him.

"How long, Ryan?"

He closed his eyes for a moment, then opened them again. She sensed he didn't want to answer but was going to anyway.

"Since right after our first anniversary."

A shudder ran through her as the memory of that night flashed vividly through her mind. It had been one of those nights he'd taunted her with moments ago, when they'd gone out to celebrate but cut it short when the anticipation and need became overwhelming. They'd raced to get home to the real celebration of their love. He'd stopped only long enough to put the car in the garage and lock the door while Lacey had gone inside to change clothes and light the candles she'd already set out in their bedroom.

Ryan had come in while her back was to the door, and in his eagerness—and that damn quiet way of moving—he'd been on her from behind before she even knew he was in the room. He had her facedown on the bed, his fully aroused body pinning her, before he realized her panic was real.

He'd stopped instantly, making the switch from fierce lover to gentleness so swiftly that it had added to her confusion. When he'd rolled over and caught her in his arms, she'd fought at first, struggled to get away, raining blows down on his chest that had to hurt despite his solid muscularity. He'd never even winced, just held her, whispering soothing words she didn't even hear until her panic began to ebb.

"I knew something was wrong," he said softly. "I knew it from the beginning. I kept thinking you'd get over it, that it was only natural for you to be wary. I'm so much bigger than you, and you weren't used to me yet...but you didn't. You kept on being as skittish as a frightened deer."

She shuddered again, trying to deal with both the ugly memories and the stunning fact that Ryan had known. He'd known, and he'd never said a word.

"But that night was the worst. I had to know, Lace," he repeated softly. "The idea that I'd scared you so badly..."

"It wasn't you." She barely managed to get the words out.

"I know that. But I didn't then. I didn't know what I'd done, only that I would slit my throat before I'd ever scare you like that again. But I had to know what not to do. It was hard, because you were a juvenile when it happened, and those records are confidential, but I pulled some strings. And then...then I understood. Why you were so wary. Why you hated people coming up behind you. Why you'd never... wanted sex that way."

"He... he didn't rape me," she said, as if it were important to make that clear.

"The hell he didn't." The words burst from him, unexpectedly furious. "There's more than one kind of rape. What he made you do to him... I wanted to kill the bastard. If he hadn't still been in prison, I might have done it. Damn it, Lacey, you were only sixteen!"

She stared at him, her shivering halted as if by the heat of his anger. Anger for her. Had she ever dared to tell him, she would have expected shock or distaste, but not this. Not the quiet acknowledgment that he'd always known, the tender acceptance of her involuntary recoiling, and now the fury at her long-ago pain.

Her mind was spinning, image after image tumbling one after the other.

Words came gushing out like water held too long behind a dam, words of that horrible night, words of fear and pain and humiliation. And then, at last, came the words of thanks she'd never given him, thanks for how Ryan had turned the ugliness into something bearable. How he had supplanted the brutal memories with gentle ones. Memories of Ryan, holding her so sweetly that night, never pushing her to tell him what was wrong, never asking her to relive what she couldn't even speak about. Ryan, waiting for days after that night before he did anything more than hold her at night, waiting without complaint until the need overcame her and she made the first move. Ryan, never again approaching her from behind without warning, even in the most ordinary of circumstances. Ryan, never again urging her to taste him as he tasted her, yet never stinting in giving to her that most intimate of kisses she had come to crave from him, only him....

He'd done it all for her, and she'd never known.

"I... I was so glad," she finished at last, feeling almost hollow inside now that it had poured from her, feeling as if something dark and malignant had been removed. "Glad that you didn't ask. I knew I could never tell you. I was sure you'd be... disgusted."

"It wasn't your fault, Lace," he whispered, one hand coming up to stroke her hair, the other gently rubbing the tense muscles of her back. "You were the victim. And nothing you could ever do would make me feel disgusted."

"Oh, Ryan..."

She'd missed this so much, this tender strength of his. She'd read an old proverb once, supposedly from some of the ancestors Ryan knew only by his own resemblance to them, that had made her think the writer must have known a man like him. *Nothing is so strong as gentleness,* it had said, *and nothing so gentle as real strength.*

It was only fair, she told herself. If she had to remember all the pain, the anguish, of their marriage, she should remember the good, too. And there had been good things in it. So many good things. And this, this gentle, wordless support, had been one of the best. This was the Ryan she'd loved beyond measure, the Ryan she had tried so very hard to hold on to, even when she'd known she was only holding part of him.

This was the Ryan she was utterly helpless to resist.

For a long time she just stood there and let him hold her. He did so quietly, his only movement that stroking of her hair and soothing massage of her back. Calm slowly enveloped her, and she felt herself relax, taking from him what he so freely gave. He'd always done that for her, loaned her his strength when she'd needed it. Even now, when the secret she thought she'd hidden from him throughout their marriage was out, he gave to her.

But then, giving had never been Ryan's problem.

With a sigh of contentment, a sound she hadn't made in a very long time, Lacey settled in closer against him. Ryan sucked in a quick breath and went still for a moment, then resumed his gentle, soothing stroking. Belatedly Lacey realized what some part of her mind had been trying to tell her, became aware of the sweetly familiar yet long-absent hardness pressing against her belly.

He'd always told her that she made him hotter faster than any woman ever had, but she'd forgotten how potent the truth of that was. And although he was clearly thoroughly aroused, there hadn't been an untoward motion or caress to betray that; he'd done nothing but hold her and soothe her so gently that she'd utterly relaxed in his embrace.

And if she told him to stop right now, he would. And that, she knew, had nothing to do with what had happened to her all those years ago; that was simply Ryan. She suspected he'd always been that way. A man strong enough to be gentle.

But she didn't want him to stop.

The realization should have shocked her, should have made her jump out of his arms instantly. It didn't. She doubted at this moment if anything could make her want to give up this languorous feeling of contentment. Not even the knowledge that she was surely headed for trouble.

Before she even realized what she was doing, she was moving, pressing herself closer against him, caressing his body with her own in the way she'd learned so long ago. Ryan groaned, his arm tightening around her, and she felt his hips move slightly in response to her movement. She felt the prod of ready maleness, and a sudden wave of heat swept over her as she remembered how completely he filled her, how thoroughly he took away that empty ache, the ache that had been with her every day of the three years since he'd walked out of this house for the last time.

Still in that dreamy state of heated memory, she moved again, shifted her position to increase the pressure on that aroused column of flesh, savoring the rightness of this, loving the liquid, melting sensation only he had ever made her feel.

Ryan went very still, and she felt his body go rigid. He took a deep breath.

"Lacey?"

His voice was tight, strained. Why? she wondered vaguely. This felt so right. It had always been right between them. When everything else was falling apart, this had always been right, this pure, fiery need for each other.

She snuggled closer to him, sighing. This time he made a throttled sound deep in his chest, and she leaned her head back to gaze up at him.

"God, Lacey, don't!"

"Don't... what?"

"Look at me like that. Like you used to. When you... wanted me."

I've always wanted you, and I probably always will.

Her own words rang in her head, the truth of them coming home to her once more with resounding fervor. She did want him. She couldn't help that.

"I told you," she whispered. "That hasn't changed."

She saw his jaw clench, heard him suck in yet another breath and hold it. "You're playing with fire, Lacey."

"I know," she said, knowing even as she said it that she was quite probably making the biggest mistake of her life. "But I've been cold for so very long."

He groaned and clutched her to him. "Ah, God, Lacey, so have I."

"And no one has ever warmed me the way you do."

She felt a shiver go through him. She leaned forward and slipped her arms around him, carefully avoiding his injured side. He shivered again, and Lacey felt once more the thrill only Ryan had ever given her, the purely feminine thrill of knowing this big, powerful man wanted her so much he was shaking with it.

"Lacey, I..." He stopped and swallowed audibly. "Please, don't... start this."

She went still. "I... you don't want...?"

"Damn." It was low, fervent and more than a bit rough. "You know I do. I've never stopped wanting you." His hands slid down her back to her hips, and he pressed her against him, against the rigid proof of his own words. "Isn't it obvious?"

"Then why—"

"You're the one who said it wasn't enough," he reminded her, his voice harsh.

Lacey sighed. "I know. I know this will only...complicate things. I know it means nothing beyond this moment. But..."

"You wanted a clean break. You're the one who told me never to come back."

"I was desperate, Ryan. I knew if you didn't go, if I had to see you again, I'd give in."

"Is that what you're doing now? Giving in? Because if it is, I don't want it, Lacey. I know what happens between us, how powerful it is. I don't want you coming to me just because it's too much for you to fight."

"It *is* too much to fight."

"You think I don't know that? You think I haven't spent every day of the past three years fighting it, aching for you, wanting you, knowing I can't ever have you again?"

"And...now that you can?"

A low, pained sound rumbled up from his chest. He closed his eyes. "God, Lace, if I thought for a minute you really meant this..."

"I do mean it. God knows why. I swore it could never, ever happen again, but I do. Even if it's the biggest mistake I ever make."

"I thought marrying me was that."

"No," she said softly. "It was never that. No matter how it ended."

"But it ended. Because this—" he slowly ran his hands back up to her shoulders "—wasn't enough."

Hearing her own words quoted back at her made her cringe inwardly. "Ryan..."

"So instead I've spent three years wondering if you'd found somebody to replace me, somebody safe, who would never make you cry the way I did."

As if anyone could ever fill the hole his absence made in her life. Still, she felt the rising tide of need ebbing. She took a steadying breath, then backed up a bare half-step. Ryan let her go, and when she looked up at him, she saw in his eyes the same mix of emotions, sorrow and regret and need mingled with relief, as if they'd stepped back from a dangerous precipice, both knowing the flight would have been incredible.

"I haven't even tried," she said quietly.

"Neither have I," he said just as quietly.

"Not even . . . your redhead?"

He gave a slow, half-shake of his head. "She was never mine. And it wouldn't have mattered, anyway. She isn't you."

Emotion shook her again, and she reached out impulsively and placed the palm of her hand flat on his chest, over his heart. She felt the steady thud, then felt it speed up, as if her mere touch had the power to alter his very life force. He'd never tried to hide the effect she had on him, and she supposed that, in its own way, was indicative of the strength of the man.

And he was wise enough, and knew her well enough, to know the stunning effect it had on her, this instant response of his body to her touch. The effect that drained away any thought of how wrong this was, how big a mistake this would be. The effect that made her think only of how long it had been since he'd held her, since he'd made love to her as only he could, as if he knew every secret dream she'd ever had. The effect that made her want nothing more in this moment than to feel it again, that wondrous, soaring sensation only Ryan Buckhart had ever aroused in her. The effect that made her consider it well worth any cost.

She raised her gaze to his face and saw in his eyes the acknowledgment of what she knew must be showing in hers. And the realization that they both knew they were about to leap off that precipice they thought they'd safely backed away from.

When at last he lowered his head to kiss her, she met him with every bit of welcome and longing that had built up in her for the past three years. Her lone wolf had come home.

And somewhere, in the back of a mind that was becoming swamped all too swiftly with sensations both remembered and new, floated a fact she'd thought of and denied more than once.

Wolves mated for life.

Chapter 7

As he lay down beside her, Ryan knew he had to be crazy. Flat, flipping insane. He should be out of here, back with the Pack, getting his damn job done. He was past due checking in at the department, and Captain Mallery would have his head for that soon. Not to mention Robards, who hated his guts and had been demanding he be pulled for weeks now, wanting to simply storm the warehouse and let the lead fly, and if half the Pack escaped to rob and loot and kill another day, so be it.

But here he was, completely out of touch. The whole damn operation could be falling apart, and he wouldn't even know.

And right now he wasn't sure he even cared. Lacey was in his arms, willingly, and no matter how he tried to tell himself this was a mistake, no matter that this was nothing better than ripping the wound in his side open again and pouring acid into it, he couldn't stop. He was too hungry for her, a hunger rooted in three long years of yearning, of missing her smile, her laugh, the sometimes razor sharpness of her wit. Three long years of reaching for her in the dark only to find emptiness. Three long years of wondering if he could tear himself apart and come back together in some different way as the kind of man Lacey wanted, the kind of man she deserved.

Just this once, he told himself. Just this once he could taste the sweetness again. He knew it wasn't forever, knew it would only make things infinitely more complicated, but he was powerless to resist the inexorable power this woman had over his heart, his soul, his body.

As he reached for her in the bed they'd shared for so many nights, sometimes talking, sometimes laughing, sometimes cursing, sometimes crying, but always whispering their love before the night was through, he wondered why she was doing this. Was it simply as she'd said, that this thing between them was too strong, too potent, to fight?

Or was she lonely? Had these past three years been as cold and desolate for her as they had been for him? She'd said there had been no one, and he believed her; Lacey didn't lie.

And then she slid into his arms, and at the first touch of her silken skin against his naked body he knew it didn't matter anymore why, it only mattered that she was here, and that for this moment, at least, she was his again. He would deal with the aftermath when it came. Somehow.

He shivered as he pulled her against him, knowing only in this moment, when his body roused fiercely to the hauntingly familiar feel of her, when his heart seemed to leap in his chest at the rightness of it, when he nearly cried out at the sweet pain of holding her again, just how raw the empty place she'd left in him still was.

"You're sure?" he asked, hating himself for whatever it was in him that wouldn't let him just push ahead, whether she was sure or not. But he could do no less; this was Lacey.

"I should be asking you," she answered, her hand delicately coming to rest on his side above the bandage. "You're the one who's hurt."

"Lady, I'd have to be dead to say no to you. But you have to be sure. I don't want any regrets over this."

He knew that was an impossibility. There was no way they wouldn't come to regret this. But he no longer cared.

Lacey's answer was to move closer, to entwine her legs with his, to press herself against him until he could feel every taut curve of her body. And then she stretched upward to kiss him, softly at first, then more fervently. Her fingers threaded through the length of his hair in the way they always had, with that stroking, caressing motion that told him she liked the feel of it, the way that had made him dread the times when he'd had to cut it.

He'd thought there would be hesitation, uncertainty, as they fumbled their way through what had once been well-known paths. But they came together as if the time between had never been, as if this were nothing more than a continuation of the passion they'd always known. Lacey's hands moved over him in the old ways, the ways he'd tenderly taught her so long ago, and she responded to his touch as sweetly, as fervently, as ever. Whatever her reasons, he could no longer doubt that she had, indeed, wanted this. Wanted this with an eagerness and longing that matched his own.

And that knowledge alone threatened to send him careening out of control. When it was added to the erotic forays of her roving hands, touching him in all the ways, in all the places, he'd been dreaming of for so long, he knew he was perilously close to the edge.

"Lace," he murmured against the silken fall of her hair, "Lace, you've got to slow down. I can't . . . I'm not . . ."

"Oh, yes, you are," she whispered, her hands sliding once more down his body to curl around him in that stroking, squeezing caress that made his breath slam out of him in a rush. "You always were."

A memory hit him low and hard, making his body clench around a shaft of pure white heat. Lacey, their first time together, staring at him, at his naked arousal, first fearfully, then with growing awe, as he guided her hand to him. She had touched him hesitantly, almost wonderingly, tracing every line, every swollen inch of him, as if he were some miraculous thing she'd never known existed. The unexpectedly arousing sensation of that tentative exploration had caught him off guard, and he'd had to stop her with a rather dazed explanation that if she didn't quit, it would be over before they began.

As it might be now, he thought, if she kept touching him like this.

He reached down and stilled her hand, then shifted slightly away from her, wishing he didn't have to, wishing he could endure her searing caresses for hours. She made a sound of protest, but it broke into a gasp of pleasure as he slid his hands back up over her ribs to cup and lift her breasts. She still filled even his big hands with that soft, warm, feminine weight, and he shuddered again as this, too, nearly made him cry out at the pure rightness of it.

He rubbed his thumbs gently over her nipples, wondering if his touch would still affect her in the same way. Her tiny cry and the sudden arching of her back gave him his answer; not even three years of distance could change the fact that in this way, Lacey was his and always would be. Just as he would always be hers, hers like no other could ever be. She might settle for less than the fire that blazed between them in order to get the comfort she needed in the rest of her life, but she would always know what she was missing. As he would know. Always. No matter where he went, no matter who he was ever with, he would never find the match he'd found in her.

He lowered his head to her breast, his lips seeking the nipple that was already taut from his fingers. The moment he moved, she lifted herself to him, a small but unmistakable movement of offering that sent that shaft of heat stabbing through him again. Her hands moved, again seeking his hair, lifting and spreading the dark length of it over her own skin as if it were one more caress from him that she craved. As it always had, the pure sensuality of the movement nearly drove him out of his mind.

He suckled her deeply, first one nipple, then the other, then holding each with his lips as he teased them to rigidness with his tongue. She moaned, a low, sensuous sound that made him frantic to hurry, to ease this gnawing, painful ache. He was vaguely aware of her hands sliding over his chest but was far more intent on the gentle undulation of her body as it responded to his touch.

But then he was slammed into awareness as she reached his nipples and, as if returning his caress, rubbed them into tautness with her fingertips. Sensation erupted through him, and he groaned low and deep in his throat; in his concentration on her response to him, he'd almost forgotten what she could do to him with the barest of caresses.

"God, Lace," he muttered. "Please…I can't…it's been so long…."

"Too long," she whispered, and with eager hands urged him over her.

With one of the greatest efforts of his life, he made himself wait, at least until he slipped one hand down over the slight swell of her belly to the triangle of sandy curls. He found them damp, and a shudder rippled through him when he probed farther and found her feminine flesh slick and wet and ready. Her hips lifted at even this slight touch, inviting, urging, and he gave in with a heartfelt groan.

He'd wanted to pull her atop him, to have her take him, ride him as she'd learned to do so well that it made him nearly erupt at the memory, but now he couldn't wait long enough. The need to drive himself into her was so overwhelming he could think of nothing else.

Her thighs parted the moment he levered himself over her, and he felt the lure of her heat as if it were a beacon leading him home. And then, before he could move to do it himself, Lacey's hands were on him, guiding him into soft flesh that parted easily for him, yet clasped him so tightly that he cried out her name at the sweet friction of it.

He tried to go slowly, knowing how long it had been for her, as it had been for him, but she made it impossible with her low moan and the way she clutched at his hips to pull him into her. He gave in to the wild need and drove forward, sheathing himself in her, savoring the way she gasped with pleasure.

"Yes. Oh, yes..."

For a moment that seemed an eternity he held still, savoring the bliss of being inside her again, of feeling that perfect fit, of knowing that in this, at least, there was no doubt, no hesitation, no question. Then Lacey shifted beneath him to wrap her long, tautly curved legs around his hips, forcing him into her to the hilt.

"Laceeey!"

It hissed out of him with all the force of the burst of heated sensation that hit him as she moved. And then he had no choice. The moment of stillness was over. He had to move, more than he had to breathe, and he did, driving deep in thrust after thrust, thinking he had never felt anything so intense as this rising, pulsing tide, had never heard anything so sweet as his name on her lips right now.

She rose to meet him, as if doing without him for even those few seconds when he drew back was too much to bear. He'd thought he'd remembered, in all those tortured, lonely nights, how incredible making love to Lacey was. He knew now that no memory could ever match the extraordinary reality. And when she clutched at his shoulders, her nails digging into his skin as she cried out his name again, when he felt the coaxing, rippling dance of her flesh around his, he hung on just long enough to try to fix the feelings in his mind so he could carry it with him to keep him going through all the time ahead without her.

But an instant later it was too much, as it had always been. He was caught up in the pulsing waves of her climax, and his body did as hers demanded and gave itself up to her in a rush of wet heat that nearly scalded him as he groaned her name, shaking with the power of his own release.

He collapsed atop her, still panting, knowing he should move, that he was far too heavy for her, but knowing as well that it was beyond him right now. Every muscle in his body was quivering, drained. He finally managed to slip to one side, keeping his arms tight around her.

"Ryan," she whispered.

He murmured something that started to be her name in turn but faded out before he could finish it. He felt her move, then felt the slow, rhythmic motion as she began to stroke his hair where it lay against his back. It was so seductively familiar, that gentle caress. How many hours had he spent, his head cradled on her shoulder, as she did this? Usually just like this, in the quiet moments after they'd once more proven that the incredible fire between them hadn't abated.

He savored it, telling himself it was all right, just for a while. He could let himself drift in that wondrous place he'd found only with her, just for a while. Maybe, just for a while, he could even pretend it was real, pretend that when he finally had the strength to raise his head she would be looking at him with love, with joy, with that quiet trust that had always been there before. . . .

Before.

Before it had all come apart. Come apart because he hadn't been there when she'd needed him most. Come apart because he hadn't been here when she'd lost their baby.

He shuddered at the memory, at the ugly, vivid images that were seared into his brain. Sitting exhaustedly on his twelfth consecutive night on a futile stakeout and hearing that damn wolf howl. Racing home to find Lacey lying sprawled at the foot of the stairs in an ominously large pool of blood, her balance betrayed by her awkward, seven-months-pregnant body. Usually he could fight the visions off, but here, now, lying with her in the bed where the son who had died that night had been conceived, they were stronger than his will to stop them.

He'd lost his unborn son that night and very nearly the woman he loved more than his life. All because of his job, because he'd put it before her, even when she'd needed him there, needed his help because his child was growing inside her.

And he knew that no matter how sweet, how breath-stealing, this night had been, it meant nothing, not when stacked up against what he'd cost her.

"Ryan? What's wrong?"

What was wrong? How could he begin to tell her what was wrong now, when he'd never been able to tell her then? All the nights she'd wept for their loss, and he'd never been able to tell her, afraid that if he gave in to his pain he would never be able to deal with hers. He hadn't been able to talk about this then any more than she'd been able to admit what had happened to her at sixteen. But she had found the courage to talk about that now. To admit how awful it had been.

Were you always this tough and I just never realized it?

His own rueful words came back to him, but only now did he realize how true they really were.

"What is it?" she asked again, pushing the strands of his hair back from his face.

"I . . . I'm sorry, Lacey."

She went very still. She was silent for a long moment, then said with a sigh, "I knew this would happen, but I was hoping we could wait at least until morning for the re-grets."

He lifted his head then, quickly. "No. I mean, that's not what I—" He stopped, letting out a weary breath as he looked at her.

"Then what?" she asked gently.

He wanted to avoid this so fiercely it was almost a physical need to run. He fought it down. If she could find the nerve, surely he could. Couldn't he?

"I . . ."

He lowered his gaze. He focused on a reddish mark on her shoulder, where he'd gripped her in his frenzy just minutes before. Even when he was loving her, he hurt her, he thought sadly.

Slowly he shook his head. "I never was any good at...talking about some things."

"Some things...like what?"

He swallowed heavily. He *could* do it. He *would* do it. He just couldn't look at her when he did, couldn't bear to see the painful memories take her over once more, couldn't bear to see her withdraw from him again as she had then, couldn't bear to see her remember how much she'd hated him for abandoning her when she'd needed him most. So he would take the coward's way out and avoid meeting those wide blue eyes that haunted his dreams.

"Things like...the baby."

She went still again, this time seeming to stop even breathing. And when she spoke, her voice held every bit of pain and withdrawal he'd feared.

"It's a little late to be sorry about that, isn't it?"

"I was always sorry."

He felt her go rigid beneath him. "You had a very odd way of showing it, then. You never said a word."

"I...couldn't."

"I thought you were...relieved."

His gaze snapped back to her face. "Relieved?"

"You kept saying you didn't know anything about being a father, you'd never had one—"

"That didn't mean I didn't want our child, Lacey!" He shook his head, stunned that she could even think that. "I wanted him! And when we lost him, I..."

His throat tightened up, and he had to swallow again to keep going. He didn't want to do it, but he knew he had to. He owed Lacey this.

"I wanted...to be a father to him. I wanted him to know who his father was, not like me. Hell, if it wasn't for my looks, I wouldn't know a damn thing about myself. I didn't want him to have to live like that. I couldn't tell him about his ancestors, but he would know me. Just thinking that made it...easier for me to look in the mirror every day."

"You never told me that," Lacey whispered, an undertone in her voice he didn't recognize and couldn't name.

"What was there to tell? I never knew who my people were. Buckhart was just a wide spot on the highway, not on any reservation, and no one had seen any Indians come through—especially any pregnant women—before they found me in that sheriff's car."

That he'd spent the rest of his life in foster homes chosen by the court system, because the law giving Native Americans the right to determine the fate of their own children hadn't been passed yet, she already knew. He'd told her before he'd asked her to marry him, feeling she had the right to know his past and how little he knew of where and who he'd come from. She'd only smiled and said it was probably just as well, because the court battles over which tribe should take him would have lasted until he was eighteen anyway. For the first time in his life he'd laughed about it, and he'd known then what a precious thing he'd found in Lacey Bennett.

Just as he knew what a precious thing he'd lost.

"I never knew you felt like that," she said in that same soft tone.

"I felt...foolish. I should have gotten over not knowing who I was long ago. But the thought of our child...brought it all back. And...healed it at the same time. And when we lost him, it was like...I'd lost myself again." He shook his head ruefully. "Now you see why I don't talk about things like that. I don't make much sense when I do."

"Ryan," Lacey said, still hushed, "why didn't you tell me?"

"What good would it have done? You were hurting so much, inside and out. I couldn't let my pain matter. It was eating me alive, but I had to be strong for you. You had to know you could lean on me."

Lacey shook her head. "Don't you see? You didn't have to be strong for me. I didn't need to lean on you. I needed to...to share the pain with somebody who felt it like I did."

"But you were already in such pain! What good would it have done for you to know that I... that at night while you slept I used to sit on the floor in that nursery we painted and cry?"

Lacey stared at him, her eyes wide with shock. "You... I... Oh, God, Ryan!"

She reached for him, convulsing into tears. He was stunned by the suddenness and power of her sobbing, and he didn't know what to do, except to hold her. It made no sense to him, that his admitting to his own long-ago tears would have this effect on her now. But then, he knew that he had mishandled everything about the death of their baby, from the moment he'd walked out of this house to leave her alone yet again. And he didn't, couldn't, blame her for hating him for it.

He held her quietly, stroking her tangled hair as she had been stroking his, until her weeping at last subsided. She tried to speak, but he hushed her; he could feel her exhaustion.

"In the morning, Lace. We'll talk in the morning."

And he held her still until he felt her relax into sleep. He wished he could follow, but he knew rest was a long way away for him on this night.

Lacey rubbed at her reddened, swollen eyes, then slipped quietly out of bed, knowing it had to be a sign of Ryan's weariness that she accomplished it without waking him. She wondered how long he had lain awake last night after the emotional scene that had drained her so completely.

She quickly gathered up the jeans and blouse she had so quickly and willingly removed last night in her eagerness to get to Ryan. She refused to regret it, she told herself firmly as she left the bedroom, closing the door behind her with quiet care. She'd expected to have second thoughts this morning—afternoon, she realized, glancing with some embarrassment at the clock—but she'd made her decision last night knowing that.

She dressed out in the hallway, then went down the short flight of stairs to the lower level. She'd gotten to the point where she rarely thought about it anymore, but after last night the memories had been stirred back to vivid life. Such a simple thing, going down a mere eight steps. . . .

She went through the routine of preparing the coffee—Ryan strength—automatically, without thought, without really seeing what she was doing.

She didn't remember much about that night. Only that heartrending moment when she realized she was actually going to fall. And later a blurred, split-second vision of Ryan's face and the realization of how badly she was hurt, made clear by the terror in his eyes. And much later the crushing, crippling knowledge that she had lost the precious life growing inside her. The baby she had wanted so much, because it would give her a part of Ryan she could hold forever, as she could never be sure of having the man himself.

At night while you slept I used to sit on the floor in that nursery we painted and cry.

Lacey shivered, rubbing her arms as if the sensation came from outside instead of within her. She didn't know which had stunned her more, the fierce, powerful reminder of just how high she could fly with Ryan, or the shock those tautly spoken words had inflicted on her. Ryan, crying? In their baby's room?

The incredible images that formed in her mind were matched only by her shock that he had told her at all. If she had had to judge by his actions, at least the ones she had seen, she would have said their unborn son's death had been merely a faint ripple in his life, nowhere near as upsetting as the time a murder suspect had been released on a technicality.

At night while you slept I used to sit on the floor in that nursery we painted and cry.

Ryan Buckhart, huddled on the floor in that gaily painted room, amid the baby paraphernalia they had already begun to accumulate as she had neared the last two months of her pregnancy, tears in his dark eyes, perhaps even streaking down his strong-boned face, was an image that made her want to begin crying herself all over again.

But he'd never told her. He'd simply gone on, stoic, silent, as if unmoved by the death of the baby they had never had a chance to name, had never held.

I couldn't let my pain matter. I had to be strong for you.

Had that really been it? Had he thought it was helping her to think she was the only one feeling this agony, this debilitating sense of loss? Had he somehow thought that by not admitting his own pain, he was easing hers?

She poured the water into the coffeemaker and set the pot in place. Rubbing her arms yet again, thinking this night had drained her energies in many more ways than the one she'd expected when she'd admitted she wanted him enough to risk the inevitable pain that would follow, she went outside to pick up the local morning paper. She'd arranged to stop delivery while she was gone, but had kept it coming until today to have something to read on the plane. As it was, she hadn't read a paper since the night Ryan had broken down her door, and her eyes were too weary and sore from her outpouring of tears to read this one now, but she would look at it later, she thought.

After, she thought suddenly, with more than a touch of grimness, she called her mother and told her that she definitely wouldn't be there by early afternoon as planned.

She sighed. Her mother would not be happy. But if she knew why—and had the slightest inkling that her daughter had spent the night naked in the arms of her ex-husband—she would be furious. And right now Lacey simply was not up to dealing with that.

Maybe she could use a cup of that Ryan-strength coffee after all, she thought wryly as she walked back into the kitchen where it was already filling the room with the familiar aroma. She tossed the newspaper, already slightly yellowed by a morning lying untouched in the California sun, on the counter and reached for a mug from the cupboard, tapping her finger on the rim while she waited for the pot to finish filling with the painfully dark brew. Then, despite her inner turmoil, she had to smile at herself, waiting impatiently for coffee that once would have taken ten times as long to make.

She set the mug down on the counter beside the paper. And froze, staring at the headline.

Three days. He'd been gone only three days. But the Pack had already slipped the leash and was wreaking havoc on the streets of Marina Heights. And the Trinity West cops were under siege.

Chapter 8

At first Ryan put her edginess down to what had happened between them last night. Lord knew he was antsy enough himself over it, knowing it had resolved nothing, had accomplished nothing, except to make him even painfully more aware of what he'd lost. He felt marginally better for having at last admitted to his own pain at their baby's death, but he doubted it meant anything to her at this late date, beyond proving that she'd been right to get rid of the man who had been the cause of it all.

But by late afternoon he realized that it was more than that. Lacey wasn't just having second thoughts, she was nervous. Nervous in a way that didn't fit with what they'd done. Unless . . .

A sudden possibility hit him. He set down his knife and the piece he'd been finishing up. A possibility that, like the idiot he was, hadn't occurred to him. He swallowed, then shoved a hand through hair still damp from the quick shower he'd taken after he'd realized he'd slept more than half the day away after the night he'd never dared hope to have.

"Lacey?"

She looked up from the remains of their toasted bagels and peanut butter. It had been about all that had been left in the cupboard, reminding him that she'd been ready to leave for her parents' house today. He would deal with that later—right now, this was more important. Much more important.

"What?" she asked when he didn't go on for a moment.

"I... we didn't take any... Are you still on the pill?"

After the miscarriage she'd been on the pill for several months. Long enough for their marriage to finish falling apart, anyway.

She gave him a sideways look. "That was three years ago."

"I know, but—"

"There was... no reason to be," she said.

Although she'd told him as much last night, Ryan couldn't deny he was, perhaps unfairly, glad to hear her say it in so many words. Except for the fact that it made what they'd done last night even more foolish than he'd already known it was.

"It's all right, Ryan," she said wryly. "My judgment may be severely impaired when it comes to sex with you, but I'm not an utter fool."

You're not the only one whose judgment is haywire, he muttered inwardly. "It's all right? What does that mean?"

"It's a bit late to ask, but there was... some scarring. I'd have to have corrective surgery to get pregnant."

She was right, he told himself coldly. It was too late. And he deserved the answer he'd gotten, an answer that only added to the pain and guilt.

"Besides," she said, her voice hovering on the edge of bitterness, "do you really think I'd risk that again?"

He winced at her tone and at the implication of her words. He couldn't blame her, he thought again. She'd almost died because of him, because of his baby. Why should he think she would ever want to risk herself again? Especially with him, when he'd failed her so miserably? Of course she wouldn't have gone to bed with him if there was a chance she would get pregnant.

He stood, started to gather the plates they'd used, then stopped.

"I'm sorry," he said stiffly, thinking he'd apologized more to this woman than he had to anyone in his life. But then, he'd hurt her more than he'd hurt anyone in his life. "You're right, this was far too late to ask. I should have made sure last night, before we..."

"You should have known I wouldn't take a chance like that," Lacey corrected.

He looked at her for a long, silent moment. "Yes," he said at last, "I suppose I should have."

He began to clear the table. He put the plates and the knives in the dishwasher, trying not to think of the day they'd installed it and one of the hoses had broken loose, spraying the room wildly. They'd both been drenched, and Ryan had learned in a rush the appeal of a wet T-shirt on a woman as nicely distributed as Lacey. That incident had ended as so many had, in the big brass bed, after Lacey had pointed out to him that she thought he looked rather nice in a wet T-shirt himself.

He opened the cabinet to shove the used napkins into the trash basket, also trying not to think about the fact that he was almost certain, although he didn't know why, that that had been the day they'd conceived the baby.

He couldn't think about that. He didn't dare.

"I should check in," he muttered, desperate for any change of subject. "Or Mallery will be in an uproar. He'll—"

The headline on the crumpled newspaper caught his eye first. The Pack, it said, on the only part he could see. He fished it out of the trash and straightened. He unfolded it and read the entire headline. And the first couple of paragraphs of the grim story beneath it.

And then he turned around to find Lacey staring at him. He read in her wide, impossibly blue eyes the knowledge of what he'd found.

"You. . . read this?"

To her credit, she didn't deny it. But then, Lacey Buckhart had never been short on nerve. "Yes."

"And then threw it away?"

"Yes," she repeated, then added, ruefully, "I see I should have burned it."

He wanted to ask why, but he doubted he would get much of an answer. Her delicate jaw was set, her chin up, as if daring him to ask. He'd learned quickly not to push when she was feeling that way. He turned back to the newspaper and the account of the violence since Alarico's arrest.

He hadn't thought it would happen so soon. He'd known the Pack would be in turmoil after the loss of their second leader in just a few months, but he'd hoped they would flounder for a while before anything happened. Obviously that had been a futile notion. From all appearances, they were on the verge of either going completely out of control or self-destructing.

He looked again at the ugly list of crimes, from thefts to robberies to assaults. Innocent people had been threatened, robbed, beaten and shot at. The local emergency room had been overwhelmed. The cops of Trinity West were fighting to regain peace in the streets, while being blasted from all sides for not somehow preventing the crime spree.

Guilt grabbed him, clawing at his gut; he should have been there to stop this. Carlos's fingerprints were all over this rampage; he was the most violence-prone of the remaining lieutenants of the Pack, and the one Ryan had judged most likely to try to take over.

He dropped the paper back on the counter and strode across the kitchen to the doorway. Without another glance at Lacey he went into the living room and walked to the telephone. He dialed a number, let it ring twice, hung up and dialed again. After three rings he heard the receiver being picked up, but no one spoke.

"It's Ryan," he said into the receiver.

"Ah. Contrary to what I've heard, I suspected we had not seen the last of you, my friend."

The voice was soft and melodious, and the image of Carny Lang was as clear as if the muscular black man was standing right there, his customary smile bright against his skin. If there was such a thing as a man who should be head of the Pack, it was this calm, well-spoken man, Ryan thought.

"What have you heard?" he asked.

"That you took a bullet when Alarico was taken."

"It wasn't serious."

"You are recovering?"

"Nicely, thank you," Ryan said with mocking politeness.

Carny laughed. "You will be returning, then?"

"Yes. And no one needs to know that yet but you."

There was a pause. "All right. You were handpicked by Alarico, so I will abide by your wishes. And I will watch this with great interest," he said.

"I'm sure you will. I'll be too busy watching my back for Carlos."

Carny laughed again, louder, longer and more genuine this time. "It's a wise man who knows which flank to protect. He has been spreading the story that you have deserted us."

"That figures."

"He is gathering those who think as he does. He hasn't the nerve to do it openly, but they've been seen meeting."

Ryan didn't question the man's knowledge; Carny simply had a way of hearing things, and they were usually right.

"Meeting where?"

"A place around the corner on Trinity."

"The old pawn shop where he holds his crap games?"

"I believe so."

"So he's recruiting, is he? I presume he's behind all this . . . stupidity?"

He knew he was pushing, on the edge of violating the Pack's code of protecting each other, but Carny had always seemed to have more sense than the rest of them.

"He has . . . expressed a desire for more authority." Ryan could almost see the man shrug. "I believe he thinks this is the way to do it."

"You're giving him too much credit, my friend. Thinking and Carlos are barely acquainted."

That laugh came again, the deep, genuine laugh that made Ryan wonder what on earth Carny was doing mixed up with a bunch of scum like the Pack.

"Perhaps," Carny said. "But I will tell you, Ryan. He has said he will kill you if you do come back."

"Thanks for the warning, Carny."

"You will need more than that. Things are extremely uncertain on Steele Street these days."

Ryan hung up, knowing how bad things must be for the usually unruffled Carny to make such a statement. And wondering what the hell he was supposed to do about it. What *could* he do? Was the Pack under whatever control he could exert better than the Pack on the loose? Should he try to interject some kind of restraint, or would it be better in the long run to simply let them disintegrate, and concentrate on damage control?

If he went for direct control, he would be up against Carlos, and he knew the man was more than a little crazy. He didn't think Carlos would have the nerve to take him one-on-one, but . . .

He twisted slightly, testing his side. It was still tender, but the shower hadn't bothered him, and he thought he could withstand anything short of a direct hit of some power. But even if he did go back and try to reestablish his position with the Pack, could he possibly get things back under control before they pulled him out?

"Ryan?"

He nearly jumped; he was so lost in thought he hadn't heard Lacey come in. He wondered how long she'd been there, how much she'd heard. He went back over what he'd said and told himself that even if she'd heard it all, she wouldn't have heard enough to get her into trouble. He wondered if he was right, or if that was simply wishful thinking.

She moved, coming to stand beside him. He glanced at her. She was looking at him as if she'd guessed exactly why he'd been testing the healing of his wound. He shifted his eyes, staring down at the phone, unable to look at her.

"Is there... news?" she asked tentatively.

"Nothing I didn't already know," he said.

Six months. Six months of the worst kind of undercover work, day after day with the kind of scum that just made him itch to get them off the street, convincing them he was one of them. Six months of living a lie, until it became so real he sometimes jumped when a police unit drove by. Six months of feeling so dirty that he often found himself standing in the shower until the water ran icy cold, trying to scrub it off. And it was all about to go down the drain as quickly as that dirty water.

His mouth twisted bitterly. "Six damn months down the tubes." He jammed a hand into his hair, shoving the long strands back from his face. "Not that it matters."

"What doesn't matter?"

He let out a long, weary breath. "I'm not sure anything does anymore."

He walked back into the kitchen, then just stood there, staring at the tile floor they'd put down, wondering why everything in his life had gotten so damned complicated since the day he'd lost Lacey.

Lacey watched him go, but what she was really seeing was that moment when he'd flexed, as if testing just how much his side had healed. As if he needed to know. And there was only one reason he would be thinking about it. He was going to go back. But at the same time, she remembered his expression when he'd said he wasn't sure anything mattered anymore. She'd never seen that look on Ryan's face before, and it bothered her. Just as the way he'd talked about his job before dinner last night bothered her.

After a few minutes he came back into the living room. He sat down on the sofa. The late-afternoon sunlight slanted through the windows, a shaft of it setting off the blue-black highlights in his hair. He gathered up his socks and boots, obviously ready to put them on.

"What doesn't matter anymore?" she repeated as she sat a careful three feet away from him. She didn't dare get any closer. It would start those singing, searing memories of last night flowing again, and she would lose track of what she was asking. And for some reason she couldn't grasp, it seemed very important to understand why he'd looked the way he had.

"Nothing."

"Was that 'Nothing matters,' or the old 'Lacey, go away, I'm not going to talk to you about this'?"

His head snapped up. "The what?"

"You heard me."

He just looked at her for a moment, and she saw something flicker deep in his obsidian eyes, something even darker, pained somehow.

"Is that... how you felt?"

"Frequently," she said, but refused to be diverted. "What doesn't matter?" she asked for a third time.

Ryan sighed and shoved his long hair back with the motion that was so familiar to her.

"Nothing," he said again.

Stung, Lacey drew back and started to get up. There was no reason to subject herself to this anymore.

"Lacey, wait. I meant that... literally."

She eased back down to her seat. "Nothing matters?"

His mouth twisted into that same bitter curve she'd seen in the kitchen. "I guess I just don't see the point anymore. It's all so damn futile."

She waited, scarcely daring to breathe. He couldn't be saying what she thought he was saying, not Detective Ryan Buckhart.

"We run around like crazy," he said, waving an arm in a sharp motion of disgust, "trying to plug all the leaks, and we don't affect what's behind the dam at all. So we catch a bad guy here and there, and if the courts don't let him go, he may do some time. But he's back on the streets before we've cleared our next case. And if he's not, ten more just like him have stepped in to take his place. We're not even running in place anymore. We're losing ground faster than we ever gained it."

Lacey stared at him. She'd never heard him talk like this. She would have sworn she never would. Not Ryan. Not the man who repeatedly drove himself to the edge for a cause she'd always been half-convinced was already lost. He'd never sounded so defeated.

And she hated it.

She couldn't believe it. She couldn't believe her own reaction. She'd always cursed the fact that he never knew when to give up, that he gave and gave and then gave some more to a system that seemed capable only of minimizing losses, never stopping the drain from those leaks he spoke of. He gave so much that she'd sometimes felt there was nothing left for her. She had always thought she would treasure the day when he realized he was giving too much, that no matter what he did it would never, ever be enough. Because no matter how much he or his fellow officers gave, they would always be outnumbered and outgunned.

And now that it seemed he had, she hated it. She hated seeing him like this, hated hearing him sound like this. And with a little shock she realized that his stubborn determination to never give up was one of the things she had most admired about him.

She watched, unable to think of a thing to say in the face of this contradiction she'd discovered in herself. He picked up his socks and pulled them on. Then he reached for the shirt she'd washed in a useless effort to rid it of his blood. Inanely, Lacey remembered that he always put his boots on last. One of the little habits that made him uniquely Ryan.

She studied his face, saw the doggedness in the set of his jaw, the tightness of his mouth. And the weariness in his eyes.

"You're going back," she whispered.

"Of course I'm going back." His gaze narrowed as he looked at her. "And I'm trusting you, Lacey. Not to tell anyone that I was here, or hurt, or that I've gone back. Or that I don't have control at the moment."

She stared at him, shaking her head in pained wonder. "After everything you just said, you're going back?"

He stopped in the midst of unfolding the shirt to pull it over his head.

"I still have a job to do."

"A job that nearly got you killed," Lacey snapped. "Again."

"It wasn't that serious. You know that."

She leapt to her feet, smothering an exasperated exclamation. "Only because you were damn lucky, Buckhart. What about next time? Or the next? That luck is going to run out someday."

Ryan rose in turn, discarding his shirt as he eyed her warily. She supposed it was a reflex with him, to use his size to point out the foolishness of crossing him, but she still didn't appreciate having to look up at him. But if he thought she was going to be intimidated by his sheer size, he was wrong. Very wrong.

The fact that the only reason she could take such a stand was an utter trust that he would never use his size against her flitted through her mind, but she refused to dwell on it, not now.

"What am I supposed to do?" he asked. "Give up? Walk away and let the Pack run riot through the streets, maybe all the way up here to Trinity West?"

And get to you? He didn't say it, but Lacey heard it as clearly as if he had. She didn't try to tell him again that protecting her wasn't his personal responsibility; she'd already seen how useless that was. But she couldn't help trying another tack.

"But if you don't believe it's doing any good anymore..."

"What I believe doesn't make any difference."

"What about your life, Ryan? Does that make any difference?"

For a long, silent moment he just looked at her. "I don't know, Lacey," he said softly. "Does it?"

He'd caught her so off guard, slipped beneath the shield of her anger and her exasperation so neatly, that before she could stop herself, tears welled up in her eyes. He'd told her once that no one in his life had ever really cared if he lived or died except for her. He'd said it not as a ploy to rouse any tender feelings in her, but merely as simple truth, as he explained why it was so hard for him to accept that she worried about him.

And the most horrible part of it was that she knew that for most of his life it had been true. It wasn't true now. There were people who cared, people like Cruz and Gage, but was it really Ryan's fault that he thought it still was?

"Damn you," she whispered.

He was beside her in an instant, his strong fingers gripping her shoulders. She lifted her hands, curling them into fists, wanting to strike out, hating herself for being such a fool when it came to this man, even as she ached inside for him once more. Instead she let him pull her to him, let him loosen her fists and place her palms flat against his chest.

"I think we established my state of damnation a long time ago," he said quietly.

"Don't give up," she whispered.

"What?"

"Don't give up. You can't think it's all for nothing. Not you. Not Ryan Buckhart."

"You always told me I never knew when to quit. Maybe I've finally learned."

She shook her head, aware that wetness was tracing its way down her cheeks, but unwilling to pull her hands free from his to wipe the tears away.

"You always said you prayed for the day I'd quit pushing so hard."

"I was wrong. You can't be anyone but who you are, Ryan."

He went very still. "But you...can't live with who I am."

"I can't live with what it means. You risk yourself so freely. You could never see... that part of you had become part of me, and you had no right to risk that."

"Ah, Lacey," he said on a long exhalation that she felt leave his chest.

"You give so much, Ryan. I know it must have seemed unfair for me to ask that you give more. But I needed more. I needed you to keep yourself safe for me."

"Lace, I'm a cop—"

"I know. And I accepted that. I know how much it means to you. Perhaps more than you realize."

She did know what it meant to him to have finally found a place where he could belong, where he'd found the family he'd never had in the kinship of the uniform. So when she went on, it was in a tone of gentle understanding.

"But being a cop doesn't mean you always have to be the one to take the chances, to risk yourself."

"It's not always me," he insisted. "Cruz defused that bomb when it would have gone off long before the bomb squad got there. And Clay—"

"I know. Three medals of valor. You learned from the best in Clay Yeager. But..." She hesitated, then plunged ahead. "He paid an awful price for being the kind of cop he was."

Ryan went pale beneath his bronze complexion. "Yes. He did."

Lacey slipped her arms around him, half-expecting him to pull away, as he always seemed to when talk turned to the man who had been his savior as much as his mentor, before Yeager's life had disintegrated into nothing more than ugly debris.

"I'm sorry, Ryan. I know you don't like to talk about him."

"You always said there was too much I don't like to talk about."

She sighed. "Perhaps I talk too much, period."

She heard him chuckle, a faint but definite sound of amusement. She tilted her head back to look up at him. One corner of his mouth was lifted in the barest hint of a smile, to match the slight laugh.

A long, silent moment spun out between them. Lacey felt the moment when it changed, felt the moment when heat began in the instant before it lit Ryan's dark eyes. She had time to move but couldn't seem to do it. And then his mouth was on hers, claiming it in the way only Ryan could, demanding yet coaxing at the same time. He traced her lips with his tongue, delved farther and tasted the soft inner lining. She opened for him because she could do nothing else, and he flicked the tip of her tongue with his own.

He tasted hot, male and faintly exotic, and she couldn't stop herself from accepting the tacit invitation when he withdrew. She probed with her own tongue over the firm fullness of his lower lip, past the even ridge of his teeth, until she found the rough, wet velvet of his tongue and stroked it. A shiver rippled through her at the taste and feel of him, so familiar yet so strange, so precious and so long missed.

He gave a low, husky groan. And then, unexpectedly, he broke the kiss. He stood looking down at her, and Lacey saw the full force of the fire she'd kindled in him reflected in his dark eyes.

She knew she should back away now, before this had a chance to go any further. Last night had been sweet, hot and achingly familiar. It had salved the torturous longing but made the time to come without him again even more torturous. If she let this happen, if she let the need for him overcome her common sense yet again, she would be ripping open a wound that had never completely healed in the first place.

But perhaps that was the only way to treat this particular wound. Perhaps it had never healed because it had festered. Perhaps she needed to sear it closed with the same heat that had caused it.

And perhaps, she thought ruefully, she was just looking for excuses. Reasons to justify what she'd wanted to do since the moment she'd seen the change in Ryan's eyes.

"It's your call," Ryan said softly, as if he'd read every nuance of her dilemma in her face. As he might well have, she thought wryly. She'd learned long ago the benefits—and price—of being married to a trained observer.

She hesitated. She could come up with a hundred reasons not to do this. A hundred reasons, from the pain and confusion it would cause, to the temptation to try to rebuild something that shouldn't have been put together in the first place. And a hundred more justifications for doing it. From the foolish thought that she might be able to burn this need for him out of herself in one final blaze, to the melodramatic yet grimly real possibility that he might walk out of this house and really get himself killed this time.

"I know, Lace. I know."

He whispered it with gentle understanding and regret. Relief trickled through her. But then he let go of her, and she thought she'd never felt so cold.

Ryan's leaving her had always made her cold. Inside and out. And it would make her cold again, so very cold, no matter that she knew it had to be. So what did it matter if she delayed it just for a little while longer? Especially when she knew this would be their last night together. She wasn't fool enough to think she could survive watching him walk away from her a third time.

In the moment when he was about to turn away from her, she reached out and touched his arm. He turned back. She opened her mouth to speak but saw by the flare of passion in his eyes that she didn't have to.

Ryan reached for her. He picked her up as easily as he ever had, despite the fact that her own muscled fitness made her heavier than she looked.

She noticed that this time he didn't ask her if she was sure.

Chapter 9

If there was an element of desperation in her lovemaking, Ryan was matching it with his own, Lacey thought. It was as if he, too, was thinking this was the last time they would ever do this, the last time their hands would touch each other, stroke each other, seek out the places so familiar, yet still so wondrous, that made them uncommonly matched in this, if nothing else.

He used everything he'd ever learned about her body to drive her mad, but she couldn't blame him, when she had done the very same thing. She touched every place, made every move, that she had ever discovered made him gasp or groan. She stroked every inch of that hot, satin-smooth skin she could reach. She let her fingers trace every curve of muscle, every hollow, until she could feel his heart pounding beneath her fingertips.

And now she tangled her fingers in his hair, loving the heavy silken feel of it as it slid over her skin. She ran her hands over his shoulders, then down along the straight, strong indentation of his spine to cup his muscled buttocks and pull him tighter into her. She lifted her head and flicked her tongue over his chest, circling his nipples until they drew up even tighter and he let out a hissing breath.

He hastened the rhythm of his driving thrusts, and Lacey welcomed the fierce pounding, crying out his name at the depth of each stroke, wishing it could go on forever and already crying inwardly because she knew it couldn't. She looked up at his face, shadowed by the thick, dark mane of his hair. She reached up and pulled his head down toward her just slightly, until his hair was brushing over her skin with every movement of his sweat-sheened body.

His gaze met hers then, and she saw the flash of understanding there. He shifted one hand to her own tangled fall of hair and threaded his fingers through it. It was a moment of sensual agreement that seemed somehow even more intimate than the joining of their bodies, and Lacey felt herself surge in response to the unspoken exchange.

She felt his hand slide between their bodies and knew it had affected him the same way, that moment of silent communion. Convulsively her hips arched upward, offering herself for the touch she knew would send her soaring. It came, his finger gently probing, then caressing, as his body continued the pounding tempo.

And a moment later her own body was gathering itself for the flight. She clutched at his shoulders, moaning. His nostrils flared, and he shifted himself slightly upward, his rigid flesh sliding over the spot he'd been stroking. She moaned, then nearly screamed as the convulsions took her, pulsing through her in hot, heavy beats that made her so sweetly aware of that part of him those muscles deep inside her were stroking in turn.

Her urge was to close her eyes; anything more than what she was feeling was too much. But then Ryan cried out her name, arching into her like a bow, throwing his head back, his long hair flowing down his back as he ground his hips against her, and she couldn't look away from the beauty of his face as the pleasure took him. As the last spasms of her body died away she felt the hot, molten rush as he pulsed inside her, shuddering over her as he said her name again in a low, guttural moan that was the sweetest sound she'd ever heard.

And the most mournful, for it was tinged with all the regret, all the acknowledgment of impossibility, she herself was feeling.

But still, when he reached for her again—and then again, and again, into the night—she went to him willingly, eagerly. She met his urgency with her own, and by silent agreement they thought of nothing beyond this night.

And even though she knew it had changed nothing, she couldn't regret having seen him like this one last time.

You expected this. You knew *it was going to happen like this. So you have absolutely no right to be angry.*

Stepping out of the shower, Lacey toweled herself off, rubbed at her hair, then with sharp, angry movements dressed in jeans and a fresh silk blouse. She grabbed a comb and began to drag it through her tangled hair, ordering herself to stop thinking about useless things she had no control over. Think about something you can do something about, she ordered herself.

She needed to make a decision now. Should she cancel her trip to San Francisco altogether and go through the hassle of trying to explain to her mother, who was already upset that she was a day late? Try to explain without telling her the real reason? She couldn't say she was sick or her mother would be on the next plane south. Nor could she say she had to go back to work. One phone call would catch her in that lie.

Lacey sighed. She'd never been much good at lying to her mother, anyway. As a child, she'd always been caught. Maybe she should just go and hope that her mother wouldn't sense something was wrong and try to worm it out of her. Her mother having a fit because she thought her daughter was involved with her ex-husband again was the last thing Lacey needed.

The first thing she needed was a distraction. And trying to keep what had happened in the past few days a secret from her mother would certainly accomplish that. But she couldn't stop herself from wondering what her mother would say if she told her what Ryan had said, how he'd felt about coming between them. Would it make any difference? Could anything change the way her parents felt about Ryan?

She nearly laughed aloud at herself then; what did it matter what they felt? Ryan was gone. Again. Gone out of her life, this time forever. She knew that. He'd only come back this time because he'd been hurt. And she found herself beginning the self-lecture all over again.

What did you think, that you'd wake up this morning and he would still be here, and you could have a leisurely breakfast while you again explained to him all the reasons he shouldn't go back to the Pack and give them the chance to really get him killed this time?

She slammed the comb down on the bathroom counter. The cluttered counter Ryan had always teased her about as the one place where she failed utterly in maintaining any semblance of order.

The memory did nothing to ease her mood. She didn't know which was worse, that she'd apparently been foolish enough to harbor some hidden hope that something might change, or that she was letting herself get worked up over what she knew had been inevitable. Ryan was gone, just as she'd known he would be, leaving no sign he'd ever been there except for the slight swelling of her lips and the lingering awareness between her thighs. Bittersweet reminders of his presence and her own reckless stupidity.

She stalked out through the bedroom, managing not to slam the door behind her. She headed for the kitchen, intent on coffee. *Her* kind of coffee today, drinkable, not so strong it made your hair stand on end. Never again would she look into a mug and have it glare back at her. Never again.

She stopped dead in front of the machine. Her mug was on the counter, waiting, and the coffee was already there, the way she liked it, not Ryan's heavy brew. But that wasn't what stopped her in her tracks.

Beside the machine was a small carving, no wider than her cup was across. With a hand that was shaking she picked it up, cradling it gently in her palm. Two tiny, bewhiskered, whimsical faces looked back at her.

Otters, she realized. Sea otters. Two of them. One male, one female, although she wasn't quite sure how she knew that, except that one had a delicate little chin and a sassy nose that made it seem a natural conclusion. The other wore an expression she could only describe as...hopeful. The pair were intertwined in an intricate way that made the carving seem even more unique than she already knew it was.

It was unique, all right. Ryan had carved a fanciful menagerie for her from the moment she had first expressed wonder and delight at the creatures he produced with that unlikely tool, his huge knife. But never before had he done this. Never had he produced something like this.

Never had he carved a pair.

The tiny duo seemed to shift, to move. Lacey blinked and realized it was her own tears that had blurred her vision. Sea otters. A species once thought to be extinct, brought back with love and care. And Ryan had left them for her to find.

What was she supposed to see in this little carving? Was she supposed to wonder what he'd meant by it? Was there hidden in the clever lines, the intricate details, the whimsical expressions, a message? Was it a hope that they, like the otters, could be brought back to life?

Her fingers curled around the tiny pair. She was filled with the urge to find him, to ask him what he'd meant by this. But she knew she couldn't. She wouldn't know where to begin to look for him, and if she even tried, Ryan would never forgive her. So what was she to do? Sit here and wait, hoping he would come back and explain, or at least contact her?

The image of herself sitting by the phone like some forlorn teenager waiting for a call that would never come made her mouth twist into a mocking grimace.

"*Bennetts, my dear, don't wait for anyone. People wait for* us."

Perhaps that was what she needed, Lacey thought wryly, a good healthy dose of her family's arrogance. Maybe that would give her back her sense of perspective.

Anything, she thought, would be better than sitting around here waiting for a call from Ryan that would never come. Or for a grim call from Cruz, or the chief, or the chaplain, that she was all too certain would come, sooner or later.

She strode back to the bedroom determinedly. She ignored the tossed bed and the memories it brought back. She finished packing her suitcase.

At the last moment she carefully tucked the pair of otters inside.

Ryan knew he was walking a tightrope, and he wasn't any too sure of his balance right now. His reappearance at the Pack's Steele Street warehouse had been met with surprise by some, disgruntlement by others and, by a few, with merely the air of an expectation fulfilled.

But then Carlos had arrived, furious at finding Ryan in the leader's office, blurting threats and wild speculations about Ryan's part in Alarico's arrest, his failure to prevent it, his part in accepting into their midst the man who had turned out to be a cop.

Ryan watched him warily, knowing everything depended on how he handled this. He was going to need every bit of luck fate would allow him.

That luck is going to run out someday.

Lacey's words rang in his ears, as her image had been dancing in his head since the moment he'd taken a last, longing look at her as she lay curled in sleep in their bed. He knew it had been the last time, no matter how this turned out. Even if he survived, it would make no difference; all the things that had destroyed them before were still there.

Carlos's angry words yanked him back. He'd better get his head back in the game, he thought grimly, or it was going to get chopped off.

"Alarico, he trusted you," the tall, gaunt man said. "Called you his lieutenant and left you in charge. But I'm not such a trusting man."

"Then you're smarter than I gave you credit for," Ryan returned, noting that, as usual, Carlos's eyes looked unnaturally wide and dark, and his skin damp. "I take that back," he said. "Still shooting up, are you? Very, very stupid, Carlos. Which means it was you behind that half-witted string of crap that's going to bring the Trinity West cops down on us like a swarm of locusts."

Carlos swore, low and ugly, then added a string of invective to emphasize it.

Ryan laughed. "Since I have no idea who my ancestors were, insulting them doesn't mean a thing to me."

"Then I'll just scalp you when I kill you, Indian. Maybe that will remind you of what you are."

"You're welcome to try," Ryan said affably, holding his hands out as if in invitation.

For a long moment, longer than Ryan would have expected he had the nerve for, Carlos met his gaze. The drugs, he thought, giving the skinny man the courage he otherwise lacked. It was easy to be brave when your fried brain was telling you you couldn't die.

But the man finally broke and, with another muttered curse, turned on his heel and stalked out.

"I still would not turn my back on him," Carny said in a tone that was mildly amused rather than warning.

"I won't. I don't even like him in front of me," Ryan said wryly.

The black man looked at him, considering. "Speculation has been . . . quite wild here. You are . . . well now?"

"Well enough." Ryan gave the man a speculative look. "Planning to take me on?"

Carny smiled widely. "Not I, my friend. I like living. Even wounded, you are not a man I would care to fight."

"Good," Ryan said succinctly.

"I cannot say as much for our friend Carlos, however."

"Carlos is a fool."

"But a fool who has some . . . influence among the other fools surrounding us."

Ryan stared at the man, curious, and not for the first time. But this time he did something he rarely did; he gave in to that curiosity.

"Who are you, Carny?"

The smile came again, that easy, wide, misleading smile. "I am who I am. Don't waste your time trying to figure me out, Ryan. You have, as they say, larger fish to fry."

Ryan smiled wryly, acknowledging the neat deflection. "How much support does he have?"

"Not so much, but it is among the most dangerous."

Ryan knew what he meant. And he wasn't surprised; a man as prone to violence as Carlos was would naturally attract others of the same ilk.

"And the rest?"

"Some are willing to go along with the succession of Alarico's choice as second in command. The rest will wait and see if you're strong enough to hold power."

Was he? Could he possibly hope to rein in the chaos? Could he, when he seemed to have lost the belief that it would do any good, that plugging up this one little leak in the dam would make any difference at all?

Don't give up. You can't think it's all for nothing. Not you. Not Ryan Buckhart.

Lacey. Of all people to tell him not to give up, the woman who had always prayed he would. The woman who had tried so hard to get him to place his own welfare first, to put the instinct for self-preservation over the instinct to act.

"If they see weakness in you," Carny said, shaking Ryan out of his dangerous—in many senses of the word—reverie, "they will go with Carlos, even knowing he is crazy."

This time Carny's tone was warning. It was far enough out of character that Ryan took heed. "And you?" he asked quietly. "What will you do?"

Carny shrugged. "I have no wish to follow a crazy man. He will get others killed along with himself, and I do not want to be one of them."

Ryan knew he shouldn't, knew it might make the man suspicious, but he couldn't help himself. Something about this man didn't fit. He didn't belong here, not in this life.

"Ever think about a different line of work?"

Carny laughed. "One with a longer life expectancy? Often, Ryan, often."

The man was still smiling as he walked out the door. And Ryan sat there for a long time, pondering. Carlos's threats, Carny's warning . . . and Lacey's words. Trying not to think about what had happened so unexpectedly between them.

And trying to keep himself from running back to her right now. He wondered if she'd found the otters, if she'd read what he'd tried to carve into them, tried as desperately as if he were carving it into his soul. Wondered if it would matter to her if she did.

But most of all he wondered what had possessed him to harbor any faint hope that, after three years, their relationship wasn't completely dead and buried. True, the sparks still flew between them, and the fire those sparks lit was the most consuming, searing thing he'd ever known. But he also knew, as Lacey had said, that it wasn't enough. Not when he seemed to hurt her by his very existence.

They pitied me for being married to. . . the man who would never share the biggest thing in his life with me.

The sound of a man tentatively clearing his throat brought him back to the present. He swore inwardly. If he didn't stop all this mooning over Lacey, her grim belief was going to become truth—he was going to get himself killed.

He looked up at the small, wiry man in the doorway. Jimmy Crawford, he realized, the ex-con who had recognized Romero and tipped Alarico off. There was something else he should remember about the man tickling the back of his mind, but he couldn't nail it down just yet.

With a conscious effort Ryan slipped back into the persona he'd established here. He'd been far too talkative with Carny, much more so than the Pack had come to expect. He was going to have to watch it. Carelessness—that was what happened when you were out of character for a while.

Out of character and back, for however short and self-deluding a time, in your old life.

Yanking his mind out of what he was very much afraid was going to become a well-worn groove, he lifted a brow at the man in the doorway.

"Me an' the boys... well, some of 'em... are wondering what you're gonna do. Some of us are broke, you know?" Crawford said.

Yeah, Ryan thought sourly. It's tough hanging on to your money when there's all that crack calling your name.

The thought of the drug made the memory he'd been trying to pin down slide into place. Lenny. Jimmy was Lenny's best friend. He wondered if that loose end had been tidied up by Romero, as well. He didn't doubt it; the man had meant to take down Eddie's killers, and Ryan had no doubt that he had. But it would be nice to know.

"You and Lenny strung out again?" he asked casually.

Crawford flushed. Ryan stood, and the flush vanished as the much smaller man paled. "I... Lenny... he's in j-jail," Jimmy stammered out.

Ryan lifted a brow and waited, silently.

"He... that cop, the one that snuck in here and busted Alarico, he did it. He found out Lenny shot that kid up with that stuff."

Rest in peace, Eddie, Ryan thought. Romero had indeed gotten it done.

"Guess you're right," Crawford said. "It don't pay to piss off the cops."

"Sucking up to me doesn't pay, either, Crawford." The man flushed. "You tell your friends that thanks to Carlos's stupidity, we're going to be sitting tight for a while. We've got to let the dust settle or every Trinity West cop out there is going to be on our butts any time we step outside. You'll be lucky if your supply of rock candy doesn't dry up altogether."

Crawford's eyes widened with horror at the thought. "You think it will?"

"You'd better stock up while there's still any around," Ryan said, his mouth twisting at the fact that this shocked the man, whereas the murder of a fourteen-year-old boy meant less than nothing.

"But we need money."

"Then get Carlos to lend it to you. He got us into this mess, going off on that rampage, stirring up the whole damn town."

Crawford wheeled and ran off. Carlos wasn't going to like this. But Ryan had bought some time. And planted the idea that the Pack was going to ground, at least for a while. Whether they accepted the idea—and him—was yet to be seen. But he'd made a start. It was all he could do.

And if he didn't stop thinking about Lacey, if flashes of hot, erotic memories didn't stop careening through his mind without warning, it was going to be all he could do to keep from going out of his mind.

Chapter 10

She was, Lacey thought wearily, more exhausted than before her supposed vacation had begun. She'd been exhausted since the morning she'd awakened to find Ryan gone. . . and a pair of hopeful otters left behind.

She lifted her suitcase off the baggage carousel, grateful for its wheels as she pulled out the retractable handle and began to make her way out of the busy terminal of the county airport. She smiled, as she always did, at the huge bronze statue of the famous actor the airport had been named after—an irony he wouldn't have appreciated, since he'd hated the noise it created while alive—and headed for the parking garage.

Five days with her mother had drained her more effectively than if she'd circled the globe in those days. She'd finally turned tail and run, leaving a day earlier than she'd planned, unable to take it any longer. Subtly—Bennetts were never obvious—the pressure for her to return to San Francisco permanently had been relentless.

Her mother had put on a glamorous show, a tempting

string of glittering parties and events that would have dazzled anyone. Her father had even joined in, telling her that if she insisted on pursuing this career, he owned enough stock in one of the city's finest hotels to get her any job she wanted there.

And they never realized, Lacey thought sadly, that they had done the very thing most guaranteed to shore up her determination not to come back. The glitter, the social whirl wearied her more than excited her, and the thought of taking a job earned only by virtue of her father's position and power made her feel slightly sullied.

But one thing had been oddly missing. Even during her most invasive interrogations, her mother had never asked her about Ryan. Nor had her father. Neither of them had even mentioned him. Never before had they let a chance pass to at least remind her how much better off she was without him.

It's your guilty conscience, she told herself wryly. They no doubt assumed he was well and permanently out of her life, that she'd probably forgotten all about him, so therefore there was no need to mention him and every reason—from their view—not to. Had they known she'd come to them practically from his arms, she doubted they would have been so generous.

She lifted the heavy suitcase into the trunk of her little red compact with an effort; it took up the entire space. There had been a time when she wouldn't have been able to lift it at all, she thought with satisfaction as she slammed the trunk closed. Which reminded her how glad she would be to get back to karate class on Monday. She hated missing more than one session, and she'd had no chance to practice on her vacation.

You don't practice with enthusiasm, you practice with resolve.

Ryan's words rang in her mind as an echo of the shock she'd felt ripple through her body. He'd known. She still couldn't believe he'd known, all that time, about what had happened to her as a girl, and had never let on. Had never pushed her to tell him, never prodded for answers to what she now saw was very betraying behavior on her part. He'd just accepted, done his best to be certain she was never frightened again and kept on loving her.

She shivered, tried to shove Ryan out of her mind for what seemed like the millionth time this week, and hastened around to unlock her car door and get started. She settled into the driver's seat and jammed the key into the ignition. She'd bought the car after the divorce was final, purposely and probably somewhat spitefully picking a small car Ryan would barely have been able to sit in.

She started the motor and backed out of the parking slot. Maybe she would call Kit Walker to see if she wanted to have dinner after their lesson Monday. She and the young police officer had found they had a lot in common after they'd been assigned as partners for the class karate exercises.

Or maybe she wouldn't, Lacey thought glumly as she pulled out onto the street in front of the airport. Kit worked at Trinity West, and it wasn't unlikely that the subject of The Pack—and Ryan—might come up. Kit knew Lacey was Ryan's ex, although she never pried. Nor had she ever given her that pitying look of understanding. She'd only pushed back a lock of her sunny blond hair and said, "He'd be a tough one to love. And a tough one to lose."

But Lacey wasn't sure she was up to even Kit's understanding presence. She'd done enough dodging in the past week to last her a lifetime. Her mother had known something was wrong, but Lacey had outlasted her inquiries with sheer, dogged determination. She'd been afraid, when her mother had blithely announced that she had selected a charming, wealthy young investment banker as Lacey's dinner partner for the Harcourts' party, that her instant recoiling at the idea had given her away, but her mother had seemed thankfully unobservant this time.

So as much as she liked Kit, perhaps it would be best to avoid any opportunities for long talks for a while. At least until she had some of her equilibrium back.

It would also, she thought as she looked at the traffic jamming the freeway, be best to avoid that mess. The Friday evening rush hour—an oxymoron if ever she'd heard one—had obviously gotten an early start. She watched the stream of cars inching along. She would stay on the surface streets, she decided.

She turned right, instead of left toward the freeway, drove for a few miles, then made the left onto Trinity Street East. And flipped the locks on her doors—this was not a neighborhood to take lightly, even in broad daylight on a Friday afternoon. She'd known that even before Ryan had lectured her on avoiding it whenever possible.

While he, of course, thought nothing of throwing himself into the middle of it.

Into the middle of this, she thought as she traversed the worst part of the Pack's territory. He lived here, walked their streets, played their evil game, all in the hopes of stopping some of their mindless violence.

Had they beaten him down at last? she wondered, as she remembered the Ryan she'd never seen before—weary, defeated. And if they had, what did it mean? Would it change what he did, here in this cesspool of anger and outrage? Would he be a little less willing to sacrifice himself? Or would he somehow lose the edge that had kept him alive?

Again she shoved the thought of him out of her mind. Or tried to. She'd thought she'd finally learned the knack, after three years without him. But in four short days he'd blasted back to the front of her mind, and she was having a very hard time getting rid of him.

So hard, she thought ruefully, that she even thought that was him standing over there on the corner.

It *was* him.

She slowed the car, staring at the men on the corner, men who would have made her lock her doors now if she hadn't already. Six...no, seven of them. And Ryan in the forefront, the posture and attitude of the men around him subtly proclaiming him the center of the group. He seemed to fit, to belong. He looked as tough, as hard, as merciless, as any of them. And as cold.

He looked nothing like the man who had held her so gently, the man who had made love to her until she forgot the ugly memories of the girl who had once been so terrified, until she forgot there was any other way to have sex except his loving, giving way.

This time she didn't have to shove the memories away; the actions of the group of men did it for her. There was something wrong, something in what she was seeing that made her stomach lurch. The men around Ryan were tense, watchful, and Ryan was moving in that way she'd come to both know and hate—hands loose, on the balls of his feet, ready to leap in any direction in a split second.

He was acting, she realized, like a man expecting an attack at any moment, from any direction. Even from within his own group. And she knew then that she was seeing what his injury and absence from the Pack had cost him.

He seemed to look her way, but there was no reaction, no recognition, in his face. She sped up, driving past without looking again, both because she hated what she was seeing, hated this firsthand glimpse of the danger of what he was doing, and because she knew she could cause him trouble if she lingered, staring too obviously. A woman alone, who didn't belong here, drew enough unsavory attention; she certainly didn't want to draw the Pack's. And she didn't want to put Ryan in the position of having to protect her when, to keep his cover intact, he should by rights be leading the charge.

She didn't realize how shallowly she'd been breathing, or how rapidly, until she felt the relief of a deep breath as she crossed over to Trinity Street West. The change in the surroundings was marked, as was the change in the pace of her heart.

And Ryan lived with this, with this tension, this hyperawareness, every day. Every hour of every day. She shivered at the idea, thinking that no matter how hard she tried, she could never really understand what he went through.

When she got home she unpacked methodically, concentrating on the mundane task of sorting clothes to rehang and clothes to go into the laundry much more intently than necessary. Only when she reached the small wooden carving did she pause. She stood there for a long time with the two otters cradled in her hand. Should she put them with the others, with the collection on her dresser? They didn't seem to fit, this only pair among them.

She'd thought, when she'd first tried to purge her life of all things relating to him, that she should burn the carvings, maybe even make a ceremony out of it, to mark the destruction of the last vestige of Ryan Buckhart. But then she realized she would have to burn the house down to accomplish that. And besides, she knew that with one look at the whimsical, adorable animals she would weaken. She'd thought then of giving them away, anything to get them out of her sight and life, but when she'd found herself worrying that they wouldn't be properly appreciated in their new home, she knew she was doomed. Worrying about a menagerie of tiny wooden creatures was a sure sign of her fragile mental health, she supposed, but she couldn't help it. She couldn't just give them away.

At last she set the otters on the nightstand beside the bed. She would decide what to do with them later. She took a quick shower to refresh herself, then fixed a light meal of soup and crackers. She should have stopped at the market and restocked her nearly barren cupboards, but she'd been far too disturbed by what she'd seen to even think about it.

At last, desperate for a distraction, she flipped on the television. She hadn't meant to watch the news, hadn't really wanted to know if the Pack's rampage had continued, but now that she knew Ryan was at least alive, she thought she could bear it.

Barely three minutes into the newscast she had her answer. The rampage had slowed. Not stopped, but slowed. The newscasters were speculating as to why, while the public information officers for Trinity West warned everyone to still be on guard, that there was every chance this was merely a temporary break.

And then she remembered what she'd seen today, the edginess, the sense of men on the verge of an explosion, and she wondered how long Ryan could hold them back. And what would happen to him when they finally broke loose completely.

She turned off the television. And sat there, unmoving, until the afternoon shadows gave way to dusk, then darkness. She felt as if she were waiting, but for what she didn't know, and didn't care to think about it.

The fact that—after the little start she gave when she first heard the noise at her back door—she wasn't really frightened told her it was this she'd been waiting for. She got up and walked through the kitchen, then opened the door still marked with the signs of Ryan's repairs.

"I'll save you the trouble of breaking it down this time."

Ryan stepped out of the shadows on the small porch. "You shouldn't have opened it without looking."

"Why? I knew it was you."

"Lacey..."

"I'd prefer to skip the lecture, if you don't mind. Are you coming in?"

"Only for a minute. I may have been followed."

He stepped inside and hastily pulled the door shut behind him. He looked healthy enough, but Lacey didn't miss the signs of strain around his eyes and mouth, the wire-drawn tension of his body. And he didn't waste any time making his point.

"Stay out of the Pack's neighborhood, Lacey."

"So you did see me."

"I did. And so could anyone else." He shook his head. "I thought you knew better. You were shocked at Caitlin poking around down there, and then you go and do this. Both of you have more nerve than sense."

"Thank you," she said dryly. "I was only there because the freeway back from the airport was jammed. I don't make a habit of driving through there."

She saw the knowledge that she'd gone on her trip anyway register, and then saw him decide he didn't have time to talk about it. Odd how much more readable he seemed to her now than he ever had before when he was working.

"But you did today," he said. "Stay away. Things are...calmer, but they're nowhere near under control. And after Romero's play, they're edgier than ever about strangers. Any outsider going through, especially a woman alone, gets reported to the Pack. It's not safe for anyone right now."

"Including you?"

His jaw tightened. "I don't have time to go through this again. Just stay clear."

"I will," she agreed easily, not seeing any point in lying just to show him that she wouldn't be ordered around. He already knew that. "I didn't like the look of those men you were with."

His mouth quirked. "I can't say I care for them much myself."

"I saw the news. You've...plugged the leak in the dam."

He shrugged, a gesture that could have meant anything. "It isn't plugged. I've only slowed it down. For what little good it'll do. And only for now. It won't hold."

"Then get out. While you can."

"And let it all go to pieces?"

"What else can you do?"

For a moment that same defeated look that had so stunned and dismayed her flickered in his eyes. "I don't know. Maybe nothing. But I have to try."

"Ryan..."

"I've got to go. I shouldn't have come at all, but I had to make sure you'd stay clear. Things could break loose again any second."

He turned and went to the door, pulled it open, then stopped and looked back at her. Driven by an urge she didn't understand, she followed him. She couldn't read his expression now, knew only that in his obsidian-dark eyes was a world of longing and regret.

"I love you, Lacey," he said softly.

And then he was gone, fading into the shadows of the night with all the stealthiness and silence of the ancestors he didn't know.

And Lacey stood there, her hand on the knob of the door, trembling as she remembered the times before when he had made sure that was the last thing she'd heard from him before he left. At first she'd thought it was sweet. Later she had laughed bitterly at her own naiveté, when she'd finally realized he wanted those words to be her last memory of him in case he never came home.

It was a long time before she could move. She stood there staring out into the night, into the darkness, as if hoping he would materialize out of the shadows and say he'd changed his mind, that staying alive was more important than attempting the impossible, than putting his life on the line to stop a group of vicious criminals who were probably unstoppable anyway.

You're a fool, Lacey Buckhart, she told herself. *He wouldn't do it when you were married, whatever makes you think he'd do it now?*

At last, fighting the numbing fog that seemed to have enveloped her, she closed the door and locked it. She ran a finger over the bare wood that still showed where the paint had peeled off when Ryan had broken his way in. His repair was sturdy, but it hadn't run to the cosmetics. The door and lock would hold against anyone smaller or less powerful than he was, but the bare wood was mute proof of what she'd always known. If somebody really wanted in, they would get in.

She'd never worried about it when Ryan was here. She had complete and utter faith in him. He would never, ever, let anyone hurt her.

Except himself. And the fact that he'd never intended it didn't make the pain any less.

She turned out the kitchen light, then walked through the house, never turning on any other lights, preferring the seclusion of the darkness. By the time she reached the bedroom, her eyes had adjusted fairly well.

She paused in front of the tall dresser, looking at the small creatures that inhabited the polished expanse of oak. The blue jay, the tiny raccoon with his bandit mask, the tiger cub Ryan had carved out of an odd piece of wood whose grain had incredibly supplied the tiger's stripes. She'd asked him about that one, how he'd known it would do that. He'd said sheepishly that he hadn't, he'd only known there was a tiger in there somewhere.

The fact that tough, cynical, hardened Ryan Buckhart was at such a loss to explain his own unexpected artistic skill had been just another of the things that drew her to him. There had to be something eminently good in a man who could take such a fierce weapon—for his huge knife was nothing less—and turn it to such a use.

She supposed, if she were feeling philosophical instead of numb, she could expand that metaphor to encompass all of who Ryan was. A man trying to take something ugly, brutal and all too often fatal, and turn the tide, change it into something else. If not something beautiful or precious, at least something . . . peaceful.

She fought a ridiculous urge to cry and wished the numbness that had filled her would stay for a while. She was going to go to bed now, even though it was barely ten. She was going to catch up on her sleep, she told herself firmly. She would relax all weekend, and she would not think of Ryan. Or the dangerous path he was walking. She had to go to work and begin her new job on Monday, and it wouldn't do to show up looking haggard, with bags under her bloodshot eyes.

She finished in the bathroom, came back and sat on the edge of the bed. She'd changed the sheets before she'd left, knowing that coming back to any hint of Ryan's unmistakably masculine scent would ruin whatever progress she might have made. She smelled nothing but the clean scent of freshly washed cotton and knew it had been the right thing to do.

And then she saw the otters on the bedside table and knew that no matter how many right things she did, no matter what she washed, no matter what she gave away, no matter what she burned, she wouldn't be able to rid herself of the memories of Ryan Buckhart. She would never be rid of them. He would haunt her until the day she died.

She felt the tears well up again, and this time she didn't think she had the strength to fight them back. She stared at the tiny pair, that sassy-nosed female and the hopeful male, until the image blurred as it had the first time she'd seen them.

She should have made Ryan take them away with him, she thought. She should have thrown them at his departing back, when he had left in that damn quiet, skulking way of his. She should have—

The jangle of the phone stopped her internal tirade and, for the moment, her tears. She wiped at her eyes, sniffed once, hoping she didn't sound as if she'd been on a crying jag, and picked up the receiver in the middle of the second ring.

"'Lo?"

"Lacey?"

Her breath caught. "Cruz?"

"You're there." He sounded relieved. "I've been calling."

"I...yes. I'm sorry, I hadn't thought to check the machine yet. I just got home from my parents'."

"You've been gone? How long?"

He sounded suddenly tense. "Since last Sunday," she said.

"Damn."

If she had not just seen Ryan, she would have been more disturbed by his tone. "What's wrong?"

"I was hoping . . . that Ryan was with you."

"No, he's not," she said honestly, glad she didn't have to lie to Cruz.

"Lacey . . . have you heard from him?"

Alarm bells went off in her head. She managed to channel her fear into a suitable tone of trepidation in her voice. "You mean you haven't?"

"He's missed two weekly check-ins now."

"What?"

Her surprise was genuine. Ryan had said he would check in, and she'd thought he'd done that Saturday morning after he'd seen the paper she'd tried to hide. Her mind raced, playing back what he'd said. *I should check in, or Mallery will be in an uproar.* Not would. Should. Vintage Ryan, meaning exactly what he said, no more, no less.

"I'm worried about him, Lacey. He's even got his pager turned off."

"I think my...premonition was just that, Cruz," she said, trying to head him off. "Just a feeling. It went away."

"After you called, I checked all the hospitals and clinics for fifty miles around. He wasn't at any of them. So if he was hurt it wasn't badly." Cruz's concerned efforts only made her feel worse. But when he added something else, guilt slammed through her. "Unless he had . . . other help, of course."

Damn you, Ryan, for making me lie to a man I like and respect. "I'm sure he's . . . all right."

"Oh, I know he's all right," Cruz said. "Physically. He's been seen back on the street, with the Pack."

"Then what—"

"He still hasn't checked in," he repeated. "And that makes the brass very nervous."

"Nervous?"

"He's an undercover cop, Lacey. It hasn't been unheard of for one to. . . get so deep he can't get out."

Lacey's brows furrowed. "What are you talking about?"

"I mean the brass is wondering. The chief trusts his people, but he has to think about the possibility."

"What possibility?" Lacey said, wishing he would get to the point.

"That Ryan's gone bad."

Chapter 11

"What?"

Lacey's yelp was incredulous. She moved the phone away for a moment and stared at it, as if it had somehow come up with this ridiculous theory on its own. Then she put the receiver back to her ear.

"Cruz Gregerson, that is the most ludicrous thing I've ever heard you say."

"You know it's absurd, and so do I, but it's the chief who gets held accountable if a cop goes bad."

"Ryan is the most—"

"I know, Lacey, I know. You don't have to tell me."

She couldn't believe he'd even said it, couldn't believe that anyone could really think Ryan Buckhart, that cop's cop, that unswerving, dedicated, give-his-life-for-the-job cop, could ever be swayed from his straight-ahead course.

"The longer he goes, Lacey, the worse it's going to get. The captain's ready to pull him out right now, and the chief is none too happy, either. He's more than a bit wary of any solo stuff lately."

"Ryan has always been the lone-wolf type, Cruz."

"I know. Hell, he doesn't even trust me, and I'm the most trustworthy guy around."

"I know, Cruz. I know."

"At least *you* do."

She could almost see Cruz's unexpectedly blue eyes rolling heavenward.

"He knows, Cruz. He just can't . . . do anything about it. It's too deep in him, never trusting."

"And it's going to land him in a lot of hot water," Cruz said warningly. "You can't imagine what things are like at Trinity West. The chief is forming a task force, ready to put an end to this once and for all. He's already called the detective division in for weekend shifts, to work up a battle plan. I just got home."

"I'm sorry."

"Never mind that. It doesn't matter. Lacey, if you hear from him, you've got to get him to come in. The bottom line here is that if he doesn't, they're going to start looking at him like a rogue cop. They'll go after him worse than if he was one of the Pack for real."

Lacey suppressed a shudder. She tried to steady her voice. "Even if I did see him, what makes you think I have any influence over what he does?"

"Because he loves you," Cruz said simply. "He always has."

Lacey sighed. "I know. But not enough. Not enough to change, not enough to let down those walls. He trusts me, but no one else. Not even you, even when he admits that you're the best friend he's got."

There was a moment of silence. "He . . . said that?"

His shocked tone didn't surprise her. Except for her, Ryan never spoke of his feelings for anyone. "He did."

She heard him let out a compressed breath. She wondered if Cruz understood now that it wasn't that Ryan didn't trust her that had driven a wedge between them. He *did* trust her. Completely. It was the fact that he couldn't let himself trust anyone else.

"I think I'm finally beginning to understand," Cruz said quietly. "Being the only person a man like Ryan trusts must be a heavy load."

She felt a tiny easing of pressure at his discernment. "Maybe it's fainthearted of me, but it's more than I can carry. If he was anything other than the man he is..."

"But he isn't."

"And I don't know if he ever can be."

Cruz was quiet for a moment, then repeated urgently, "He's got to come in, Lacey. I haven't told anyone that he...might have been hurt, and I'm doing my best to stall the captain, to reassure him, but Robards is already pushing to have Ryan declared over the line."

Robards. The old-boy cop, the man with the buzz-cut blond hair and heavy jowls. With the ever-present fat stub of a nasty-looking cigar clenched between teeth yellowed by years of the habit. With an attitude that made the people who had to work for him call him a dinosaur, while he did his best to make life miserable for them all.

And with a festering, fierce hatred of Ryan Buckhart, rooted in prejudices so deep no one wanted to plumb them.

"He hates Ryan," she whispered.

"I know. Fortunately the captain and the chief know it, too. I think that's the only reason they're holding back, giving Ryan a little more time. But it's going to run out, Lacey. If he reports in now, there's a chance to salvage this. If he doesn't, and damn soon, he's going to be hung out to dry."

"Cruz, you know he hasn't gone over. You know he's trying to do the job—"

"I know that. But this is one time when doing it his way, alone, isn't going to work. Robards is pushing to go after the Pack in full force. He wants to lead the charge, and I think half his reason for being so eager is that he's hoping Ryan will go down in the cross fire."

Lacey's breath caught in her throat.

"If you see him, Lacey, you've got to tell him. This time that lone-wolf act could get him killed."

Cruz's ominous words echoed endlessly in her head long after she'd hung up. She sat on the edge of the bed, the tiny otters still in her hand, hearing the sentence over and over.

This time that lone-wolf act could get him killed.

It wasn't fair. She wasn't supposed to be worrying about this anymore. She was supposed to have left this behind the day she'd signed the final divorce papers. And the fact that she had never really stopped worrying about him, had only managed to hide it, even from herself, for the past three years, didn't make it any easier to accept. Ryan had always been the lone wolf, and she was afraid it went straight through to the core.

In other words, "Don't interfere with my solo heroics," she thought bitterly. She knew he didn't look at it that way, that he didn't do it to be a hero. It was only that he knew just one way to do the job—his way—and the fact that it was the way most likely to get him killed didn't matter. He wouldn't let it matter.

She swung her feet up on the bed and leaned back against a pile of pillows. She held the otters up, staring at them for a long time, tracing each line with a gentle finger, marveling with an odd sort of detachment at the intricacy he achieved with the big, overpowering knife.

Just as, she thought wearily, he used his big, powerful body to play hers as gently as a harp. She wondered if it was that simple, if the incredible union they created when they made love was what made it so hard to let go. Was it simply that, simply a stubborn belief that anything that good had to be accompanied by the same perfect meshing in the rest of their lives? She knew better, didn't she? She'd had friends in relationships where the sex had been spectacular but they'd had little in common out of bed. And the words about loving someone but not being able to live with him hadn't become a cliché by accident.

Eventually she dozed, but fitfully, her light sleep made restless by ugly dreams that woke her up with a start and a spurt of adrenaline that took time to ebb. It was a roller-coaster kind of sleep, broken and unrestful, peaks and valleys, and when dawn began to streak the sky she felt more tired than when she had first lain down.

She looked once more at the small carving she'd held through the night. At the pair she couldn't help thinking had been meant to convey a message much deeper than their playful expressions might indicate.

She knew she needed more rest, but she also knew it was not going to come now. So she gave up and, yawning, rose and walked out to the kitchen.

Stay out of The pack's neighborhood, Lacey.

She wasn't sure what had made his warning race through her head once more, as clearly, as loudly, as if he were standing there again. She shook her head, as if that could rid her of the echoes. There might, she thought, be something to Ryan's lethal-strength coffee after all.

She didn't quite go that far, though, stopping a couple of scoops short, but it was definitely stronger than she was used to. She had the feeling she was going to need it.

Stay out of the Pack's neighborhood, Lacey.

She changed her mind and added another scoop. Maybe the extra caffeine would stop this ridiculous tape recording in her head. Of course, it could be worse. She could have Cruz's ominous warning echoing in her head.

Again she caught herself waiting impatiently for the coffeemaker that was already going as fast as it could. She shuddered at the first sip of the hot, dark brew. The second went down a little easier. The third seemed almost smooth. She supposed she should worry about that. But right now all she could worry about was this crazy feeling that she should do something. Anything.

As if there was anything she could do. There was no way she could reach him, and he'd made it clear that he wouldn't be back here again. Especially if he thought he was being followed.

For the first time the significance of that hit her. Followed by whom? By the Pack? By other cops, who'd been told by Robards he was a renegade? An inner chill chased away the warmth she'd gained from the coffee. Suddenly Cruz's warning seemed even more urgent.

And she felt even more helpless. There was nothing she could do. Except wait.

She set her coffee mug down. There wasn't enough caffeine in the world to overcome this. When he'd never told her what he was doing, was this what he'd been trying to protect her from, this sickening feeling of powerlessness? Even knowing the little she did, she was so afraid for him. And there was no way to reach him. She couldn't exactly send up a flare and hope he would see it. Nor had she any certainty that he would listen if she did somehow reach him.

She felt lost, able to do nothing but wait, always wait....

Stay out of the Pack's neighborhood, Lacey.

Again it played through her mind. But this time she remembered her own answer.

I will.

She'd promised him. She'd promised she would never again go through the Pack's territory.

And never had she ever broken a promise to him. Even when things between them had been at their strained, painful worst, she had never broken a promise to him.

Any outsider going through, especially a woman alone, gets reported to the Pack.

Maybe she had that flare after all. The question was, did she have the nerve to fire it?

Ryan felt like a man who'd clipped the fuse on a stick of dynamite just a bit too short and now wasn't sure whether to drop it and run or try to put it out.

The rumblings were coming from all sides now, and they were getting louder. The men who had been willing to accept him were getting restless at the inactivity. The men who had been waiting to see were looking at him with more and more doubt. Carlos's faction was becoming more vocal, more tenacious in their loud and unsubtle suggestions that Ryan shouldn't be running the show.

After the loot from the spree Carlos had initiated, the shortage of money because of the stand-down Ryan had enforced only added fuel to the fires of dissension. Then Jimmy Crawford's arrest yesterday, for holding up a convenience store on Trinity Street West to get money for his habit, had made things even worse.

Mutiny was in the air on this pirate ship, and the first order of business was to scuttle the captain.

He leaned back in the chair Alarico had once occupied, swinging his feet up to the desktop as he admitted to feeling a reluctant admiration for the man who had managed to keep this band of cutthroats under some kind of control. Of course, Alarico had been more cutthroat than any of them, and they'd known it.

He'd also kept them busy. A burglary here, a car theft there, the regular dealing of drugs from grass to crack, the occasional assault to remind the neighborhood it was wisest to keep the Pack on their good side with regular payments . . . and, when necessary, murder.

Ryan knew he was walking a fine line here, trying to judge at what point the members of the Pack would become so restless, so eager to caper, that they wouldn't question his violation of the cardinal rule of never having them all together at the warehouse at one time. Not to mention that he had to come up with a plan that would seem feasible to them, both in logistics and the payoff. Knocking off a liquor store, or even a bank, wasn't going to be enough of a distraction. He needed something bigger.

What he needed, Ryan thought wryly, were the kind of connections Romero obviously had, helping him con Alarico into believing he could help him get his hands on a fortune in jewelry from the wealthiest citizens of Marina del

Mar. But Ryan didn't have those. Hell, right now he didn't even have another cop to back him up.

He thought instantly of Cruz, remembering Lacey's words. *The guy who's been there for you, and for me, no matter what.*

It was the truth. Cruz had always been there. Through the times he'd been hurt, through the hell of his breakup with Lacey, Cruz had always been there.

And you still don't trust him.

The rest of her words rang in his ears, as well. And he knew they were true. But he didn't know what to do about it, how to make himself do something his gut warned him against at every turn.

Automatically, he pulled a small block of soft pine wood out of a drawer and reached for his knife. He had it unsheathed and halfway into position over the wood before an all-too-familiar thought stopped him. Had Lacey found the otters? Did she like them? Had they made her smile the way she always had over his amateur efforts?

More important, had she understood? Not only the meaning of the otters, but that there were two of them?

He had to believe that she had. Lacey was quick, bright, perceptive. She would know what he'd meant, even if he wasn't exactly sure himself, beyond a desperate need to make absolutely certain that there was no hope for them, ever, before he gave up.

And he had to stop thinking about her. It was going to get him killed.

He'd had to work harder at keeping her out of his mind since he'd come back to the Pack than he'd had to work at anything in the past three years. Since the last time he'd had to put her out of his mind. And it was taking far too much of his attention at a time when he needed to watch not only his back but all sides, as well.

He knew he was already in trouble. Knew that not checking in was a transgression even the generally supportive Mallery wouldn't accept. Nor would Chief de los Reyes, even though he was a rarity among chiefs these days, a man who had been a street cop long enough not to have forgotten what it was like. Especially if they found out Ryan had been shot and hadn't reported it. Although he wasn't sure why they hadn't already known. Romero must have realized he'd been hit and included that information in whatever report he'd made. And even though the Marina del Mar detective hadn't known Ryan was a cop, there wasn't anyone else close to answering his description—there weren't many six-foot-two Indians in Marina Heights.

He wasn't even sure what he thought he was accomplishing. He was going to have to call in eventually. And when he did, even if he managed to avoid their finding out he'd been hurt—assuming they truly didn't know, for some unaccountable reason—and pulled him for that reason, he was still faced with having to either lie about the situation to his superiors or admit just how close to exploding the stick of dynamite was. And if he did that, he knew Robards would win the battle and they would move now, too soon, while the men were still scattered, lying low as he'd ordered them to in his efforts to stem the vicious rampage that Carlos had instigated after Alarico's arrest. If that happened, the Pack might be slowed for a while, but not destroyed, and the cancer would only grow again, reforming around the next man ruthless and powerful enough to become the nucleus for the evil they did. The cops would have gained nothing.

Unless, of course, he got himself killed in the process; Ryan was sure Robards would look on that as a plus. He'd often wondered if one of his superior's ancestors had been killed by one of his own; the man's hatred was palpable enough to be felt. It made Ryan want to stroll into the man's office one day dressed in Native American garb, complete with war paint, maybe with a tomahawk added for color. If he'd had any idea what tribal dress would be rightfully his, he might have done it. But adopting one just for the sake of doing it had never seemed quite right to him.

Realizing his thoughts were out of hand when he found himself spending even this much time thinking about Ken Robards, Ryan turned his attention back to the small block of wood. And suppressed the urge to chuckle when he found himself consumed with the need to produce a walrus with a brush haircut.

He'd found the yellowed tusks inside the little block, and considered and discarded several options to present to the Pack as the next big job, when Carny appeared in his doorway. The man adopted a casual posture, leaning against the doorjamb, but Ryan had come to know him well enough to recognize a sense of purpose, no matter how well hidden.

Ryan didn't stop his minute movements with the knife, but he lifted a brow at Carny. The man shrugged.

"Know anything about a little red car with a Marina del Mar Resort parking sticker in the window?"

Ryan's hands froze, then resumed moving, but he doubted the observant Carny had missed the pause. The black man's next words proved it.

"I thought so. Looks like the same car that caught your eye the other day. Same pretty lady driving it, too. Looking very nervous."

"What about it?" he asked, wondering if he'd managed to sound at all casual.

"It was cruising Steele Street for about fifteen minutes. Back and forth. Seems to be gone now, but a couple of the men have been discussing ways to find out exactly what the lady wants, if she comes by again. And perhaps give her something she doesn't want."

Ryan nearly sliced off a fingertip with his own wicked blade.

"I thought you might be interested, my friend," Carny said in the tone of one whose suspicions had been confirmed. Then he turned away.

"Carny?" The man looked back over his shoulder. "Let me know if they see her... it... again."

Carny nodded, and Ryan saw something flicker in the man's chocolate eyes that absurdly made him want to nod back. "I'll do what I can to distract the children," he said.

Ryan did nod then. "Thanks."

And then the man walked out, leaving Ryan once more pondering the mystery of Carny Lang. Pondering Lang because it was much easier than figuring out what in hell Lacey thought she was doing.

He'd told her to stay away. He'd told her how dangerous it was. She'd even agreed. And she couldn't possibly have any business down here. So why the hell was she here, not simply driving through on Trinity Street, the main drag many people used, but driving Steele Street, notorious as the home of the Pack's headquarters? Was she crazy? She had to know she would stand out in this neighborhood as much as he had among her parents' social set, the few times he'd encountered it. She was damn lucky the men who'd seen her had waited this long. What the hell had she been thinking?

Anger kicked through him. Was she that determined to show him that he didn't run her life? Would she do a crazy thing like this just to prove she didn't have to do anything he said? Was teaching him that she was now utterly independent of him worth that much to her?

He'd risked a great deal, her safety and his own, to warn her. And then she went and pulled a fool stunt like this. How stupid could—

He cut off his own thoughts. Lacey was many, many things. But stupid had never been one of them. Nor did he believe it was now.

Stay out of the Pack's neighborhood, Lacey.

I will. I didn't like the look of those men you were with.

Their exchange rang in his ears, pounding home what he knew he should have realized right away.

She'd promised. And Lacey had never, ever broken a promise to him. Except her wedding vow, but he knew he couldn't count that. She would have kept that vow, as well, had it not caused her more harm than good. She was an honorable woman, down to her soul. If she gave her word, it was gold. It had always been gold. As pure and precious as the woman herself.

And she wouldn't break that word out of anything less than desperation. Not Lacey.

But what could possibly make her so desperate, desperate enough not just to break her word but to risk herself like this, when she knew the danger here, when she knew how close things were to exploding into chaos? What could be so damn important to her?

He knew the answer his subconscious was trying to fling at him, but he didn't dare accept it. If he believed for an instant that it might be concern—he didn't dare even think the word love—for himself, the man who had brought her here to this morass of viciousness, he would be sorely tempted to walk away, to leave this all behind, let the chips fall where they might, and try to salvage some kind of future with the woman he loved more than his life. But he knew he couldn't dare think that. He wouldn't be able to take the anguish when he found out, as he inevitably would, that it wasn't true.

He might believe, however, that she had been trying to reach him. For whatever reason. Perhaps Trinity West had been pressuring her, guessing he might have contacted her. Even Cruz, perhaps. Cruz knew better than anyone that although Ryan had stayed out of Lacey's life, he'd never really managed to put her out of his heart.

He had to stop this. He could speculate for hours about the whys. But that wouldn't change the fact that Lacey had come here, had tempted a very cruel fate, and he had to see that she never did it again. No matter what her reasons. Warning her obviously hadn't worked. And scaring her hadn't worked, either. She'd come anyway, albeit, if Carny was right, very nervously. But he shouldn't be surprised. Her courage had always managed to overcome her fears.

He didn't know what to do. Just as he didn't know what to do here. It was getting to be a habit, a habit he didn't like.

Indecisiveness had never been a trait of his, and he didn't care to make it one now.

But he didn't care much for his limited options, either. He could try to warn Lacey again, although what made him think it would take any better than it had last time, he didn't know. But perhaps, if she had been trying to reach him, once she'd passed whatever message it was along, she would stay home. And safe. But if he went to see her again and Carlos was truly having him followed, he could destroy that safety in the very act of trying to preserve it. He was good at losing a tail, but if they used more than one or two men, no one could be sure of shaking them all. And he'd already risked contacting Lacey once; going to her again would only double the odds of them finding her.

And a phone call was out of the question. The Pack's warehouse didn't run to standard phones, which were too easily tapped, and the cellular phones were far too easily monitored. He was sure Carlos was doing just that; one of his cronies had already done time for copying cellular phone numbers.

His only other option was to do nothing. But he discarded that idea almost as soon as it formed. It wasn't really a choice. It wasn't a choice because he knew Lacey. He knew she wouldn't give up. She never gave up on what she felt she had to do.

He was swamped by a sudden feeling of isolation. He'd always run alone, had preferred it that way. But now, faced with the reality that he didn't even have a safe way to contact Lacey, he felt alone in a way he never had before. And for the first time in his life he felt the urge to share the burden, because once he'd added Lacey's welfare to the load, it had suddenly become overwhelming.

But he was in too deep now to call for help. He should have done it long ago. Cruz would have helped. Maybe even Gage, if he'd asked. They would have helped and kept it quiet if he'd told them why. Wouldn't they?

You trust Cruz to cover for you, and maybe to teach you street Spanish. You trust Gage to warn you when Robards is on the warpath. You trust them to help their brother cop. It's Ryan Buckhart you don't trust them to help.

Well, it was Ryan Buckhart who needed help now. Only now that he'd finally admitted it, he couldn't ask for it.

He was on his own. As usual. A lone wolf to the end. And that this might really be the end was a possibility that didn't escape him. But he refused to dwell on it. If he went down, he went down. If he lost his career, he would live with it. If he lost his life, so be it. Only Lacey mattered.

And he would do whatever he had to do to make sure she stayed safe.

Chapter 12

He stared at the house for a long time from his concealed spot in the overgrowth she'd fostered. The rectangle of light from the kitchen shot out across the backyard, adding a yellowish streak to the wash of moonlight. He'd half-expected Lacey to let the garden run loose after he'd gone, but she'd kept it as it was, profuse and a little wild, yet controlled by the removal of weeds and some occasional judicious cutting back.

He'd teased her that the yard, with its semicontrolled wildness, was as much trouble to keep up as if they'd mowed and pruned like most people. But he understood her preference. In the spring it was riotous, an explosion of color as the blooms burst to life; in the summer it was green, dotted with the fewer summer flowers; in the fall some of the plants turned to rich autumn reds and golds, and in the winter it lay quiet, storing up energy for the next spring's eruption.

That the very quality she loved about it was the thing that made him nervous—too many places of concealment—was something he'd dealt with in his own way, making sure the doors and windows were as secure as they could be. It was a trade-off, he'd decided—Lacey's pleasure against security—and he'd made the balance as even as he could.

He'd loved this house, in a way he'd never expected to love anywhere he lived. He'd trained himself early on never to become too fond of a place, because he knew he would always be moving on to the next foster home whenever, as always happened, the people taking care of him grew tired of the task. Or the court decided he would be better off somewhere else. Or he was simply too much trouble.

But here, with Lacey, he'd let down his guard. When they'd first found the older house, she'd been doubtful. As they'd walked through the house, with the levels and angles he'd found so fascinating, he'd tried to tell her what he saw there, without much hope that she would see it. He understood. She'd grown up in what was, in his eyes, no less than a mansion. But she had seen what he'd seen, and before they'd even finished looking at the place, she was off and running with ideas. And she'd made it into what he'd never in his life had. A home. A place he would have been happy to stay in for the rest of his life.

But it had been Lacey who had made it that way, and without her, it meant nothing.

He shifted position again, careful not to lean too far toward the bougainvillea, with its too-frequent, too-sharp thorns; he'd already argued with Lacey's peppermint-striped roses and lost. He'd made three approaches to the house, from three different directions, moving in spurts—swiftly, then slowly, then stopping altogether—hoping to trip up a follower. He knew it was futile if they'd already determined his destination, but he had to try.

The light in the kitchen went out, casting the yard back into stark, moonlit silver and shadows, and he edged forward slightly. He wasn't going to risk the door this time. There was too much open ground to cover, and he didn't want to be spotted. But he could reach the bedroom window, which had always been one of the things that bothered him, without having to cross more than a couple of feet without cover.

If, he thought wryly, he could get over there without scratching himself to death on various thorns and branches. And without waking the entire neighborhood with all the rustling noises he was making. The bushes were a bit further out of control than he'd thought.

A light came on in the living room, and he hoped she would stay there for a moment, long enough for him to get inside. He didn't want to scare her to death by coming in on her unexpectedly.

When he was at last in the shelter of the corner of the house, out of sight from three sides, he gave up on concealment and went for speed. He raced up the slight embankment that made the house's split levels necessary and was up on the balcony of the bedroom in moments. He knew Lacey spent a lot of time out here, looking out over the profusion in the yard, and he could only hope she hadn't yet secured the French doors for the night.

She'd looked at the doors and seen beauty. He'd seen only ease of entry for a burglar. He'd done his best, adding a dead-bolt lock in an unexpectedly low position, then hiding it with molding that looked purely decorative. That would at least slow down someone with a glass cutter, who would be expecting the lock to be in the usual place above the knob. By then, he'd figured, he would be awake and waiting for the unlucky bastard.

Of course, he'd thought that about the kitchen door, too, and he'd taken it down with his first attack. Not quietly, but he'd done it. He hoped he didn't have to take down Lacey's beloved French doors the same way.

His mouth twisted wryly. Here he was, hoping Lacey hadn't used the dead bolt, yet at the same time knowing he would be furious with her for not doing it.

She'd fastened the latch, but not the dead bolt. He supposed that was something. But he changed his mind when the fastening gave easily under only slight pressure. He was going to have to do more fixing around here. If she would even let him set foot in the place after this was over.

And if, of course, he was alive to do it.

He slipped into the room, pulling the door closed behind him silently. For a moment he stood in the shadowed room, breathing shallowly, until his eyes adjusted. It had been dark outside, but even the moonlight had been brighter than the darkened room. All he could see was the glow of the numbers on the clock radio on Lacey's side of the bed. The side she still slept on.

He shoved the images that thought gave rise to out of his mind and waited. Gradually the shapes became clear, the neatly made-up bed he tried not to look at, the nightstands, the dresser....

The dresser. Where she still kept the collection of his carvings, those absurd animals that he'd hidden from her at first, afraid she would laugh at his silliness, only to one day, shortly after their marriage, find her holding one he'd thrown away. She'd been utterly charmed by the tiny raccoon's bandit-masked face, so charmed that he'd found the nerve to carve the blue jay next and had presented it to her with his explanation. She'd responded to the simple chunk of wood with as much delight as another woman might to a gift of a diamond necklace. More. And had proceeded to delight him in an entirely different way that night in bed, taking the lead for the first time, tentatively but definitely, until he thought he'd carved his way straight to paradise.

When he'd seen the animals still there the first time he'd awakened back in their bed, he'd been stunned. More than stunned—he'd been sure she would have gotten rid of them. The fact that she hadn't had been what had inspired him to gamble with the otters, to take the chance that she hadn't quite buried their marriage completely yet.

His stomach lurched sickeningly. It hadn't been that, had it? She hadn't come to Steele Street, risked herself, because of the silent message of hope he'd left her?

Before he had time to dwell on the possibility, he heard light footsteps coming down the hall. He dodged to one side, where he would be partially hidden by the dresser, where he could give her some warning before she saw him.

She walked into the room and flipped on the light. He blinked at the sudden brilliance, but nothing could erase what he'd seen in that first moment—Lacey, her hair tied back with some kind of cloth fastening, her long legs bare and taut and fit beneath the hem of the T-shirt she wore.

His shirt. One of his old white police academy shirts, with Buckhart stenciled across it. Worn and soft from countless launderings in the eight years since he'd used it in the academy, it clung to her, emphasizing the slight sway of her breasts beneath it, the hem flirting with the feminine curves of her hips. He wondered if she was naked beneath it, then cursed himself for wondering as his body surged in response to the mere thought.

His shirt, he thought again. She was sleeping in one of his shirts. Had this just begun? Or had she dug it out after last week, as...as what? Reminder? Consolation? Penance?

She reached up to pull at the band holding her hair back. Ryan's breath left him in a rush as the movement lifted her breasts and her nipples peaked the worn cloth of his shirt.

"Lacey," he breathed, knowing he had to let her know he was here, while at the same time wishing he could just watch her forever.

He heard her stifled gasp as she spun around.

"Have you *ever* heard of coming to the door and knocking like a normal person?"

She was startled by his unexpected appearance, Ryan noted, but not surprised to see him. So he'd guessed right; her appearance had been a message of sorts.

"Nothing in my life is normal right now," he said wryly.

"Nor mine," she returned, a little sharply.

"I know," he said gently. Then, with a wry grimace to match his tone, he said, "You rang?"

She smiled suddenly, and his breath left him again. He'd meant to lecture her on her recklessness, but it seemed pointless now. His entire life seemed pointless without this woman in it.

"I knew you'd understand," she said.

"I'm here," he noted unnecessarily. "Why?"

She raised delicately arched brows. "No lecture?"

"About how stupid it was to go down there? About how angry I am that you did it? No. You already know that. Just like I knew you wouldn't break a promise without a good reason. All that matters now is what that reason is."

She seemed to become suddenly aware of her state of undress. She sat down on the edge of the bed, curling her long legs up under her and pulling the shirt down over her knees. He didn't bother to tell her that nothing could lessen the impact of the sight of her in his shirt. Nor did he move. He didn't dare get any closer to her—and their bed—than he already was.

"Cruz called me."

His mouth tightened. But at least this was better than thinking she'd come charging down to the Pack's turf because of the otters. "I thought that might be it."

She looked up at him, her vivid blue eyes troubled. "You're in trouble, Ryan."

"I figured that, too."

"You haven't checked in."

"No."

"Why?"

"A lot of reasons. None of which anybody at Trinity West is going to buy."

"Cruz would."

"Maybe. But it's gone beyond him being able to help now."

For once she didn't argue with him, and that alone worried him. "What did he say?"

"He said..."

She stopped and averted her eyes. His brows furrowed; she rarely avoided meeting anyone's gaze, especially his. "Lacey?"

"He said . . . they think you might have gone over."

"Might have . . . what?"

She looked up at him again then. "Gone bad. Switched sides. Whatever you want to call it."

He gaped at her. "They think I . . . ?"

"I told Cruz that was ludicrous. He agreed. He didn't believe it for a second. But with you not checking in, and the Pack running amok, the brass is getting nervous."

"But who—"

He cut himself off as the obvious answer came to him.

"Yes," she said, her tone acid. "Robards planted the idea. That arrogant, pompous, lying bigot."

Ryan blinked, then grinned despite himself. "So how do you really feel about him?"

"The man is trying to sell Captain Mallery and the chief on the idea that you've gone over the line, and you're joking about it?"

"No. I'm just glad it . . . means something to you."

"Of course it does. He's slime, and anybody who'd believe him is just plain stupid."

"I don't think the captain or Chief de los Reyes would appreciate that assessment."

She blushed slightly. Ryan knew she thought a great deal of Chief Miguel de los Reyes, who had come in at a time of crisis and managed to pull things together at Trinity West, until the department had gained the best reputation in the county for doing the impossible with nothing.

"Well, maybe not stupid," she amended. "Cruz did say that they know Robards hates you, so they weren't in a hurry to believe him."

He didn't think his expression changed, and he knew he hadn't moved—he was leaning against the wall as if it were the only thing keeping him from joining her on that bed—but she went on as if he'd relaxed.

"That doesn't mean you're in the clear. He's still pushing, and he may wear them down. And Cruz also said the captain's ready to pull you right now, and the chief isn't happy with you, either. He's considering calling in a task force to go after the Pack and try to put them out of business for good."

"Robards has been pushing for that for a long time."

"Cruz had an opinion about that, too," Lacey said. "About why Robards is so anxious to storm the Pack."

He read her look, the bitter anger in her eyes. "He's hoping I'll get myself killed in the process, no doubt."

Her eyes widened. "Then it's true? He hates you... that much?"

He lifted his free shoulder in a shrug. "Or so close it doesn't matter."

In a smooth, graceful motion she sat up on her heels. "Ryan," she said urgently, "you have to come in. Cruz said there's a chance it'll work out if you do. But if you don't, they're going to label you a rogue cop. They'll go after you like you really are one of the Pack. He's trying to stall, but..."

She was looking at him so compellingly that he wanted to go to her, wanted to go to her so badly it hurt not to. He leaned harder against the wall, telling himself he didn't dare leave its support. It took every ounce of discipline he had to concentrate on what he was saying, and even then, he knew he was telling her too much.

"Lacey, I can't. I've got to have more time. If they go in now, they'll get nothing. Everybody's too scattered, too wary after Romero's move and Alarico going down. I've got to have time to pull them all together. By tomorrow I'll have most of them reporting to the warehouse, but I want them all. And I'm so damn close...."

Close to either bringing down the Pack or being brought down by it. And if he was a second too early or too late, he would end up fulfilling Robards's fondest wish. And that was something he truly didn't want to do, not least because of the woman who was sitting in front of him, wearing a shirt with his name stenciled over breasts that even now his hands itched to touch. He curled his fingers so tightly that his nails dug into his palms.

"Call Cruz," she begged. "Please, Ryan, at least call Cruz. You know he wouldn't betray you. You have to know that. He doesn't even know you were hurt."

He frowned. "Do they... really not know? What about Romero? Why the hell wouldn't he have told them?"

"I don't know."

"Damn."

That was the main reason Ryan hadn't called in. He'd assumed they already knew he'd been hit in the fight at Alarico's arrest, and the minute Captain Mallery had heard that, he would have been pulled.

"Ryan..."

"I can't, Lacey. Not yet. I'd either have to lie or admit things are a whisker away from blowing. And if I do that, Robards will win. They'll come in now and get nothing."

"Except maybe you out alive," Lacey snapped.

"Lace—"

"It's time to give up the lone-wolf act."

He remembered that feeling of isolation that had flooded him, remembered how alone he'd felt. "I wish... I wasn't in too deep to do that," he said.

She looked startled that he'd admitted even that much. He couldn't blame her; he'd never done it before.

"That's my point," she said. "It always has been. It's when you're in deep that you need help the most."

"I can't. It's too late. I won't take anybody else down with me."

He saw her delicate jaw tighten and knew he'd said the wrong thing, as far as his ex-wife was concerned.

"It's not too late. It's never too late. You're already in hot water up to your neck, Buckhart. Call in now and you might be able to salvage something. Cruz will help, and you know everybody but that scummy Robards is reasonable."

He sighed. He was Buckhart again. That erased the tiny flare of hope that had hit him when she'd said it was never too late. He never could seem to stay out of trouble with her for long.

"Since when are you worried about my career? I thought you'd be glad to see me quit."

"Quit, yes. But not get thrown out. Besides—"

She stopped, shaking her head.

"Besides what?"

Her chin came up. "If you keep going like this, you'll end up dead. Either at the Pack's hand or because of Robards's bumbling. Or his intention."

His breath caught. Had she told Cruz that the biggest danger he was facing was being attacked from within? If Cruz knew that, there would be no holding back that task force.

He tried to smile, but it felt a little wobbly. "You've become a cynic, Lace."

"I had a good teacher."

His smile turned sad. "I never meant to do that."

"You did a lot of things you never meant to."

"I know." He took a long, deep breath. "Is that it? You wanted to tell me just how much trouble I'm in?"

"And to try—in vain, I see—to get you to see reason."

"Would you really want me to pull Cruz into this hot water with me?"

"He'd jump, if you gave him the chance."

"Lacey..."

"Never mind. I know you won't. Or can't."

He shifted his shoulders and shoved himself away from the wall. "I'm sorry, Lacey. I wish—"

"I don't want to hear it. You'll never change. I should have remembered that."

Her gaze flicked sideways. Instinctively Ryan looked in the same direction. His stomach knotted when he saw the otters sitting on the table beside the bed. When he shifted his gaze back to her face, she was watching him.

"Lacey—"

"Don't." She cut him off, scrambling off the bed to face him. "Just don't. Nothing's changed. You still can't trust anyone else. And I can't carry that load, Ryan. I can't be everything to you. I'm not that strong."

He knew she was right, that he'd made her everything, that he'd given her all the trust he had to give. He'd never thought of it as a burden too great to carry, the burden of being the only one he trusted.

"You're the strongest woman I know," he whispered.

"Even if that's true, I'm still not strong enough. Neither are you. No one is strong enough to walk utterly alone in this world. Especially not in your world. But you—" Her voice broke, and he saw her breasts rise under his shirt as she took a quick breath. "But you can't see that. And you never will, will you? You'll *die* before you see that."

"God, Lacey."

He took a step toward her. She threw up her hands and backed away. He stopped.

"Don't," she repeated. "Don't touch me. I lose all common sense when you touch me."

"I didn't...mean it that way."

"It doesn't matter how you mean it, it always ends up the same way."

His mouth twisted. "Any other time, I'd take that as a compliment."

It came out more flippantly than he'd wanted, and she drew back. "Take it any way you want," she said, an undertone of hurt in her voice, "as long as you take it and leave."

"Lacey, I didn't mean that the way it sounded."

"I don't think you know what you mean."

That was something he couldn't argue with. "I'm sorry," he said. "I didn't mean to sound...like a smart ass. It's just that this..." He swallowed tightly, but made himself go on. "This... hurts."

She stared at him, something in her expression that he couldn't read. He knew he should have been gone long ago, for the longer he stayed, the more danger he put Lacey in. But right now nothing seemed more important than this. He closed his eyes and let his head loll back wearily on his shoulders, suddenly wishing he could just run and leave his entire godforsaken life behind and start over. Maybe then he could learn, could be what she wanted.

"I . . . know what *you* mean," he said at last. "But I wish I didn't."

He straightened then, to find her still looking at him in that odd way. Nervous, he supposed, afraid that he was going to turn this into a scene like those that had marred the end of their marriage.

"It's all right, Lace," he said softly. "I understand. I was a fool for even hoping. You're right. I'll never change. I can never be . . . what you need."

He reached toward her, then stopped, knowing that if he touched her, it would tear him apart to leave. He set his jaw and dropped his hands to his sides.

"I'm still trusting you not to tell anyone. Everything depends on that. And don't ever pull anything like that jaunt down Steele Street again, Lacey. No matter how good you think your reason is."

He walked past her to the French doors.

"And throw the bolt on these doors."

He left her standing there, watching him with that odd look in her eyes. He closed the door behind him and walked to the railing of the balcony, then slipped over it and dropped down to the embankment below.

And thought that if he'd dropped straight into hell, it would have been easier.

Chapter 13

Lacey sat on the edge of the bed, wondering if she was facing yet another sleepless night. Then she laughed—of course she was. She hadn't slept for more than an hour at a time since the morning she'd awakened to find Ryan gone. Just as she hadn't slept when he'd first moved out of this house. He'd haunted her then, just as he was haunting her now.

You're right. I'll never change.

She'd said it. She'd thought it more often than that. But somehow hearing Ryan say it about himself, hearing her own words repeated to her, was different. They sounded different.

They sounded wrong.

They sounded wrong because he *had* changed. She had proof of it. The Ryan she'd known would never have admitted that he was hurting. Just as he never, ever would have admitted that he'd been wounded as deeply as she'd been by the death of their unborn son.

I had to be strong for you. You had to know you could lean on me.

When all she'd really wanted was for him to cry with her, so she would know she wasn't alone in that sea of crippling agony. He hadn't been cold, he hadn't not cared, he'd just been . . . wrong in what he'd thought she needed.

Did you ever tell *him what you needed?*

Her own voice, stark with realization, echoed in her head. She *hadn't* told him. She'd expected him to know. To read her mind and sense what she needed. Her grief had been so overwhelming that she'd been unable to think about anything else, even telling her husband the only way he could help her.

Would he have been able to do it then? Or only now, after the past three years? Had he learned somehow in those years they'd been apart that hiding your pain wasn't always the best or right course?

And if he *had* somehow learned that, then was it possible he just might be able to learn even more? To learn that trusting someone didn't mean weakness, didn't mean losing control—it just meant you'd found a kindred spirit, someone you could trust to act as you would act, if you could.

I wish I wasn't in too deep to do that, he'd said when she'd told him it was time to drop the lone-wolf act. Had he meant it? He'd never said anything like that before, had never, ever indicated he wished he wasn't so alone. Had he changed there, too, or was she reading too much into this?

And if she was, why? She glanced over at the otters. Had she, too, harbored some foolish hope that there was still a chance for them? Hadn't she gone through enough hell? Hadn't she fought this battle over and over and over in her mind and always come to the same bitter conclusion, that no matter how much she loved Ryan Buckhart, she simply could not live with him, with who he was and how he chose to isolate himself?

Well, he'd given up those hopes now. There had been nothing more than resigned acceptance in his eyes when he'd left her this time.

And for the first time, leaving her, he hadn't told her that he loved her. And the loss of those sweet words, words she told herself she didn't, couldn't, want anymore, hurt her with a severity she'd never expected.

Would she never get over this man? Would she never be able to stop comparing every other man who came into her life to Ryan Buckhart and find them sadly wanting? Was she some kind of sick, confused woman who was fixated on her ex and unable to let go? She'd thought she had. She'd been proud of how far she'd come in three years, that she sometimes went days at a time without thinking of him. As long as she didn't see a police car, a man with long, dark hair, or look at those silly wood carvings, she was fine. She didn't think of him at all. And when she did, when one of those reminders popped him into her mind, she'd become very good at pushing him out again.

And then he'd come bursting back into her life, literally, and she'd been weak enough, foolish enough, to let herself fall victim to the powerful magnetism between them. Even knowing how hard it was to fight, she'd fallen, and now she—

The phone jarred her out of her misery, and she reached for it gratefully, even knowing it probably wasn't good news at this late hour. And the minute she heard Cruz's voice she knew she was right.

"Lacey? Have you heard from him?"

"Now what, Cruz? Has Robards convinced the captain and the chief to put a price on his head?"

"Almost. But..." He paused as Lacey heard a plaintive "Daddy" in the background. "In a minute, Sam. You should be in bed, anyway."

"But the puppy." Lacey heard the girl's voice more clearly this time.

"He'll be fine, honey," Cruz said, obviously over his shoulder. "The vet said so. He just needs to rest. And so do you. Now scat. Back to bed."

She smiled as she listened. She hadn't seen Cruz's precocious daughter in . . . had it really been nearly four years? She'd been unable to face the bright-eyed, sunny-faced child after the loss of her baby, and then she and Ryan had fallen apart. She hadn't felt truly comfortable with children or with Ryan's old friends since then, although Cruz had always told her that she was welcome anytime.

"Sorry," Cruz said back into the phone. "I didn't want to call you from the station. Robards has been hanging over me like a swarm of hornets, and I wouldn't put it past him to have tapped my office phone."

Lacey wouldn't put it past the man, either, but she didn't want to think about the arrogant swine now.

"How is Samantha?" Lacey asked. She knew she was dodging the inevitable, but she needed a moment to brace for whatever grim news Cruz had.

"She's fine," Cruz answered. "Aside from bringing home every stray creature within a ten-mile radius."

"She inherited her father's soft heart," Lacey said, trying to picture the little girl at . . . would it be ten now?

"Maybe," Cruz said, sounding embarrassed. "She sure didn't get the animal thing from her mother. Ellen hated anything other than cats and dogs, and she wasn't real sure about dogs."

Not for the first time, Lacey marveled at Cruz's calm when he spoke of his ex-wife. Not every man could speak so neutrally about the woman who had walked out and left him with a three-year-old girl to raise alone, without a word, simply vanishing until divorce papers had arrived a year later. There were moments when Lacey knew the past haunted him, and when Samantha was away at camp in the summer Cruz disappeared without telling anyone where he was going, but on the whole he seemed remarkably unscarred by his wife's desertion. And so did Sam.

Cruz had done his best with the little girl, and when Lacey had last seen her she'd been a bright, confident six-year-old, secure in her father's love and, as her father was wont to say, far too clever for her own good.

"I suppose," Cruz said, his tone wry, "that all this diversion was to subtly let me know that if you had heard from Ryan, you aren't going to tell me?"

"It wasn't just diversion. I did want to know about Sam. I've...missed her."

"I know. She misses you, too."

She waited for the accusation, that it was no one's fault but her own that she hadn't seen the child, but it didn't come. She should have known better; that wasn't Cruz's way. She steeled herself, then made herself go on.

"What's wrong, Cruz? Has Robards really got them believing that...garbage? About Ryan going bad?"

"It may not matter," Cruz answered grimly. "We picked up some information that may make it a moot point."

"What do you mean?"

"Trinity West patrol busted a guy trying to knock over a convenience store a couple of days ago. Small-time hood named Crawford. He was strung out really bad, and when they caught him and he realized he wasn't going to get his fix, he started babbling. Talking up a storm."

Lacey already didn't like the way this sounded. "Talking...about what?"

"The Pack."

"He's...one of them?"

"Sort of. He's been on the inside, in any case. And what he was saying doesn't look good. Since the leader went down a couple of weeks ago, things have been going from bad to worse. He says the Pack is splitting into two rival factions and is about to explode."

She didn't have to ask, but she did. "And I assume one of those factions is...Ryan's?"

"From what we hear. Crawford wasn't real generous with the details, but he said half the Pack is out for the big Indian's blood. We don't know who's on what side, and at this point the chief doesn't really care."

Something she'd heard flitted around the edges of her mind, but she couldn't remember it right now. And Ryan's words, playing back in her head, distracted her.

I've only slowed it down. For what little good it'll do. And only for now. It won't hold.

Was this what he'd meant? Did he know what a dangerous tightrope he was walking? Of course he did. Part of the reason he was so good at what he did was his knack of assessing the situation.

His reaction to something she'd said flashed through her mind—the startled glance he'd given her when she'd told him that if he kept going like this, he would end up dead. Either by the Pack's hand or Robards's bumbling. Or his own intention.

Oh, yes, he knew. He knew quite well what he was up against. And in that instant he'd been afraid she knew it, too. But why? Why afraid? What did he think she would do?

"The chief wants him out, Lacey," Cruz said, cutting off her thoughts. "Now. He's not wasting any more time, and he's not going to cut Ryan any more slack. He doesn't quite buy Robards's line yet, but he's through waiting. He's ordered up that task force. We're to report at 0600 hours. And be ready to move by noon."

Lacey swallowed tightly. "And then what?"

"You know I shouldn't tell you."

"I know. And if anyone ever asks, you didn't."

He sighed. "We're supposed to hit the warehouse in full force. SWAT team backing us. Round up whatever we can of the Pack."

"What if...they're not there? You said things have...quieted. Maybe it's because they're lying low. Scattered."

There was a pause. "I won't even ask what made you think of that. But, damn it, Lacey, if you know something, tell me! De los Reyes doesn't want to move until he knows exactly where Ryan is, but Robards is pushing for a full frontal assault, and the devil take anybody who gets in the way. Including Ryan."

"You mean especially Ryan."

Cruz didn't bother to deny it. "Yes. He'd consider that a bonus. That's why we have to get Ryan out of there, or at least warn him."

"He...knows how much Robards hates him. He'd expect this of him."

"You *do* know something, don't you? He's been there, or been in touch?"

"Cruz, I...I can't."

"Damn. I never figured that you, of all people, would support him in this solo game of his. I thought you had too much sense."

She heard him let out an exasperated breath that she sensed was driven more by worry than anything else. Cruz cared, he genuinely cared, and it made it all the harder to deny him what he wanted.

Then he spoke. "Did you ever stop to think that maybe part of the reason things have quieted down on the streets is because the Pack has had other things to think about? Like just how they're going to kill Ryan without him taking half of them with him?"

He paused, as if waiting for her to react. She couldn't; she couldn't even breathe. She hadn't thought of that, although she saw now that she should have. But Ryan had trusted her; how could she betray that trust?

"It was bad enough watching you go through your divorce, Lacey," Cruz said, his voice taking on an angry edge. He was a quiet, calm, coolheaded man, but right now he sounded like a man who'd been pushed a hair too far. "I don't want to watch you go through his damn funeral."

She barely managed to bite back a whimper.

"Think about it, Lacey," Cruz said in a sharp tone he'd never used with her before. "And when you recover your common sense, you call me. I'll be here."

He hung up, and Lacey slowly did the same.

She had never felt so torn. Not even when she'd had to decide that she couldn't go on living as she had been and had finally filed for divorce. Then she had been wrestling with many of the same things that swamped her now—her word to Ryan, her anguish over the way he did his job, his inability to trust anyone else and the burden of him trusting her. Only her. It made the obligation more sacred at the same time that it made it almost impossible to carry.

But then she had only been facing the end of their marriage. Now she was facing the very real possibility of Ryan's death. Probability, she corrected grimly, because he had the Pack after him on one side and a cop more than willing to see him die on the other. What did any of the rest matter, when stacked up against that? The pressure building inside her expanded, making it hard to breathe.

I'm still trusting you not to tell anyone. Everything depends on that.

Ryan would expect her to keep her promise. He'd sworn her to secrecy, and he would expect her to do as he'd asked. She'd already broken one promise to him by going into the Pack's territory to send up that flare. If she did it again, he might lose the trust he had in her. And then he would be completely alone, truly trusting no one. The pressure swelled even more, until she could have sworn she felt it crushing her heart.

He survived that way before he met you, and he's survived the last three years that way, she told herself. She had to believe he would survive this, too.

But what if he didn't? What if he was killed, and she could have prevented it? Could she survive with that knowledge in her heart?

"Damn you, Ryan Buckhart," she sobbed out, the pressure unbearable now.

How could he do this to her? How could he put her in this position, of being the one to decide what to do? How could he, when he had to know it meant lying to a man she cared about, a man who cared about Ryan, whether Ryan believed it or not? How could he, when he knew it could mean his life?

I won't take anybody else down with me.

A fine excuse for what he wanted to do, anyway. As if he were some old-time gunfighter, riding into town alone and, if he lived, riding out still alone.

The irony of it struck her when she realized that one of his ancestors, whatever nation they might have been, would have picked off that lone gunfighter with ease. She laughed aloud, ironically, then made herself stop, fearing she was on the edge of hysteria.

I won't take anybody else down with me.

Yes, that was Ryan's creed. He had some very stiff-necked, rigid ideas about honor and loyalty. And he wouldn't easily forgive her if she broke his trust.

Forgive her?

Her own thought echoed in her head as if she'd spoken it aloud. And the absurdity of it struck her hard.

Forgive her? Had she truly just worried about whether Ryan would forgive her if she broke her promise? Was she really concerned that he might hate her for breaking her word? This was the man who had just walked out of her life again. Walked out, after returning just long enough to shake her so badly that she didn't know what she thought or wanted or needed or had to do anymore. Just long enough to remind her of the hell she'd gone through before by giving her a taste of the sweetness that had almost made it worth it.

Almost.

Ryan had walked out of her life once more. And she knew this would be the last time. So what on earth did it matter if he hated her for breaking her word?

Yes, he had his own inflexible ideas about loyalty and honor. But she, thank God, was a woman and therefore could separate practical necessity from the luxury of maintaining personal honor, a luxury Ryan was too stubborn to admit he could no longer afford.

And if the cost of saving his life was having him hate her, then so be it. She could be as stubborn as he was, if necessary. She would never have survived even two years with him if she hadn't been.

She glanced at the clock, a little startled to find it reading almost midnight. She'd been wrestling with this for nearly an hour.

But now she was through. She'd made her decision and was prepared to live with the consequences. She could survive Ryan hating her. She didn't think she could survive him dying because she hadn't done anything to prevent it.

She reached for the phone.

Cruz answered on the first ring. She didn't waste any time on niceties.

"He's been here twice. Since the first time."

"The first . . . ?" A moment's pause, then she heard the detective let out a compressed breath. "How bad?"

Lacey blinked. "What?"

"Your premonition, Lacey. How bad was he hurt?"

Lacey grimaced. "It depends on who you ask. It looked ugly to me, but he acted like it was a mosquito bite."

"That's Ryan," Cruz acknowledged. "But I figured he must be okay when you acted so oddly when I called you the last time."

She sighed. "You knew all along, didn't you?"

"Suspected," Cruz corrected. "And I was damned mad at him for putting you in the middle."

"I haven't been very pleased with him myself," she said, her tone a shade away from being grim. She was able to keep it that way only by virtue of the relief she was feeling at having made her decision. "He's *not* crooked, Cruz."

"I know that, Lacey. You know I never believed that for a moment. Now, what happened?"

"He was shot. The night the Marina del Mar detective arrested Alarico."

"What?" Cruz sounded astonished. "Romero never said anything about anyone being shot."

"Ryan didn't know that. He assumed you all knew. That's why he wouldn't check in."

"Because he knew he'd get pulled."

"Yes. And it was... fairly superficial. For Ryan."

"Damn. There was blood at the scene, but Caitlin said it was hers, that she'd cut her leg when they were holding her. Romero backed her story. So we didn't check."

"You... know her?" A spark of the old jealousy shot through her, heedless of the knowledge that she had less reason than ever to feel it now.

"Yes," Cruz said. "And there's no reason in hell I can think of that she'd lie about this. As far as she knows—and Romero, for that matter—Ryan was Alarico's right-hand man."

"He...got hurt saving her. The bullet was meant for her."

"I see," Cruz said, sounding like a man to whom everything suddenly made sense. "That explains why both of them... carefully left that out of their story, then."

"Then it's true? They're... together?"

She could hear Cruz's smile in his voice. "Oh, yes. Very." Then, his concern back, "He's really all right? Mobile?"

"Oh, he's that, all right," Lacey said dryly. "Twice now he's skulked back in here like the best of burglars."

"Why?"

"Once to warn me because I made the mistake of simply driving through the Pack's territory."

Cruz coughed. "Well, he always was... protective."

"You have a flair for understatement, Cruz."

"And the second time?"

"I, er, did it again."

"What?"

"I...sort of cruised Steele Street. After you called last time."

"Why the hell would you...?" His startled yelp trailed away. "Damn. No wonder he came after you again. You wanted him to." He laughed then. "You pushed his buttons like a master, didn't you?"

"If I was that good, he wouldn't have gone back."

There was a moment of silence before Cruz said quietly, "He did go back?"

This was it. Lacey took a deep breath and dived into the icy waters she'd decided were her only choice.

"Yes. Even though he knows they're after him. He said something to someone on the phone, about watching his back and somebody named Carlos."

"Carlos? *He's* leading the opposition?"

"I can't be sure, but that's the impression I got. You know him?"

"By reputation only. He's not...someone you'd want to know personally." She heard him let out a breath, could almost hear him thinking rapidly. "What you said, about the Pack being scattered? I presume that came from Ryan?"

"Yes. He said they were lying low, I think after all the trouble Carlos stirred up."

"What else?"

"He said he won't check in now, because he knows if they have a clue how close things are to exploding, Robards will win. They'll make their move now, before he has a chance to get all the Pack together."

"And if we wait, they may kill him."

"He knows that, too."

"Damn it, why didn't he call me?"

"He said he...wouldn't take you down with him."

"Stubborn son of a—"

"I know. But I think...maybe...maybe this time he wanted to. But he thinks it's too late."

"Well, he's right about that. I think I can convince the brass that he hasn't gone over, but there's no way I can stop the sweep. They're going to hit the whole neighborhood, take what they can get."

"He said most of them would be at the warehouse tomorrow—no, today, now. But that it wasn't enough. He wanted them all."

"When?"

Lacey tried to remember if he'd given any clue, but could think of nothing. "I don't know. That's all he said. Except that...the man he was talking to on the phone seemed to be warning him. And Ryan called him...Carny, I think. That's all I know."

"All right. It'll have to be enough."

"Cruz...you'll be there?"

"I'll be there."

"Beside Robards?" she suggested.

Cruz gave a harsh laugh. "You learn fast. But I think behind him would be better."

"With your gun out," Lacey said bitterly. "I wouldn't trust that man not to shoot Ryan himself."

"I'm not sure I would, either. He'd trade his own mother for a commendation."

Trade. Something poked at Lacey. Something important. She closed her eyes, trying to remember. After a moment she had it.

"Cruz, wait. There is something else. When Ryan was talking on the phone, about that Carlos, he said something about someone meeting . . . at an old pawn shop."

"Pawn shop? There's a place that used to be a pawn shop on Trinity, near Steele, but the Pack's headquarters is still that warehouse, as far as we know."

"But it was the same conversation, so it must be . . ."

"Carlos's faction? Meeting in the old pawn shop?" Cruz asked, almost to himself. She could practically hear him thinking. "That means we'd have to try to take both places simultaneously. That could get dicey. Are you sure?"

"As sure as I can be. They could hardly meet under Ryan's nose, could they?"

Cruz chuckled. "Want a job here in detectives, lady?"

"No," she said, very solemnly. "I just want Ryan safe, Cruz."

"I'll do my best, Lacey."

"That's good enough for me. And it's good enough for Ryan, even if he can't admit it."

She hung up knowing she'd done the right thing, the only thing she could do.

She knew he would do just that, his best. And Cruz Gregerson's best was very good indeed.

She knew there would be no sleep for her tonight, at least not now. She thought some hot chocolate and the most boring movie she could find might help. She thought for a moment and decided she would be more comfortable if she was dressed and ready, just in case. In case of what, she wasn't sure, but right now even small comfort wasn't something she took lightly.

She pulled on a pair of heavy socks, trying not to think of the way Ryan had always teased her about her cold feet, just before he proceeded to warm them, usually in a very...inventive way. Then she took a pair of soft, faded jeans from a drawer and pulled them on. Automatically she began to tuck in her T-shirt. And stopped dead as it struck her for the first time that she had been wearing Ryan's shirt, with his name emblazoned across her breasts, the entire time he'd been here. And although it was too late now, she pulled it off and replaced it with a much safer Marina del Mar Resort T-shirt.

She walked through the living room, heading for the kitchen, thinking that after all this, she was going to be in simply marvelous shape to start her new job on Monday. She'd worked her way up from her college days on the switchboard to lead concierge, and now that she'd finally made it to the front office, she was going to be too exhausted to enjoy it.

But hopefully not too exhausted to do the job at all, she thought, yawning widely as she pushed her hair back from her face. That would make a fine impression on Mr. Darby, the general manager.

She went into the kitchen and flipped on the light. A split second later she heard a sound from the back door.

Ryan? Again? She would have sworn he would never come back. Not after the way he'd left. She walked toward the door. Before she reached it, it burst open with the sound of splintering wood, in the same way it had the first night Ryan had come to her. And now, as then, a man burst into the room.

Only this time it wasn't Ryan. It was a total stranger.

And he was holding a gun on her.

Chapter 14

Ryan paced the small office that he'd inherited by default. That action alone was unusual; he wasn't a pacer by nature. He usually turned to his carving as an outlet for a surplus of nervous energy, but he didn't dare pull out his knife right now. He would be too likely to slit his own throat.

After three years he would have thought he was used to the idea of doing without Lacey. He'd thought he'd accepted it as finished the day the final papers had come through. It had taken him a long time to adjust to the hole she'd left in his life, but he'd expected that; you didn't cut out a vital part of yourself and expect to keep functioning as you always had.

After a while he'd even managed to stop hating himself for being who he was—the man Lacey couldn't live with. He never stopped blaming himself, but at least he began to put away his gun at night instead of leaving it close at hand in case it got to be too much and he somehow found the nerve to put a permanent end to the pain.

For three months he'd lived out of a motel room just

down the road from Trinity West. Cruz had offered him a room, and Gage Butler had offered him a couch, but he'd turned them down. He didn't want any witnesses to what he was certain was going to be an ugly process, that of learning to accept that Lacey wasn't ever going to be there for him again.

And it had been. It had been the ugliest thing he'd ever gone through. He'd been so used to not having love in his life. He'd grown up without it, knowing only cruelty at worst, the limited caring of overloaded but sincere foster parents at best, or, most frequently, an indifference that fell somewhere in between. He hadn't thought he'd missed anything worth having, but then Lacey had come into his life, had taught him what it meant to be loved. Had made him come to need it, to depend on it . . . and then had taken it away.

No, he told himself as he spun on his heel and reversed his path across the room. That wasn't fair. She hadn't taken it away. It would have been easier if she had. And that had been the most bitter pill of all. Down to the day the divorce was final, Lacey had never once said she didn't love him anymore. Only that she couldn't live with him.

He stopped midstride, almost staggering under the pressure. He felt as if he was about to jump out of his skin. He felt that if he didn't do something he would go crazy, run out of here screaming.

He felt like that kid he'd once been, certain he was being shifted from place to place because there was nothing about him that made anybody want to have him around for long. No, he felt worse than he had then, because Lacey had proved that even if somebody loved him, they still couldn't live with him. There was something basic, something fundamental, wrong with him. There had to be. Lacey was the most loving, giving person he'd ever known, and if even she—

"Damn."

He muttered it fiercely, under his breath. He was losing his mind. He'd been through all this three years ago, and he would be damned if he was going to go through it again just because he'd made the mistake of going to her when he'd been hurt. And she'd made the mistake of not throwing him out on his butt the moment he'd arrived.

Why hadn't she? Why hadn't she done just that, or followed through on her threat to call the paramedics, or Cruz, or anybody at Trinity West?

He shook his head, as if that would help him rid his mind of the useless speculation. He'd already caused enough trouble by reading too much into her actions, reading in them a hope that perhaps their relationship wasn't quite extinct yet. It didn't matter why she hadn't thrown him out then; she'd done it last night, bluntly and without equivocation.

Take it any way you want, as long as you take it and leave.

It couldn't be much plainer. She hadn't added the words "And don't ever come back," but she didn't have to. It had been more than clear in the tone of her voice and the rigid posture of her body.

So accept it, he ordered himself. Accept it and get on with your life. You've done it before, you can do it again. And you damned well better do it soon. Many more sleepless nights like last night—and far too many other nights in the past two weeks—and Carlos won't have to take you down, you'll crumble on your own.

He glanced at the small clock on what had been Alarico's desk. After ten. Yet Ryan felt as if it was four in the morning and he'd been up running for a week.

He knew he needed rest, sleep. His head was pounding, his eyes were gritty and tired, and his side was aching more than it had since right after he'd been shot. But he'd spent the night thrashing on the couch here, images of Lacey destroying any chance at rest. When he'd finally given up this morning and gotten up, one look in the mirror in the small bathroom had told him that today would be a good day to try to strike fear into the faltering members of the Pack—this face would be enough to scare anyone.

"You look like a pothole on the proverbial road to hell."

He whirled around to see Carny in the office doorway, looking at him amiably, a black beret perched at a jaunty angle on his head, an envelope tucked under his left arm.

"Thanks. I've got a mirror."

Carny lifted a brow. "Still intact?"

In spite of everything, Ryan wanted to laugh. His mouth curved into a wry grin, and he shook his head. Whoever Carny Lang was, surely he could manage something better to do in life. But if he managed to pull off a miracle, Ryan thought, Carny would go down with the rest of them.

Ryan opened his mouth to speak, then shut it abruptly when he realized he'd been about to suggest Carny find somewhere else to be for the next week or so. He was stunned at himself; never would it have ever occurred to him to warn a member of the Pack that things were going to be either falling apart or put to an abrupt end soon.

"You must be very tired, my friend," Carny said softly. "You're not usually so easy to read."

For a split second Ryan just stared at him. Then every bit of mental armor he possessed snapped back into place.

"Ah. That's the Ryan we all expect." Before Ryan could even begin to speculate on this exchange, the man went on. "I have a message for you. I don't think you're going to like it."

Ryan frowned. "What message? From who?"

"Carlos. He wants a meeting."

"A meeting?" Ryan's frown deepened. This wasn't Carlos's style, asking for meetings—he came in shooting.

"It does sound rather...civilized, for our incautious friend," Carny said, agreeing with Ryan's tone and expression.

"Too civilized."

"Yes. And he wants you to come to him."

Ryan's brows lifted. "Does he, now?"

Carny nodded. "At the old pawn shop. In an hour."

His brows rose higher. He wouldn't have thought Carlos had the brains or the balls to try to pull a power play like this one. Summoning the head of the Pack like some flunky. The man must be very sure of himself. Ryan wanted to know why. What made Carlos think he would dance to his tune?

"Now, what do you suppose he's got up his sleeve that has him convinced he's calling the shots?"

"The cheese in the trap?" Carny said. "I'm not sure. But I believe this may be part of it." He pulled the envelope from beneath his arm and held it out. "He sent this along with the message."

Ryan took it, stared at it for a moment, then glanced at Carny. He felt an odd and unexpected sense of affinity with the man, but he wasn't about to trust an unknown quantity now, when things were about to come to a head. The man shrugged, then took the hint and left.

Ryan opened the envelope. His stomach lurched when he saw it contained a single photograph, from an instant print camera. A photo of Carlos's trump card, his hostage to guarantee Ryan's cooperation.

Lacey.

"Man, you're crazy! That big Indian isn't gonna fall for this! He's smart."

"I tell you, he'll be here. She means something to him."

"But I don't want to fight him. He's too damn quick with that knife."

"Maybe this wasn't so smart, goin' against him like this."

"Yeah, maybe we should just back off. He said he had something big in mind, bring us lots of cash."

The man Lacey had quickly realized was Carlos whirled on the group of men clustered off to one side of the large, dimly lit room that smelled of dust and mildew. The rather grand-looking pillars, more decorative than functional, gave the place an almost gothic air that Lacey found ominously appropriate.

"I'm the boss here," he snarled at the group. "And don't you forget it."

"All right, all right," the smallest man said, backing up a step. Carlos, it seemed, wasn't any too certain of his hold on these men, she thought. And things had gotten nothing but worse since he'd sent one of them off with that photograph they'd taken of her, sitting on this painfully hard chair with her hands tied in front of her. She knew the picture's destination, and the thought of what Ryan would do when he saw it made her cringe inwardly. They were going to use her to lure him here, that much was obvious. Her only hope was to stall.

"Who d'ya think she is?" asked a tall, bulky man with a neck so thick it made him look as if his small head was perched directly on his shoulders. He'd been the one who had broken down her door, and she noticed with some satisfaction that the marks she'd left on his face with her nails were still bleeding. He was looking at her intently, and not kindly. She schooled her face to impassivity.

"If you'd had the brains to look around the house when you grabbed her, Victor, we might know that now."

"Hey," the man protested, "you didn't say nothin' about that, you just said to go get her. And that was tough enough. Bitch clawed me like a wildcat."

"Never mind." Carlos wiped at a nose that seemed to be constantly running. He was tall, thin to the point of gauntness, and there was a feverlike brightness in his small eyes that made Lacey very nervous. "She'll tell us who she is, and what she is to Ryan, soon enough."

Like hell she would, Lacey thought.

"Maybe she's his sister," Victor suggested.

"Damn, Vic," the small man said, "look at her. She look like an Indian to you?"

Lacey didn't care for the way Carlos was looking at her. He seemed to have a tendency to sway from side to side, and he put her in mind of a coiled snake following its prey with its beady eyes just before the strike.

"She ain't wearin' no wedding ring," a chubby man with a thick mustache offered after studying her tied hands.

Carlos glanced at the man and laughed. "Ryan isn't the marrying kind. But maybe she's his girlfriend. Wouldn't surprise me to know he gets hot for the rich, white-bread, snooty lady type." He looked back at Lacey. "That it, sweetheart? The Indian get off sliding between your lily white thighs?"

The man made her desperately want to wash, but she kept her expression even. Carlos stared at her, then smiled, a cold smile that held nothing less than cruel amusement.

"What are you to him? Why did he sneak into your house? Uh-uh," he said when her chin came up. "Don't deny it. Tubby here saw him go in. And come out. Saw him talking to you as he left."

"I hate that name," the chubby man said. "Just because I'm your cousin doesn't mean you can call me names."

"Shut up," Carlos said without looking at the man.

"Hey, you're the one who came to me, remember? Said you needed somebody this Ryan had never seen before to follow him. I helped you out."

"Shut up," Carlos repeated. Then, to Lacey, he said, "Talk!"

"Make up your mind," she said, her tone biting as she spoke for the first time.

With a movement so swift Lacey barely saw it coming, Carlos backhanded her across the face. Pain seared through her cheek, and she tasted blood. So much for stalling, she thought. She wasn't foolish enough to think she could stand much of this.

"Puta," Carlos snarled.

"Not smart, Carlos," she said when the pain had receded slightly.

Carlos drew back as if she'd startled him. "You're a cool one, I'll give you that. Are you this cool in bed? Is that what he likes? A cold ice princess?"

Lacey knew he wanted her to get angry enough, or embarrassed enough, to let something slip, but all she wanted to do was laugh in his face at the idea of any woman being passive in bed with Ryan Buckhart.

And cry at the thought of it being any woman other than her.

"Does it make him feel like less of an Indian to screw you?"

Anger surged in her. She'd had enough of this. More than enough. First Robards, now this slime. She uttered a crude suggestion, a phrase she'd never used in her life.

Carlos smiled again, and Lacey regretted giving him the satisfaction of having driven her to futile threats. She was even more suspicious than ever when Carlos seemed to change his approach. He rubbed at his chin with a hand that Lacey noticed was none too steady.

"We just want to talk to the Indian," he said coaxingly. "Make him see reason."

She could tell by the reaction of the others that this was not the man's usual tack, but she didn't really need that to let her know he wasn't the least bit sincere. Even if she hadn't already known, she wouldn't have trusted the man's oily assurances. She had no doubt that his only goal was Ryan's death.

She stared back at the man, realizing now, even more than she had the day she'd seen Ryan with men like this on the street, what it must be like for him. No wonder it had always been so hard for him to come down after living with this high-wire tension, no wonder he'd stayed away from her when he was working undercover—one moment out of character and these jackals would be on him.

And she felt a bitter irony that what he'd most feared, her being used against him, had come to pass.

Unless she could convince them that the weapon they thought they had was useless.

"All he has to do is step down," Carlos said easily. "And he can walk away."

She knew better than to believe that. She could read the much more deadly intent in the man's reptilian eyes. She took a deep breath and said in the steadiest voice she could manage, "I can't help you with that. He's never listened to a thing I say."

She saw satisfaction flicker in Carlos's eyes as she at last admitted she knew Ryan. "We make progress," he said.

She laughed, surprised at how strong it sounded. "Hardly. If you've got some idea of him listening to me, you're sadly mistaken. Ryan doesn't listen to anybody, but especially not to his ex-wife."

Carlos blinked. She'd startled him with that. He truly hadn't known who she was. Perhaps he really was as stupid as Ryan believed. She braced herself to go on, praying that by sticking as close to reality as she could, she could give her words the ring of truth.

"Why do you think we're divorced?" she said, with her best attempt at a sneer. "Because he never gave a damn about anything but his so-called work. He's the most stubborn, bullheaded man on the planet. And he'll never change."

She'd accused Ryan of all those things to his face. And at the time she'd meant them. All of them. But now, stacked up against the thought of him dead, they didn't seem to mean much anymore.

"You might as well just let me go," she told Carlos. "I don't mean a damn thing to Ryan."

"But you did once."

"Maybe. I'm not sure. And I don't care."

She waited, scarcely daring to breathe, waiting for him to ask the obvious question. If she meant nothing to Ryan, why had he come to her? She could see the man thinking; from his scrunched-up face it appeared to be a painful, unfamiliar process.

Thinking and Carlos are barely acquainted.

She could only hope that Ryan had been right.

"Boss!" Victor yelped. "Somebody's coming!" The thick-necked man leaned forward to peer out the window of the old pawn shop. "It's Ryan!"

"Son of a bitch," Carlos snarled as he looked at his watch. "Can't the damn Indian tell time? I said an hour."

In spite of her apprehension, Lacey smiled. "I told you he doesn't listen to anyone."

A moment later she saw Ryan stride past one of the big pillars. Dressed all in black, he seemed to dwarf everybody in the room, even Victor, by sheer presence alone. The only touch of color about him was around his forehead—a pure white bandanna that held back his long hair.

He was alone, but he stood there as if he had an army at his back. And the men in the room reacted as if they saw that army, backing up in that slow, shuffling way that spoke of instinctive, unconscious reaction. It didn't matter that they were no doubt all armed—she'd seen a couple of lethal-looking automatic pistols, and Carlos himself had his own within reach on the table beside her. All that mattered was that Ryan overpowered them all by his sheer presence.

Carlos grabbed her by one arm and yanked her to her feet. Her wrists, already rubbed raw by the nylon line they'd used to tie her, screamed a protest. She bit back an exclamation of pain. Carlos shoved her ahead of him, past the line of retreating men and into the light.

Lacey nearly gasped aloud at the look that flashed in Ryan's eyes the moment he saw her. It was fear, pure, genuine fear. She'd never thought to see such a look in Ryan Buckhart's eyes. She saw his jaw tighten, sensed him go rigid with tension. She saw his gaze narrow fiercely as he took in the blood on her lip and the bruise that was no doubt forming by now.

And then it hit her. She *had* seen him look like that before. Once. It had been lost in the confused mist of memories of that time, but now it snapped into focus with vivid clarity. Ryan, on his knees beside her, calling her name, agony in his voice and that same horrible fear in his eyes. The night she'd lost their baby.

At night while you slept I used to sit on the floor in that nursery we painted and cry....

God, she'd been such a fool. She'd expected him to read her mind, to plow his way through the silence of her anguish and somehow heal what could never be healed, while she had never once seen that he was hiding his own pain behind the stoic mask he'd shown to the rest of the world, but never before to her.

"What do you think you're doing, Carlos?"

Ryan's voice was low and harsh. And she heard the fear for her ringing in it, although she doubted anyone else did. And she knew she had to act, or Ryan was going to do something stupidly heroic and noble, like give himself up in exchange for her.

He took a step toward her.

"He thinks," Lacey said quickly, before Carlos could gather his wits after Ryan's unexpected early appearance, "that you give a damn about the ex-wife who threw you out. I told him he was wrong. I explained that you hate me just as much as I hate you."

Ryan stopped dead. His brows furrowed. Then the fear faded from his eyes as he looked at her. His glance flicked to Carlos. Then, with a slow, almost loving movement, he reached to the sheath at his waist and drew out the big knife, the polished, finely honed blade glinting as it moved. Lacey felt every man in the room go very still.

"You should have believed her," Ryan said in a voice she'd never heard from him, one that sent a shiver of pure trepidation down her spine. "She threw me out. Of my own home. No woman does that to me."

He ran his thumb over the razor-sharp edge of the knife. It was so quiet now in the room that she swore she could hear every ridge of his thumb scraping over that deadly blade.

He stared directly at her, his gaze zeroing in on her throat. "I'd like nothing better than to see her dead."

Chapter 15

Ryan kept moving his thumb over the blade. He knew every eye in the place was on his hands. Except for Lacey's. She was looking steadily at his face. He saw the faintest hint of apprehension in her eyes, and he knew he'd come on just a little too strong. He held her gaze, putting everything he could of reassurance into his look. After a moment he saw the fear fade from her eyes.

"Just what were you planning, Carlos?" he asked, never taking his eyes off Lacey. "Somehow I doubt that you were going to give me this bitch as a gift."

"Go to hell, Ryan," Lacey snapped, sounding so genuinely angry he blinked.

Recovering, he looked at Carlos. "Did you really think you could use her? Against me?" He shook his head, assuming a pitying expression. "You always were a fool, Carlos."

Carlos flushed, and Ryan saw him tense.

"Don't try it," he recommended, as Carlos glanced at the MAC-10 on the table beside Lacey. The man stayed where he was. So did the others in the room. He had his own weapon, a 17-round Glock, tucked at the small of his back, but he didn't want to use it, didn't want to even introduce the idea of gunfire, not when Lacey was in the room.

And then Lacey was at it again, distracting them all, acting as if this was a normal setting and she wasn't standing there with her lip swollen and her hands tied in front of her.

"I should have blown your head off when I had the chance last night!" she exclaimed. "Maybe I could have collected that life insurance. I should get something for the hell of being married to you."

Damn, Ryan thought. Where had that come from? She'd sounded like every man's nightmare of an ex-wife. And she'd managed to take his threat and run with it, explaining away why he hadn't killed her last night if that was what he was so set on doing. If he hadn't known she'd taken herself off as beneficiary—although he had put her back, without telling her—on his insurance, he would have sworn she meant every word.

"I think they frown on paying off murderers," Ryan said.

"Murder? When all I did was shoot a burglar?"

Ryan snorted. "Good luck proving that."

Lacey's chin came up. Ryan felt a wobble in his stomach that threatened to spread to his knees as she gave him a look that more than matched the most superior, down-the-nose stare her mother had ever given him.

"You always were an arrogant son of a bitch," she said, in a cold, disdainful tone that matched that stare.

He suddenly felt as if he was standing in her parents' cold, black-and-white-tiled foyer, knowing before he even opened his mouth that he was doomed to their eternal condemnation for daring to even think about marrying their precious daughter, let alone actually doing it.

He stared at Lacey. Something flickered in her gaze, and he suddenly realized he *was* facing her mother. She'd chosen a part she could play because she knew it so well. And she'd seen it recently, on her visit. She was baiting him purposely, although what that purpose was he wasn't quite sure.

He only knew that she had to have one, and right now he had little choice but to play along.

"And you," he returned, "are the most conceited, smug, snobbish bitch that ever walked. I don't know why the hell I married you."

"Don't think I haven't been asking myself the same thing!" she retorted. "No woman in her right mind would marry the likes of you."

"Which explains why you did!"

In spite of the fact that they were still treading on very dangerous ground, Ryan found himself having to stifle a rueful smile. They had never argued like this. Ever. They sounded like the worst kind of bickering divorced couple who despised each other. Carlos was gaping at them, and the rest of his crew were all snickering. The shock of the beyond-taciturn Ryan snarling at a woman, like a not quite domesticated dog, must have been highly entertaining to them. He hoped so.

He also began to hope, to think that there was a chance they might get out of this alive. He could distract Carlos. He doubted the others would try to take him, and then—

Lacey called him a name he would be willing to bet she'd never said in her life. He called her something worse back. She matched him with another. And with every word they said, his heart, his gut, was screaming out the opposite. It all seemed so petty now, the reasons for the divorce, the things that had come between them. They were both here, dancing on the edge of death, and beside that nothing seemed important enough to have driven them apart. He should have done as she asked. He should have changed, no matter what it took, no matter how long it took.

She hadn't asked for so very much, just that he remember he carried a part of her with him, and if he died, that part of her died as well. She'd only wanted him to learn to trust. If he'd learned it sooner, he wouldn't be alone here now, trying to save them both.

"And another thing, you sneaky, house-breaking coward! If you ever come near me again, so help me—"

She took off on another tirade that was so unlike her as to be comical. Lacey never fought like this, nastily. Even if they did argue, she wanted it over and done, and she would walk away to calm down before she would ever get involved in a long, drawn-out battle.

Long. Drawn out. With no hope of backup or help. His own thoughts, playing back in his mind, because . . . why? She had to have a purpose for dragging this out, he thought again. And then it hit him.

She was stalling.

She was stalling, and there was only one reason she would do that.

Damn you, Lacey Buckhart, he swore silently.

She'd given him up.

He should have known. He should have known she would do it the minute he was gone. She'd been too angry, too upset with him. He never should have left her alone. Hell, he never should have gone to her in the first place; he'd been followed like a rookie fresh out of the academy. And by one of Carlos's men, at that.

The only question was, who had she called? Cruz was the most likely choice, but what would he do? Would he turn the information over to the brass? Which meant Robards. If a task force came barreling in here, was he going to have to expect trouble from all sides? No, he thought, they wouldn't be coming here. They would head for the warehouse. They had no way of knowing about this place. Did they?

And what would Carlos's men do? Would they really follow the crackhead's orders? Were they committed, or just bored and tired of being broke?

He glanced at the man, who seemed so taken aback by this unexpected hitch in his plan to use Lacey as a lever that he wasn't functioning well. Or his last hit was wearing off. Or he was even stupider than Ryan had thought.

Whatever it was, Ryan knew this was his only chance to try to salvage something from this. And if the cavalry was really on its way, maybe he could string this out just long enough. . . .

"Shut up, bitch. I have to talk to this idiot," he said to Lacey, accompanying the epithet he never would have used in front of her with a barely perceptible nod. She caught it, and with a perfect impersonation of a woman fuming at having to stop her tirade but afraid not to, she subsided.

He turned his gaze on Carlos, the knife still in his hands, and still sliding his thumb over the edge, as if to be sure it was sharp enough to slit the man's throat. Carlos swallowed, his prominent Adam's apple moving visibly.

"I think you should know," Ryan said, his voice utterly flat. "I've heard from Alarico."

The other men in the room tensed. Even though he'd been in jail for nearly two weeks, the mention of their former leader's name still had the power to hold their undivided attention. Alarico had held total control, and no one, not even Carlos, had ever dared go against him. They knew what the penalty would be. And if they hadn't known before, Alarico's cold-blooded murder of fourteen-year-old Eddie Salazar had made it clear.

Ryan was counting on their fear of the man.

"He knows who set him up, Carlos. Who helped that Marina del Mar cop weasel his way in here."

The other men shifted uncomfortably. Carlos looked merely confused. "Who set him up? That cop set him up."

"But the cop had help. From the inside."

The intentness of Ryan's gaze finally seemed to register on the man. "What are you looking at me like that for?"

"He knows you were in on it, Carlos."

"Me!" The man's startled yelp was almost pitiful. "What are you talking about?"

"You wanted him out of the way, didn't you? So you helped that cop, told him what he needed to know to get Alarico to accept him."

"That's crazy!" Carlos glared at him.

"You didn't have the guts to take him on face-to-face, so you set him up so the cops could take him down."

"I didn't!"

He looked around at the men who had elected to follow him against Ryan. They were silent, considering, their eyes going from Carlos to Ryan, calculatingly. Carlos turned back to Ryan, sputtering.

"You're just trying to worm your way out of this, Indian! You knew I was too strong for you—"

"Strong? You're a coward, Carlos. You want to lead the Pack, but you haven't got the brains or the guts. Otherwise you would have challenged Alarico in the traditional way, man-to-man, instead of scheming behind his back."

"You can't prove that!"

"Can't I?" Ryan said in that deadly quiet voice. "Isn't what you've done here proof enough? First, like a coward, you set up Alarico to get him out of the way. Then you go against me, the chosen successor, but again you don't have the *cojones* to do it face-to-face. You have to split the Pack, con these men—" he gestured at the gathered group, who were now looking at Carlos somewhat suspiciously "—into doing the dirty work you won't do yourself."

"I'm not conning anyone! They're here because they don't want you running the Pack any more than I do."

"Then I hope they have their affairs in order. Because you'll sell them out as easily as you sold out Alarico. As easily as you sold out Crawford."

"Crawford? What are you talking about?"

Hell if I know, Ryan thought. He was making this up as he went along. Only the fact that Crawford was safely locked away made him think he just might get away with it. He only needed it to work once.

"He knew, didn't he? He's the one who recognized the Marina del Mar cop, and he knew you were in on it. That's why you set him up to get caught on that robbery."

"That job was his idea, not mine!"

The men were getting restless now. They'd seen betrayal from within before, and Ryan was counting on their being ready to believe in it again. Carlos had always had a big mouth, bragging to anyone who would listen, and he had a habit of sending others to do his dirty, risky work. Ryan hoped they would remember that.

"And that boy, the one who informed on us. You were his source, too, weren't you?"

"I never even talked to that kid!"

Ryan knew that was probably true. He was running a pure bluff here. But the only man who could deny what he was saying was also nicely locked away, thanks to Romero.

"That's not what Lenny says."

"Lenny?" Carlos was practically squeaking now. He was plainly nervous, and the others saw it. And as Ryan had hoped, they seemed to interpret it as guilt. They began to circle, like the sharks they were, as if they scented blood.

"He and Alarico are in the same lockup, didn't you know? No, of course you didn't. You're not smart enough to figure that out."

The circle tightened. Ryan never took his eyes off Carlos, although he knew where the others were. Carlos was looking around wildly, as if seeking support among the passive faces. Finally he turned back to Ryan.

"What the hell would Lenny know? He killed the kid!"

"Exactly. He was there when the boy died. And he gave you up, Carlos. The kid copped that you were his contact."

"He couldn't have! I wasn't!"

"With his dying breath, *pendejo.* You don't lie when you're dying."

"I don't care what you say you know. I never did it. Any of it."

Carlos sounded desperate now, Ryan took one step toward the man, and Carlos scrambled back as if he'd taken a swing at him. A rumble went around the room at this evidence of fear, and then, while that thought was fresh in their minds, Ryan played his trump card.

"Prove it," he said.

Carlos was sweating profusely now. "H-how?"

Ryan lifted his knife until the gleaming blade was level with Carlos's throat. "Fight me. Man-to-man. As it should be. Kill me one-on-one, as the tradition says, and the Pack is yours."

There was a rumbling again from around the room. Ryan heard it, heard the general sound of assent. But he'd also heard one slight, barely audible sound of protest.

Lacey. She'd been quiet throughout, as if she realized he couldn't afford any distraction in this. But as if his last words had broken her resolve, a tiny sound had escaped her.

He won't do it, Lace, he thought, wishing he could send the message to her somehow. *He doesn't have the guts.*

"Well, Carlos? I'm waiting for an answer. Will you fight me like a man for control of the Pack? Hand to hand? As it should be? As it has always been?"

Carlos swallowed. "I'd be crazy to fight you when you've got that damned knife of yours."

"This?"

Ryan lifted a brow as he looked at the blade in mock astonishment. Then, with a swift flick of his hand, he sent the blade slashing through the air. Carlos swore, throwing his hands up as if they could protect him from the deadly weapon. There was a thunk as it hit and stuck in the worn, dusty floorboard, dead center between Carlos's feet. He jumped back, and there was the sound of mocking laughter from the gathered men.

Ryan nodded at the knife. "It's all yours," he said, looking and sounding utterly unconcerned. "If," he added in a tone that matched the sound of the men's laughter, "you can pull it out, that is."

"Son of a bitch!"

Carlos bent for the knife, clearly intent on disemboweling Ryan with his own weapon. Ryan stood ready, on the balls of his feet, hands loose, just in case.

Carlos couldn't get the knife free. The laughter from the men turned to sneers. Carlos struggled for a second longer, but Ryan's strength in planting the knife was beyond the skinny man's ability to overcome. He straightened and backed away from it as the sneers became boos and catcalls.

Then four things happened simultaneously. The crashing sound of doors being broken down. The appearance of a dozen heavily armed, flak-jacketed men from all sides. The unmistakable sound of the command to surrender issued through a bullhorn.

And Carlos diving for his gun.

The minute she heard the commotion Lacey knew Cruz had arrived. At least, she prayed it was Cruz, although she knew it was much more likely he was at the warehouse. She didn't recognize the voice blaring through the bullhorn, issuing a warning so corny as to be a cliché, that they were surrounded and should give up.

And then she saw Carlos move.

The man's skinny hands grabbed the deadly-looking automatic pistol as though he was a drowning man reaching for a life preserver. Lacey cringed instinctively as shots rang out from all over the old building and chaos erupted in the dark, dank room that had once been the site for people pawning pieces of their lives for ready cash.

But she damn well wasn't selling hers.

She saw Carlos crouch behind the table, looking, searching the crowd of milling, jostling men. With an unerring eye she spotted Ryan's tall, powerful shape amid them. With some swift hand and footwork he cleverly stopped the escape of those who were trying to flee without tipping his hand to the others. He was holding his gun, even fired it a couple of times, but she saw he was only doing it to scare the fleeing Pack members into changing direction, right into the waiting hands of the task force.

He had his hands full, surrounded by panicking members of the Pack trying to flee from the advancing officers. Shots still came from those trying to fight, and the answering fire from the task force rifles made the room echo.

And then, from the corner of her eye, she saw Carlos raise his weapon.

He was sighting in on Ryan.

She screamed Ryan's name, but her cry was lost amid the chaos. Carlos smiled with gloating satisfaction as his finger slipped down to the trigger.

Without hesitation, without thinking of how easy it would be for the man to turn the weapon on her, Lacey launched herself headlong at him.

In the instant that she collided with him, a rapid succession of explosions far too close to her right ear nearly deafened her. She went down to her knees, stunned. She heard a scuffling, but it was only a faint sound through the ringing in her ears. A little dazed, she looked around. She felt off-balance, but she saw Ryan still standing, looking toward her, as if he'd heard the shots. He started to move, as if to come to her.

"You bitch! I'll kill you! I swear it."

Carlos's enraged shout seemed to penetrate even the buzzing in her ears. She thought vaguely that she should react, in case he meant that literally, right now.

Then Victor's huge bulk suddenly loomed up behind Ryan. She shouted a warning, not knowing if the man was a threat or not, not knowing if any of the Pack had yet tumbled to the fact that Ryan was helping them into the arms of the task force. Ryan whirled, whether because he'd heard her or because he'd sensed the big man's approach, Lacey didn't know. For a moment the two men—Ryan taller but Victor heavier—seemed to grapple, but they could have been merely arguing over escape routes. Lacey couldn't tell from her vantage point.

She suddenly realized she was all alone. Carlos had vanished. Along with his gun.

And then she saw something that made her stomach clench. To her left, barely three yards away, coming in through the back door of the building, was a short, heavily jowled man, a cigar stub between his teeth. He wore a police vest like the others, but it strained to cover his paunch. A black cap was pulled low over his brush-cut hair.

And he was holding an automatic rifle that looked to Lacey at the moment like the deadliest weapon in the world.

Because this was Robards. And his eyes were moving rapidly, searching the milling and still combative group. She still heard some shots from across the room as at least one stubborn Pack member refused to give up. Robards never looked that way.

And Lacey knew then he wasn't looking for members of the Pack.

Her heart racing, she dodged back behind a pillar, where Robards couldn't see her. As she did, something caught her eye, a metallic glint near the floor to her right.

Ryan's knife.

She glanced at Robards; he'd spotted Ryan. She saw him look around, his gaze stopping on each member of the task force, as if counting his men.

Or as if accounting for where they were and whether they could see him, she thought suddenly.

She moved quickly, crouching beside the knife. Its point was driven a good inch and a half into the wood of the floor, and she marveled anew at Ryan's fierce strength, to have done this with a mere flick of his wrist. She used it to her advantage, glad she didn't have to try to handle the thing and cut her bonds at the same time.

The blade sliced through the thick nylon cord as if it were merely a slender thread. She stood, pulling the pieces of cord away from her raw wrists. She knew that if Carlos hadn't had the strength to pull the knife loose, chances were she didn't, either. But she did have something he didn't appear to have—a functioning brain.

She moved to the edged side of the blade and kicked out with her foot at the handle, hard and swift, as if she were striking at an opponent in her karate class, driving the handle back and the cutting edge forward. The razor-sharp blade dug through the old wood, giving her a half-inch or so of play, and when she reached for it, she got it free with one quick yank.

And then she headed for Robards.

Chapter 16

Ryan borrowed a pair of handcuffs from a young cop he didn't even know and slapped them on Victor's thick wrists. Ryan's heart was still hammering, and he was having a hard time slowing it down. He'd never felt that way before, no matter how dangerous or touch and go the operation was, and he hadn't expected ever to feel this way, even taking down the Pack.

But then, he'd never done his job with Lacey only a few feet away. With bullets flying, and some of the wilder Pack members not caring much what they hit. He'd let out what breath he'd had left in relief when, out of the corner of his eye, he'd seen her dodge behind one of the large pillars near the back door; it was the safest place in the room amid all the confusion.

And he still couldn't figure out how they'd known about this place.

"That's the last of them, buddy."

He glanced at Cruz Gregerson, who would have looked quietly lethal in dark clothing, a bullet-proof vest and dark baseball cap, even without the automatic rifle he was carrying. Ryan couldn't think of a thing to say, not now, not when the adrenaline was still pulsing through him.

"I just got word. They got everybody at the warehouse, too. No injuries to our guys."

Ryan nodded. They'd done better than he'd hoped.

"Listen, Ryan. We've got to talk. And you've got some fancy explaining to do to the higher-ups. But I think you have something else to do first," Cruz said wryly. Ryan lifted a brow, and Cruz gestured past him. "You'd better get her away from Robards before she slits his throat with that hog-sticker of yours."

Ryan whirled. And then stood stock-still, gaping. Lacey had the paunchy lieutenant backed against the pillar he'd seen her dodge behind before. She was, as Cruz had said, holding Ryan's knife in front of her. She was nearly as tall as the other man, so the shiny silver blade was uncomfortably close to his face. As Ryan started toward her, he saw her run her thumb over the edge of the blade, as he had when confronting Carlos.

And Robards looked nothing less than terrified.

"I'll keep everybody clear," Cruz said with a wink of understanding.

Ryan allowed himself a moment to savor the pleasure of watching the bully being intimidated. And he felt a pure, sweet pride well up inside him; she was the most incredible woman in the world. He'd assumed she'd been hiding behind that pillar, when in fact she'd been watching his back and keeping Robards off it.

"Has no one ever told you what a filthy, disgusting habit this is?" Lacey was saying conversationally as he got to within earshot.

No sooner did she finish what was obviously a rhetorical question than she moved the knife in a quick sideways motion in front of Robards's face. The blade flashed. The man yelped. And half the stub of his fat cigar fell to the floor, sliced off neatly.

Robards spotted Ryan then and spat out what was left of his cigar to shout, "Buckhart! This broad of yours has gone crazy! Get her away from me!"

Ryan came to a halt beside Lacey. She glanced at him. His jaw tightened at the sight of the swollen side of her mouth, but she smiled, just slightly, and he let it go. For now.

He crossed his arms and looked down at Robards, his expression carefully neutral. He had to keep it that way; otherwise, he would break out in raucous laughter and put an end to what little might be left of his career right here and now.

"You asking me for help. . . sir?"

"Get that thing away from her! And then I'm going to arrest her for assault on an officer. With a deadly weapon."

Ryan glanced at the floor, where the two pieces of the cigar lay. Then he looked back at Robards, still neutral, as if he were of no more import than the severed cigar.

"Assault on a cigar, maybe."

Robards swore. Lacey waved the knife slightly, and he subsided. She smiled sweetly at him. Ryan knew that smile, knew the hapless soul she turned it on would be better off if she just used the knife on him. He settled back to watch, grinning inwardly.

"I have been kidnapped, tied up, hit and in general traumatized," she said, not sounding in the least injured but thoroughly angry. "I am not only a victim here, I am a private, taxpaying citizen, not one of your cops. And I doubt any court in the world would blame me for being a little confused."

"Confused? You're crazy, lady, holding a knife on an officer of the law. You—"

"I thought you were a bad guy."

"What?"

"What was I supposed to think? That a man in your physical condition, casually smoking a cigar under these circumstances, was a *cop?*"

Ryan nearly laughed at Robards's startled look. Lacey glanced at him as if she'd sensed how close he was to losing it, and shook her head slightly. He knew she was right. She, as a private citizen, could get away with things that would get him hung out to dry. And by her expression, she was about to turn that to full advantage.

"But...you *know* me! From when you were married to him," Robards protested, jerking his thumb toward Ryan.

There had been just the faintest bit of derision in that last pronoun, and it made Ryan stiffen. But when he saw Lacey's delicate chin shoot up he knew that she'd heard it, too. And he made himself wait.

"Sorry, I don't remember you at all. I guess you didn't make much of an impression." Lacey gave him a scornful look. "Not nearly the impression you made here today, staying back where it was safe, hiding while the real police were out there risking their lives to get the job done. I'm sure your superiors will be interested to hear that."

"I wasn't hiding! I—"

"I know what you were doing." Ryan finally spoke, his voice as deadly quiet as when he'd been dealing with the Pack. For this man was as much a jackal as any of them, only more dangerous, masquerading as one of the good guys. "What you wanted to do. It would have been easy, wouldn't it? To claim I'd been hit in the cross fire?"

Robards paled. The swift narrowing of his eyes gave him away, trumpeting the truth of Ryan's words.

"Ryan?" Lacey spoke quietly.

"What?" he answered, without taking his eyes off Robards.

"Wouldn't it be just as easy to claim *he'd* been hit in the cross fire?"

Ryan's head swiveled around then, and he stared at her as Robards sputtered.

"You...you *are* crazy! Buckhart, she's crazy! You'd never get away with it!"

Ryan saw the glint of devilish amusement in her eyes and found himself wanting to grin, all his rage draining away. Lacey had always been able to do that for him, and he knew it had been the only thing that had kept him sane. And he knew now just how much he'd missed it.

With his expression schooled back to impassivity, he looked back at the lieutenant.

"Why not? Two witnesses, one a cop, the other a civilian not even connected to the department anymore, and we both tell the same story?" He gave a melodramatic sigh. "That's the pity about vests, you know. They don't do anything to stop a round between the eyes."

"Are you threatening me?" Robards blustered.

"No more than you were threatening me," Ryan said coldly, and saw by the sudden fear in the man's tiny eyes that he understood. "Yes, you're right to be afraid. You've always thought I was a savage, haven't you? Well, maybe, just maybe, you're right."

Robards's eyes flicked from Ryan to Lacey and back, like a cornered rat. There would never be a better time, Ryan thought. He knew he would never be able to prove the man had wanted him dead, but Robards was scared now, and now was the time to strike.

"I'll make you a deal, Robards," he said. "You stay off my back, and I'll stay out of your way."

"And if you're nice," Lacey said in a mockingly sweet tone that matched her earlier smile, "I might be persuaded not to mention how you just stood back and didn't even help your own men when they were under fire."

God, I love you, Ryan thought as she neatly put the finishing touch on Robards's undoing.

"All right," the man snapped. "Just get her and that damn knife away from me."

"Knife?" Lacey sounded completely startled. She looked at the huge blade in her hand as if in shock. "Oh, dear. Where did this come from?"

Ryan couldn't help himself then; he laughed out loud. Lacey joined him as Robards snarled. Ryan reached out and took the knife from her, then slid it back into the sheath at his waist. The moment it was out of sight Robards glared furiously at them both, then turned on his heel and exited the way he'd come in, through the back door, much faster than Ryan would have given him credit for being able to move.

When Lacey looked back up at him, the laughter was fading from her expression, and he saw her draw herself up. He knew she had to be emotionally if not physically exhausted after what she'd been through, but still, she was gathering herself as if the fight weren't over. As if she had to get through this before her fragile remaining energy ran out.

"I know you're angry with me," she began.

"You're darn right," he agreed, an echo of the jolt of fear that had nearly paralyzed him when he realized what she'd done going through him again. "Jumping Carlos like that. You could have gotten yourself killed. What the hell were you thinking?"

"Look who's talking," she said, coming right back at him. "And that's not what I meant. I meant angry at me for calling Cruz." She sounded defiant. "But I don't care. I will always put your safety above anything else, and if that goes against your stubborn ideas about loyalty and honor, then so be it."

Ryan felt a rush of tenderness that nearly took him to his knees, sweeping his anger before it. How could he ever have let her slip away from him, for whatever foolish reason?

He reached out and gently gripped her shoulders. "I'm not angry that you called Cruz, Lacey."

She blinked. "You're not?"

He shook his head. "I knew, as soon as I stopped to think about it for a moment, that you'd do exactly what you did."

She stared at him as if stunned. "You knew?"

"The minute I realized you were stalling, I knew there had to be a reason. Then it all fell together."

"And that's when *you* started stalling, isn't it?"

He nodded. "I just didn't expect them to hit here, too. I didn't know they even knew about this place."

"I...told them."

It was his turn to blink. He released her shoulders and frowned. "What?"

"You mentioned it... on the phone the other day."

His brows lowered farther. "But I never said anything about this being Carlos's meeting place. Carny did."

"I know. But you were talking about him, and then later you said 'meeting,' and then you mentioned this place."

"And from that... you put this together? And told Cruz?"

She nodded, a little hesitantly, as if she weren't convinced he wasn't angry but was facing him down anyway. He had the sudden thought that she had enough strength to give to him, if he needed it, that he could take strength from her as well as give it. He'd never thought that before, and it shook a very deeply held perception inside him.

Something else was tugging at his mind, but right now this was more important. More important than anything. Ryan took a deep breath, knowing he owed her this, at the very least. He reached out and lifted her chin with a gentle finger.

"I'm sorry, Lacey," he said solemnly. "I've always underestimated you, haven't I? I thought I was protecting you, but you never needed it, did you? You've always been tough enough. I just didn't see it. Until now."

She gave him an almost shy smile, but her tone was as solemn as his. "And I... now I know how it happens. I never thought, when I saw Carlos take aim at you. I just knew I had to stop him."

"And you did. I owe you my life, Lacey. And for more than what happened here today."

"Er, kids?" Cruz Gregerson's voice, sounding very reluctant, intruded on their intense moment.

"Can't it wait?" Ryan said gruffly.

"'Fraid not," Cruz said reluctantly. "Somebody seems to be missing."

Ryan glanced over his shoulder. Cruz's blue eyes were troubled. "Missing?" Unexpectedly, a sense of relief shot through him. "Carny?"

"The guy who warned you? What's he look like?"

Ryan didn't question how Cruz knew. "Black man. Five-ten or so. About my age. Really buff."

Cruz's mouth twisted. "Apparently more than one is missing, then."

So they hadn't gotten him. Or Carny had somehow managed to smell that something was up and bail out in time. Ryan couldn't manage to be upset over that.

"This is where the opposition was meeting, right?" Cruz asked, dragging him back to the matter at hand.

"You know that already," Ryan said, giving Lacey a smile that was also a salute. "So what do you—" He broke off suddenly as it hit him. The thing that had been tugging at the edges of his mind since he'd slapped the cuffs on Victor, the last of the bunch.

The last minus one.

"Carlos," he hissed.

Cruz nodded. "We've got everybody loaded into the paddy wagon, and he isn't there."

"Damn. He'll go underground." Fury surged through Ryan. "And there's no way to track him. All his buddies will be in the slam. He's going to be on his own."

"And therefore unpredictable," Cruz said.

In more ways than one, Ryan thought, remembering too clearly Carlos's shouted threat to Lacey after she'd careened into him, spoiling his only chance to shoot Ryan in the back.

"What about his family?" Lacey asked.

Cruz shook his head. "None locally. Our records show they're all back east."

"Well, not all. His cousin's here."

Ryan looked at her. "What?"

"His cousin. He's the one who followed you to the house. Carlos called him in because he needed someone you'd never seen before, so you wouldn't recognize him."

Well, maybe he hadn't quite been tricked like a rookie, Ryan thought. But that also meant maybe Carlos wasn't quite as stupid as he thought. But then, there was a difference between intelligence and caginess, and Carlos had been around long enough to have learned some of that.

"This cousin... did you hear his name?" Ryan asked.

Lacey grinned. "Not his real one, no. But Carlos called him Tubby."

Cruz grinned back at her. "Tubby? I'll bet he likes that."

Ryan wasn't feeling particularly amused about anything at the moment, not when the man who'd hurt Lacey, who'd tried to use her as a tool against him, bringing his worst nightmare to life, was running around loose.

"So all we have to do is track down this cousin," Ryan said. "And convince him to tell us where Carlos will go."

"That could take some time."

"Why?" Lacey asked. Both men looked at her. "You said you got everybody except Carlos, right? So he should be out in your paddy wagon."

Ryan blinked. "Are you saying he was here?"

She nodded. "Short, round man. Thick mustache. Plaid shirt and khaki pants."

"The wailer!" Cruz exclaimed. "He's been whining he's innocent since we scooped him up." His grin widening, Cruz leaned forward and hugged her. "Lacey Buckhart, you are a wonder."

Yes, she was, Ryan agreed silently.

"He's probably not used to this," Lacey said. "He didn't seem like he was very... experienced."

"Sometimes," Ryan said quietly, "experience isn't necessary."

Lacey looked at him, caught his double meaning and colored, as if pleased.

"I'll go make sure he's there," Cruz said hastily.

Before he got a yard away Ryan stopped him. "Cruz? Bring him back in here, will you?"

"In here?" The other detective studied Ryan for a moment. "Good cop, bad cop?"

Ryan nodded. Cruz grinned again, nodded and hurried off.

"Good cop, bad cop? I've always wanted to see this," Lacey said. "Gee, I wonder what part you're going to play?"

"You're not going to see it this time. This isn't a game, Lacey."

Her smile faded. "Do you really think you have to tell me that, after the past twenty-four hours?"

He felt as if he'd slapped her. He let out a breath. "I'm . . . sorry. It's . . . a habit."

"Break it," Lacey suggested wryly. "And if you think I'm going to sit quietly in a corner after what I've been through today . . ."

Ryan sighed. She *had* earned this. And just because it went against his most basic instinct to let her become part of this, it didn't mean he had to give in to that instinct. He had some changing to do if he was going to have any hope of showing Lacey he was serious, and it might as well start here.

"All right. If you're going to be here, you might as well have a part to play."

She looked utterly startled. Then, slowly, she smiled. And Ryan knew he would do a lot more than bend what he'd always thought of as an inviolable rule to get a smile like that from her.

"What do you want me to do?"

"When Cruz gets him here, we'll sit him in that chair," he said. "Just look at him and nod. Say something like 'Yes, that's him.'"

"Make him feel isolated and picked on?"

"Sort of." He grimaced. "And could you look a little less gleeful? A bit shaken, maybe?"

Lacey laughed. Ryan sensed she was running on nerves by now, but as long as they held out long enough, it would be all right. Then he would take her home, make sure she went to bed. And then he would go after Carlos.

"I'll be suitably distraught, I promise. Ryan?"

"What?"

"He's kind of short. Maybe you should make him sit on the table instead. His feet won't even touch the ground."

He stared at her, then slowly began to smile. "Damn. He'll feel like a little kid."

"Especially next to you."

"You're a cruel woman," he said, his cheerful expression belying his words.

"I was a psychology major before I switched to hotel management, remember?"

"Psychology's loss," he said, then looked over his shoulder as Cruz led the clearly agitated man over to them.

Cruz released him as soon as Ryan was within reach. Without a word Ryan grabbed a handful of the much shorter man's shirtfront and swung him around toward the table. The man yelped but didn't try to pry Ryan's hand loose, as if he knew it would be a wasted effort.

Still moving silently, Ryan grabbed the man's upper arm. Despite his considerable bulk, Ryan lifted him as easily as if he were a child and deposited him on the table. The man Carlos had called Tubby gaped at him and cowered away as Ryan stood over him.

"You're a cop," the man said, realization dawning slowly over his round face.

Ryan said nothing. As he'd intended, his silence was an effective tool.

"You can't hit me! I'll sue for brutality!"

Ryan glanced at Lacey. Wrapping her arms around herself, looking credibly shaken, she stepped forward. She nodded, a little jerkily, as if she were barely managing not to tremble.

"Yes, that's him," she said. "That's the one."

The man's eyes widened fearfully. "The one? What one?"

"Thank you," Cruz said politely. "That's all we needed to hear."

"Hey, I didn't do anything to her. And if she says I did, she's lying! I never even touched her. I just pointed out the house."

"You can leave now," Ryan said ominously. "You won't want to watch this."

Lacey shivered and turned away, as if she couldn't bear to look at the man any longer. Or as if she were afraid of what was going to happen.

Lacey Buckhart, you are a wonder, Cruz had said. And that, Cruz, my friend, is an understatement.

Ryan moved so close to the man he literally towered over him. Sweat broke out on Tubby's forehead.

"Wait a minute," he said urgently. "I haven't done anything! I'm not one of them, I'm innocent! All I did was follow you! You can't just—"

"You aided and abetted in kidnapping, assault and extortion." Cruz ticked off the crimes on his fingers, his voice almost regretful as he looked at the man pityingly. "And you picked the wrong man to do it to," he added, looking at Ryan as if he were half-afraid of him, too. "Half the time even we can't control him."

Slowly, aware of the frightened man's eyes on his every move, Ryan pulled out his knife.

He had read once about genetic memory and the theory that it passed down instincts and memories and learned behaviors over generations. He'd wondered if it was that or early Hollywood that had planted the fear of a big Indian with a knife in so many minds. He'd hated it even as he used it, often, for his own purposes. Used it because it worked.

Tubby broke at the first slide of his thumb over that razor edge. He couldn't talk fast enough, and he gave up Carlos's probable location so quickly Ryan couldn't quite believe it had been that easy. But it was logical. Carlos's cousin—whose real name, it turned out, was Luis—had arrived from the East Coast only a couple of months ago, and already Carlos had made himself at home, stealing anything small and portable he could sell to support the crack habit that was becoming more out of control every day.

"I moved out here because Carlos talked big, and I thought he would help me. Instead, he steals from me, his own cousin!" the man whined indignantly. "And he'll go there now, to steal what's left and sell it, while I sit in jail, when all I did was a favor for him!"

Cruz lifted a small, hand-held radio from its holder on his belt. He spoke into it. A moment later the young officer Ryan had borrowed the handcuffs from appeared and, on Cruz's instructions, led the terrified but untouched man away.

"Let's go," Cruz said when the officer and his prisoner were out of earshot. "With any luck, we can be there waiting for Carlos when he shows up."

Ryan shook his head.

"Why not? Hot pursuit, right?" Cruz said, referring to the case law that allowed law enforcement officers more leeway if they were in pursuit of a recently seen suspect. "Let's get moving."

"Cruz... I'm already in deep."

"I know. Mallery's steamed, and the chief is waiting for an explanation that better be damn good. But what better reason to put it off for a while than to round up this clown? Let's go."

Ryan shook his head again. "I'll go."

Cruz went still. "*You'll* go?"

"I can't get in much more trouble. You can."

"I see."

Cruz folded his arms over his chest, and his usually friendly demeanor disappeared. His eyes went cold. This was the man who had defused a bomb with mere seconds to spare.

"I thought you might have learned something," Cruz said softly, glancing over at Lacey. "But I guess not."

Ryan didn't want to, but he couldn't stop himself from looking at Lacey, as well. She stood a bare five feet away, but from the expression on her face she might as well have been on the moon as far as he was concerned. The look she gave him held a world of pain and disappointment.

Still running alone, eh, Buckhart?

It's time to give up the lone-wolf act.

You still can't trust anyone, even your closest friends.

All the things she'd said to him rang in his head, loudly, persistently, repeatedly.

He looked back at Cruz, but more of Lacey's words were still swirling in his mind.

You still can't trust anyone else. And I can't carry that load, Ryan. I can't be everything to you. I'm not that strong.

Ryan looked back at Lacey once more, but this time it was his own thoughts that haunted him.

He had some changing to do, if he was going to have any hope of showing Lacey he was serious, and it might as well start here.

And he knew then, as she began to retreat from him as surely as if she were physically backing away, that this was the moment that would set the course for the rest of his life. If he failed her now, if he insisted on the old ways, there would be nothing left of them.

He turned back to Cruz. "This water I'm in up to my neck is pretty damned hot," he warned. Then he had to swallow before he could get the rest of the words out. "But...if you're willing to risk getting scalded...I'd appreciate the help."

Cruz drew back a little and looked at him assessingly. "No more lone wolf?"

Ryan took a long, deep breath, then expelled it slowly, wishing it would ease the pressure of doing this thing that was so foreign to him.

"Sometimes," he said finally, "wolves hunt better in packs."

Cruz grinned suddenly, and Ryan saw him throw a wink in Lacey's direction.

"And I've got a damn thick hide, Buckhart. It's going to take more than hot water to scald me. Let's get going."

It hadn't really been so hard, Ryan realized, now that it was over. And he could even admit he would be glad to have Cruz's help. The man had a cool head and a quick mind, and he was damn good in a pinch. Ryan found himself smiling and was amazed at the relief he was feeling.

And then Lacey blew it all away.

With that stubborn tilt to her chin and that determined note in her voice that he knew all too well, she looked up at him and said, "I'm going with you."

"Like hell you are," Ryan snapped.

"If you think I'm going to sit quietly at home, after all I've been through, and not even see the end of this, you're mistaken, Buckhart."

He groaned. He'd finally buckled, done as she'd asked, done *everything* she'd asked, and still he was back to "Buckhart." What the hell did the woman want from him?

Cruz burst out laughing. "Brother, if you could see your face!"

"Shut up, Gregerson," he growled.

"I *deserve* this," Lacey said firmly. "I'll do whatever you say—I won't even get out of the car—but I want to see that piece of slime get his."

Ryan doubted if she realized her fingers had crept up to the bruise on her face. He'd guessed it had been Carlos's doing, but now he was certain.

"She's got a point there, partner. None of this would have come together without her. She told us about Carlos, gave us the info on this place and backed Robards into a corner while you were... otherwise occupied."

Not to mention putting on the performance of a lifetime to keep them both alive long enough for Cruz and the cavalry to arrive. And manipulating Robards into a corner he couldn't get out of, a move that just might make his own life a whole lot easier. But the very idea of her in harm's way still made him cringe inside.

"You advocating taking a civilian along on what could turn into a shooting expedition?" he asked Cruz.

"Nope. But I am advocating just rewards."

He looked back at Lacey. "You'll stay put? Where you're told?"

"I will."

"No matter how good a reason you think you have for moving?"

Her chin came up at the reminder of her trip to Steele Street. But she met his gaze levelly as she answered, "Yes."

"I have got to be out of my mind," he muttered.

"Probably," Cruz agreed cheerfully.

Ryan glowered at him. "I never realized you were the reckless type."

"I've been watching you too much," Cruz retorted. "Besides, I've got a lot of faith in Chief de los Reyes. He'll understand."

"Yeah," Ryan said dryly. "He'll slap that suspension on us very understandingly. If he doesn't decide to fire me outright."

Cruz's gaze flicked to Lacey, then back to Ryan. "You might just need that suspension time off, partner."

Ryan felt heat rise in his cheeks, a rarity only Lacey had ever caused. Cruz's words reminded him that there was a great deal left unsettled between them and no guarantee it could be fixed. But somehow he knew that shutting her out now, when she truly did have the right to see the end of this—from a safe distance, of course—would make it that much harder.

"All right, all right," he snapped. "Let's go."

Old habits, Ryan thought, were hellishly hard to break.

"It's the only thing that makes sense," Cruz insisted. "He gets one look at you and he'll take off or start shooting. We can't risk that," he said, nodding toward a couple of children riding their bikes down what seemed to be a quiet, residential street, past an elderly woman pruning a rosebush. "But he won't know me."

"We don't even know if he burned my cover," Ryan protested.

"Does it matter? Whether he knows or not, he's not going to welcome you with open arms."

"What makes you think he'll welcome you?"

Cruz's mouth twisted. "I'm still working on that part."

They were sitting in Cruz's big four-wheel drive, knowing Carlos could smell an undercover police car at first sniff.

They were parked around the corner from Luis's house, as far away as they could get and still maintain a line of sight on the residence. A quick recon from a safe distance had turned up a broken window in the back of the small, older house, and Cruz had caught a glimpse of movement inside.

After Ryan spotted a shiny brown coupe decorated with elaborate pinstriping parked behind the house, they were sure who was inside. The too-recognizable vehicle had been an affectation of Carlos's that Ryan had always thought exemplified the man's stupidity.

They'd also quickly determined that there was no way to approach the house without being seen by anyone who happened to glance out. It had clearly been empty and neglected long enough for most of the shrubbery that could have provided cover to die back. They were going to need a diversion.

Cruz had suggested calling for backup on his car phone, but he'd done it with the air of someone who didn't expect his idea to be accepted. And when Ryan had said, "We don't have time to wait for them," Cruz had merely nodded acceptingly. Then he'd brought up his idea of simply going to the front door. And instinctively, Ryan had objected to that, too.

The minute he'd said it, he'd known he was reacting in the old way. The lone-wolf way. And he knew Cruz knew it. More important, he knew Lacey knew it, although she didn't say a word.

"Look," Cruz said now, "I'll think of something when I get up there and see how he reacts."

"If he even opens the damn door," Ryan muttered.

Cruz grimaced. "No wonder you work alone. You're a pain in the butt, you know?"

Lacey chuckled. It was the first sound she'd made since she'd climbed into the back seat, pushing aside the assortment of dog toys and an empty hamster cage. Cruz had apologized for the clutter, but Lacey had merely smiled and said this was the kind of clutter she liked.

Ryan twisted in the front passenger bucket seat and gave her a sideways look. "Think that's funny, do you?"

"I just think Cruz is very astute," she said.

"As are you," Cruz said with a gallantry that was only half-teasing.

A sharp jab hit Ryan somewhere near his stomach. It took him a moment to realize it was jealousy, and he groaned inwardly at the irony of it. Jealous of Cruz, of all people, who had been such a friend to them both. And over his ex-wife, when he wasn't sure they would be any less ex than they had been when all this was over.

"Do you think we could get back to the subject here?" Ryan requested, knowing he sounded sullen but unable to help it. "Before he rabbits on us?"

"I'm open to any ideas that make sense," Cruz said amiably. "But I don't think Carlos is going to open the door for an encyclopedia salesman."

"He might," Lacey responded, "if that salesman had something he wanted."

"Such as?" Ryan asked, not liking the look on Lacey's face.

"Me," she said.

Chapter 17

It was odd, Lacey thought, how Ryan had always seemed so unreadable about his work before. She'd assumed it was because he was so used to hiding his true reactions that he did it automatically. But now his thoughts seemed so clear to her as she watched the emotions warring in his face.

Shock, protest, incredulity and fear were all there, and she wondered if she'd changed, somehow becoming more adept at reading him—Lord knew she'd spent enough time in the past three years playing back every moment she'd spent with him in her head—or if he had changed, letting things show that he never had before.

"No!" he said suddenly, sharply, as if it had taken a moment for the exclamation to get past his shock.

"You don't think he'd open the door for a stranger who was bringing him the woman he's probably maddest at in the entire world?" she asked, feigning innocent ignorance of his true meaning.

"That's not what I meant, and you know it," Ryan said.

"Protecting me again?" she asked.

"You don't need protection, you need a keeper!" He jammed a hand through his hair, tugging a few long strands free of the restraint of the bandanna. "If you think for an instant that I'm going to let you set yourself up as...as bait for a pig like Carlos, you're out of your mind."

Lacey glanced at Cruz, who immediately threw his hands up defensively. "Oh, no. Don't put me in between you two. I've been there before, and I didn't like it much. It gave me gray hairs."

Lacey looked pointedly at Cruz's pure black shock of hair, only marginally less dark than Ryan's.

"Okay, figurative gray hairs," he admitted. "But I mean it. I'm not getting involved in this."

"But it would work, wouldn't it?" she insisted. Although she regretted putting Cruz in the middle, she knew she was right.

"Lacey," Ryan said warningly.

She glanced at him. "I know you don't want to hear it, but it *would* work." She turned back to the uneasy Cruz. "We'd have to make it look like I wasn't with you willingly. You could say his cousin told you to bring me here. He'd come out, wouldn't he? And I wouldn't be alone. You'd be there, and Ryan could be in position already and maybe get behind him. Between the two of you, nothing would happen to me."

Cruz cleared his throat. "I—" He stopped at Ryan's warning glare.

"You know it would work, Cruz," Lacey said.

"I know it's crazy." Ryan seemed to relax slightly, but tensed again when Cruz added, "But it's just crazy enough that it might work with a crazy man like Carlos. It's got all the elements, bait, surprise—"

"Forget it," Ryan snapped.

"Was that directed at her or me?" Cruz asked.

"Both," he said in the same tone.

Cruz shook his head. "I really don't like being caught here, buddy. So I'm going to say two things, and then I'm out of here while you two thrash this out. First...I understand how you feel. I don't like the thought of her being anywhere near him, so I can guess how sick the idea makes you. And I agree, even though it might work, it's crazy. She's a civilian, and we could lose our badges for using her. But it's your call, and I'll back you all the way. Second . . ."

He paused, looked at Lacey for a moment, took a breath, then met Ryan's gaze head-on.

"Second, I'd die before I'd let anything happen to her."

He yanked open the door and slid out of the driver's seat before Ryan could react. He let the door fall back but didn't push it shut, then walked away, across the street, where he would be out of earshot but could still see the house.

And still Ryan stared after the man, his eyes wide with shock.

"Surprised?" Lacey asked gently. "You shouldn't be. That's the kind of friend Cruz Gregerson is, if you give him the chance."

"I . . ." He shook his head, as if in bewilderment.

"You do it for total strangers, Ryan. Risk your life. Why is it so hard for you to believe a friend would do it for you?"

"I . . . don't want him to."

"Of course you don't. Neither do I. I don't want you to risk yourself, either. And do you think I *want* to get anywhere near that piece of slime again? But he hurt a lot of innocent people in that crime spree he started. He needs to be put away where he can't ever do it again. We have the chance to do that."

"We'll do it. But you're not getting anywhere near him."

"What are you going to do? Break in and try to take him by force? Pray you get to him before he shoots a few innocent bystanders, like those kids, or that little old lady?"

"I'll think of something."

"Like what? Present yourself as a target and hope that while Carlos is shooting you, Cruz can pick him off?"

"That's better than handing him *you* as a target!"

"Why? He's a lot less likely to start shooting at me on sight. I'm sure, charmer that he is, he'd have other things in mind for me first. He's the type."

It made her nauseous—and brought back some buried memories—to think about what those other things might be, and Ryan looked as if she'd just kicked him in the belly.

"Damn it, Lacey! I won't send you in there!"

"Afraid of losing your badge?"

"Hell, it's probably already gone. But if it isn't, that just might do it. The chief does more than frown on using civilians."

"Even if it's a volunteer?"

"This isn't like back at the pawn shop, where you only had to confront a disarmed man, already in custody. Carlos will be armed, and he's too damned ready to shoot. He's on the run, he'll be nervous and, even as dumb as he is, it could only take him a minute to figure out he's being set up."

"But Ryan Buckhart only needs ten seconds," she said, softly quoting the phrase that had become a maxim at Trinity West.

He let out a compressed breath, in the manner of a man whose own reputation had come back to haunt him. For a long moment he just looked at her, and Lacey thought she had never seen such a battle of emotion and will so plainly displayed. Either she truly had gotten better at reading him, or he really wasn't hiding anything from her now.

"What was it you said back there?" he asked her finally. "'I will always put your safety above anything else'? Well, that works both ways, Lacey. I won't let you do this. Not even to prove to you that I know you *could* do it. Because I do know. You could. But I can't. Even if it means you don't believe I've changed at all. Even if it means...destroying any chance we might have, I'd rather have you alive and hating me than dead."

She stared at him. *Destroying any chance we might have...* "I could never hate you," she said, a little numbly after this unexpected confirmation that he truly did hope things weren't over between them yet.

"We'll think of something else."

"We may not have time, partner." Cruz was back, opening the door soundlessly and sliding back into the driver's seat. "Carlos just carried a load of stuff out to his car. Looks like he's getting ready to make tracks. We have to move now."

Ryan swore—a soft, low, heartfelt sound. "He'll probably make a couple of trips. If we can get into the house in between—"

"He's already made one," Cruz noted. "He's headed back inside for the second. We can't count on him making a third. And if we go for the house and he leaves now, we could lose him by the time we get rolling. And I'd say we've got about thirty seconds to decide."

"We've got to do it, Ryan," Lacey said.

"I'm not letting you go in there!"

She could sense Cruz looking as the tension crackled between them, as tangible as the blade of Ryan's knife.

"Wait," Cruz said suddenly. "I've thought of something."

He laid it out for them swiftly, keeping one eye on the house. Ryan still wasn't happy, but he reluctantly agreed. The two men got out of the car, and Lacey quickly slid between the bucket seats and into the driver's side. She started the motor, then turned to watch the two men. Cruz was off to one side, the only one daring to risk being seen, since Carlos wouldn't recognize him. Lacey couldn't see what he was looking at from her angle, but when, a bare minute later, he lifted a hand and pointed at her sharply, she put the big vehicle in gear and pulled away from the curb.

In the moment when she was out of sight, around the corner and heading toward the alley that led behind the houses, she became aware of how rapidly her heart was hammering, that her breathing was coming in quick bursts. And Ryan *lived* like this, probably most of his time undercover, she thought in awe.

Then she made the turn into the alley and could think of nothing else but what she had to do. She was past the second house when she realized she could see the back of the big brown coupe.

The trunk was open, and she could see what looked like plastic grocery bags, full of oddly shaped objects, piled inside.

She slowed, her eyes searching for any sign of Carlos. Or Cruz. Or Ryan. She saw no one.

She slowed even more. And then she saw Carlos, loaded down with more of the grocery bags, these holding what looked like clothing. The slime really was cleaning out his cousin's home while the man languished in jail.

He stopped moving. Lacey's heart leapt—had he seen her already? But he merely shifted one of the bags that was slipping and continued to the back of the car. He was apparently oblivious to her presence. She frowned. It wasn't possible to miss seeing Cruz's big blue four-wheel drive.

He got to the back of the coupe and turned to load the bags into the trunk. By this time she was close enough to see the rear of the house. She saw Cruz dodge back to press himself flat against the wall as Carlos turned. The skinny, wild-eyed man was almost facing him. All he had to do was look up and he would have Cruz dead to rights. She couldn't see Carlos's gun, but she had little doubt that it was handy. And then she saw Ryan, coming around the other side of the house, stopping as well as he realized the man was facing them.

She felt a lurch that involved much more than just her stomach. Carlos had the car between him and them, had cover, while Cruz and Ryan were going to be right out in the open. And any second Carlos could look up and see that. She had to do something. Fast.

Swallowing, hoping she still had a voice, she rolled down the window and tapped lightly on the horn. At the faint beep, Carlos, still bent over the trunk, looked back over his shoulder.

"Hello there, Carlos," she said in the brightest, most cheerful tone she could manage. "Nice to see you again."

He straightened sharply, hitting his head on the raised trunk with an audible thunk. Despite her nerves, Lacey couldn't help the little snicker that escaped her. Fury reddened Carlos's face, and as he took a step toward her, she belatedly realized she hadn't followed Ryan's most stringent instruction—to keep moving.

She did so now, slamming down on the accelerator. The big 4×4 had more power than she was used to, and she ended up sending a nice spray of gravel from the side of the alleyway into the air, peppering both Carlos and his fancy car. The man let loose a string of curses in Spanish. She recognized only one, but his meaning was evident. She risked a quick glance in the rearview mirror in time to see him reaching into his waistband. She wondered if her slow reactions were going to get her killed and Cruz's truck shot to pieces.

But she got to the end of the alley intact and unhurt, and risked another look. Carlos was facedown on the ground, Ryan on top of him. She saw what appeared to be the gun she'd seen at the pawn shop tossed aside. With a sigh of relief she slowed down, then began to maneuver the big vehicle around to return to the scene.

When she'd completed the turn and started back down the alley, she began to wonder if she'd relaxed too soon. She saw Cruz with his hand on Ryan's shoulder, trying to get him off Carlos. Ryan had the man's right arm bent behind him, and even from here she could hear Carlos wailing.

She sped up, then hit the brakes as she got there. The truck skidded slightly on the gravel, then stopped. Ryan looked over his shoulder at the sound. He straightened slightly, and Carlos subsided to a whine as Ryan eased up. Lacey threw the gearshift into Park and reached for the door handle, then stopped as Cruz shook his head at her.

"Take a breath," Cruz said to Ryan, reaching into his back pocket and pulling out a pair of handcuffs, which he handed over. "I'll call for transportation."

Ryan didn't seem happy, even though he was almost literally sitting on the man they'd been after, and Lacey had the sinking feeling Carlos wasn't the only target of his displeasure. But he took the cuffs and began to slap them on Carlos's bony wrists.

When Cruz got to her side of the truck and opened the door, she looked at him nervously.

"You did great, Lacey," Cruz assured her. "That was a gutsy move, calling out to him like that. Gave us just what we needed, ten seconds to get to him."

Relief swept through her; at least Cruz didn't think she'd blown it. "Then what's wrong with Ryan?"

"You mean besides the fact that he almost broke the arm Carlos hit you with?" Cruz asked as he reached past her for the phone.

Lacey's breath caught. It was primitive and more than a little wild, and she knew she should hate herself for it, but a spurt of grim satisfaction shot through her.

"Yes," she said after a moment. "Besides that."

Cruz smiled, a knowing, pleased smile as she accepted Ryan's reaction without flinching. But his smile quirked at one corner as he answered her query.

"You know Ryan. He doesn't handle the idea of you in danger very well."

Lacey sighed. "I know. He's going to be a pain about it, too, isn't he?"

Cruz dialed, then looked back at her as he waited for the phone to ring on the other end. "I think you can always count on him worrying about you, Lacey. No matter if you're together or not."

As the call was answered and Cruz began to talk, Lacey looked over at Ryan again. He was crouched beside the handcuffed Carlos, just watching, his dark eyes hooded and unreadable. Lacey sighed. This was Ryan at his most stoic, most remote, and she didn't know if she could deal with it.

Some of the neighbors were venturing out now, both attracted by and wary of the commotion Carlos had made. Cruz finished his call and went to reassure them, after advising Lacey to stay put and not add to Ryan's mood. For once she obeyed without question.

By the time the marked unit arrived to take Carlos, she was in a high state of tension. Ryan hadn't even looked at her, not once since he'd checked over his shoulder when she'd first come back. And although the officer who had been pressed into service as transport driver looked at her curiously as he pulled up beside Cruz's truck, Ryan never even glanced her way. Not even when he was barely a yard away, putting the muttering and glaring Carlos in the caged back seat.

She saw Cruz look from Ryan to her and back again. He cleared his throat audibly. Ryan looked at him.

"I'll ride in with our friend here and start the paperwork. And," he added wryly, "the explaining. Bring my truck back to Trinity West, will you?"

Lacey knew he was doing this intentionally, to give her and Ryan a chance to talk, but she wasn't at all sure she welcomed his consideration this time. By the look on Ryan's face, she judged he wasn't any more certain than she was. As the marked unit pulled away, Ryan simply stood looking after it.

She saw him square his broad shoulders and felt a pang at the realization that he found facing her so hard. Slowly he turned around. His dark mane of hair was loose and flowing. Somewhere in the tussle with Carlos the bandanna had been lost, and his left cheekbone bore a red graze that told her Carlos had connected at least once.

And suddenly it was too much. "Don't say it!" she exclaimed. "Just don't say it. I know you told me to just drive by, just to let him see me, and then get out. But he wasn't looking."

"I told you to just keep going, no matter what," he said, his tone ominously flat.

"I know, but he was facing right toward you. All he would have had to do was look up and he'd have seen you. And he had the car for cover while you and Cruz were sitting ducks out in the open. I had to do something."

"So you greeted him like an old friend."

"I was scared, and that was all I could think of."

Something flickered in his eyes, and he crossed the three feet between them in a single stride. He yanked the door open. Lacey stared at him but didn't cringe. Ryan had never, ever hurt her, and she refused to believe he would now, no matter how angry he was. But she'd never seen him like this, so soon after a fight and an arrest, so soon after the adrenaline had peaked, and she didn't know what to expect.

"Move over," he ordered. She considered protesting the dictatorial tone but thought better of it and scooted into the passenger seat. She felt a moment of trepidation. Ryan Buckhart's blood was up, and she suddenly knew why he was so effective in his job. Nobody in their right mind would cross him now.

But she would. She could. The thought came out of nowhere, but she knew it was true. She could cross Ryan with complete safety, even now, when he was so close to the edge. Because he would never, ever hurt her. No matter what the provocation.

At least, not physically. But he could tear her heart out, rip her emotions to shreds, and never know he was doing it. With a stifled shiver of apprehension she settled back in her seat as he shifted the truck into gear.

Ryan drove silently, concentrating on the task as if it weren't an automatic thing, as if it really took all his attention. He sensed Lacey's glance when he drove past Trinity West without even slowing, but she said nothing. She'd said nothing since he'd taken the wheel and left the alley in a spray of gravel as large as the one she'd thrown up at Carlos.

He had to suppress a shiver at the memory; just the thought of how she'd so casually rolled down the window and taunted a man who needed far less excuse than that to kill made him shake. For a moment he'd thought he wasn't going to be able to move at all, but then instinct had kicked in, and it had been over so quickly he didn't even remember much about it.

Except that he'd wanted to kill Carlos, not just for hitting her, although that enraged him nearly beyond control, but for simply being a threat to her.

He'd wanted to, but he hadn't. Once more he'd kept the leash on the beast that sometimes raged inside him. And he felt a sudden sense of relief. If he could control it then, when Lacey's life had been threatened, he was as sure as a man could ever be that he could always control it, for nothing could be worse than that.

He drove out of the Trinity West district, over the city line into Marina del Mar. Lacey glanced at him again, but she still didn't speak. Nor did she speak when, after they'd left even Marina del Mar behind, he finally pulled off the road into a small dirt clearing on a bluff overlooking the Pacific. He parked and turned off the motor. And at last he turned to look at her. She met his gaze but still said nothing. It was a moment before he could speak, but when he did, the words came tumbling out as if this were merely a continuation of their talk in the alley.

"Scared?" he said, his voice tight. "*You* were scared? Damn it, you scared the hell out of me. When he started toward you, I swear... if you'd been one second later hitting the gas, I would have shot him."

"I'm glad I wasn't, then. You're in enough trouble."

"I know," he said ruefully.

She gave him a considering look. "Maybe it won't be so bad. You've always said Chief de los Reyes is a good man, a fair man. And Cruz will back you up, even if it gets him in trouble."

"I know he will."

She blinked. "You do?"

"You were right about him, Lacey. He's the kind of man you trust with your life." Or, he added silently, your reason for living.

He saw her lips tremble as she took in his words. "You really believe that? You really... trust him?"

"I trust him." He shook his head. "That lone-wolf approach of mine is all right...if you're truly a lone wolf." She gave him a puzzled look, and he went on softly, "I'd been one for so long, gotten so used to it, that I didn't recognize... when I wasn't one anymore."

Her eyes widened. "Ryan...?"

"I've never been so scared as when I saw Carlos within killing distance of you today. Twice. Except for the one other night when I thought you were going to die because of me."

"Because of you? What are you talking about?"

"I should have been there for you. I never should have left you alone that night."

She frowned. "You mean... the baby? Ryan, you were working—"

"And I could have gotten out of it, if I'd really tried."

She gave him an incredulous look. "What were you supposed to do, stay home with me the whole time I was pregnant? It would have driven us both crazy."

"But if I'd been there, if you hadn't been alone..."

He had to stop, had to force the words through a throat tightened with remorse and guilt. He couldn't meet her eyes, so he stared at his hands, big, strong, powerful hands that had been so useless the night she lay bleeding from the loss of their child.

"Instead I was sitting on my ass on a wasted stakeout. Then I heard the wolf, and I knew... God, Lacey, you nearly died. I nearly lost both of you, and all because I was too damn stubborn and arrogant to let someone else do the job."

"Ryan—"

"I knew you hated me afterward, and I can't blame you for that. I should have been there, but—"

"My God," Lacey breathed, cutting him off. "I never... You've felt this way all this time? Like it was somehow your fault and that I blamed you for it?"

He made himself meet her gaze. "How could you not blame me?"

Her eyes were wide now, moist with the sheen of unshed tears. "I *never* blamed you, Ryan. Ever. Not for what happened."

"But you were so... distant afterward."

"Because *you* were," she exclaimed. "You were so detached, so remote, and I couldn't reach you. I thought you didn't even care that our baby had died. You never let it show, never told me. I thought I was all alone, and it hurt so much, and you wouldn't even talk about it!"

Ryan felt a shudder go through him. This wasn't the time, still running on adrenaline, that he would have chosen to do this, but he'd come too close to never having the chance to say this to worry about choosing a right time or place now.

"I couldn't," he said. "I loved that baby from the first moment I felt him kick in your belly. I built a world for him in my head, the kind of world I'd never had, with parents who loved him and each other. When we lost him, I felt... like it was one more judgment on who I was, what I was. That I... somehow fate had figured out I wasn't fit to be a father, that—"

"Ryan, no! You can't really believe that. The one thing I knew, the whole time I had our child growing inside me, was that he was going to be the luckiest boy in the world to have you for a father. Because I knew you would want to make sure he had everything you never had. I knew you would love him and hold him and teach him and..."

The tears began to overflow and stream down her cheeks. She didn't sob, only took an occasional gulping breath; it was as if her passionate emotions had turned liquid and simply been too much for her to hold back.

Silently Ryan held out his arms, hoping against hope. She went to him without hesitation, scrambling onto his lap despite the complication of the steering wheel, and he hugged her tightly. He saw now what he'd put her through in his misguided attempt to be strong for her. In her mind he'd gone from the husband who loved and anticipated their child as much as she did to an uncaring, silent stranger who wouldn't admit he felt a thing at that child's death before it had ever lived.

She wept quietly in his arms for a long time, and Ryan felt a burning in his eyes and the trickle of moisture down his own cheeks, relieving a pressure he'd carried around inside him for so long he hadn't even realized it until it began to ease. Instinctively he wanted to wipe away his tears before she saw them, but he would have had to let go of her to do it, and the trade-off wasn't worth it. He swallowed heavily, thinking he was going to start bawling if he didn't get himself together.

And then Lacey tilted her head back and looked up at him, and the look in her eyes when she saw his face made him forget any thought of hiding what he was feeling. She lifted a hand and touched the dampness on his cheeks with a tenderness unlike anything he'd ever felt before, even from her. This, he thought a little dazedly, this had been what she'd needed from him in those days after the baby's death. The irony was that it was exactly what he'd felt like doing, but he'd assumed she needed him to be strong because she'd been so devastated.

"I'm sorry, Lace," he whispered, his voice tight and low. "I didn't understand. I thought I was doing the best thing, and instead I let you down completely."

"I should have been able to ask for what I needed," she said, her voice equally soft.

"Neither one of us knew how to deal with it," Ryan said. "And we... lost each other because of it."

He took a deep breath to steady himself. "I thought... it was me. My job. And the way I did it."

Lacey sniffed back the next wave of tears. "Only partly. I think... I thought your job had made you that way. Tough. Uncaring. Untrusting," she said. Then, looking at him steadily, she added, "But you've truly changed, haven't you? You really trusted Cruz today. Completely."

"Yes." His mouth twisted wryly. "And it wasn't easy."

"I know," she said softly. "But you did it."

"I had to," he said. "It wasn't just my life at stake, it was yours, too. And I believe him when he says he'd die before he'd let anything happen to you." He hesitated, then plunged ahead. "Just like I would."

For a long, silent moment he waited, expecting her to say no to his declaration, to tell him that she didn't want that or anything else from him. He'd spent the past week trying to force himself to accept that, to accept that had it not been for Carlos's interference, he never would have seen her again after leaving the house last night.

But Lacey didn't answer him. She studied his face, until he wondered what she was looking for, wondered if he should pray she found it...or didn't.

"Did you mean it?" she said at last.

"Mean...what?" *That I love you? That I'd die for you? I meant all of it.*

"The otters. Did you mean what...I think you meant?"

There it was. Right there in front of him. All he had to do was tell her the truth and he would have his answer. The answer he would have to live with for the rest of his life. And he was more afraid to face it than he'd been afraid of anything in his life.

"You kept them," he said. "The animals. I thought you would have thrown them away. Burned them. Something."

She didn't answer him, just kept that steady blue gaze leveled on him. He let out a breath, knowing he was dodging her question, knowing she knew it, too. His stomach tightened at the irony of it. She'd been kidnapped, hurt, had covered his back during a near firefight, had helped him get Robards out of his way for the foreseeable future, had set herself up as the diversion that had enabled them to take down Carlos without a shot, and here he was afraid to admit the simple truth.

"You've got more nerve than I ever thought of having, Lacey Buckhart."

"The otters. Did you mean it?" she repeated.

"I meant it," he said with grim determination. "I meant it with every cut of the knife, Lacey. I hoped you'd see it, but I was afraid of what would happen if you did. That you'd say no, that we were still over, that there was no hope we could come back...like they did. That you'd given up on us. On me."

For a moment she just looked at him. It took every bit of courage he had to meet the steady gaze of those blue eyes he so loved.

"The otters came back from the edge," she said softly.

He nodded. He opened his mouth to speak, then knew he would never be able to get a single word past the tightness in his throat.

"Can we?"

"I..." He had to swallow and try again. "God, I hope so."

She straightened suddenly. "You called me Lacey Buckhart."

He blinked, confused. "Just now," she said.

"I... Yes. I did." Was she upset at that? Had she gone back to using Bennett, and he hadn't known? "I didn't think...I mean, I thought..."

"I'd rather you didn't."

He stopped breathing. *There's your answer, Buckhart,* he told himself. *Start learning to live with it.*

"At least," she added, reaching up to touch his face, "until it's rightfully my name again."

He nearly gasped, feeling as if she'd just nailed him dead center with one of those vigorous kicks of hers. He stared at her.

"Lacey, I—"

"I love you, Ryan Buckhart. And I love you even more because you were willing to change for me, to go against a trait that's buried in you so deep you can't even remember when it started."

"You...do?"

"I don't think I ever really stopped loving you. I just...for a while it seemed the price was too high. But I understand that better now. Why you do what you do. And I see that...I need to change, too."

"Then we can... try again?"

"And get it right this time."

He grabbed her then and pulled her hard against him. "I love you," he whispered fervently. "And this time we'll get it right."

Epilogue

"He is . . . incredible looking."

Lacey smiled at Kit Walker, who was looking classily sexy in a short-skirted blue silk dress. Ryan had been surprised to see her there, startled when he'd discovered that she and Lacey were close friends, and more startled at the fact that Kit had never once, in all the times they'd run into each other at Trinity West, mentioned knowing Lacey. Kit had mockingly accused him of thinking all women chattered, and, unintimidated, sent him off to refill Lacey's empty champagne glass.

"Yes," Lacey agreed, "he is."

"And he's on his way back, so I'll see you later," she said. "Congratulations. Go for it, girlfriend!"

Lacey wasn't sure exactly what Kit had been referring to, but she certainly couldn't argue with her observation. Ryan Buckhart in a tux was quite something to behold.

Even her mother had had to admit that the combination of size, power, grace, long, dark hair flowing free tonight and the elegant formal wear made a striking image.

Of course, the fact that Ryan had taken her mother aside and politely but firmly explained the facts of life to her—that he was here for good, and she could deal with it or not as she chose, but that he hoped she would, for her daughter's sake, grow up and get over her prejudices—might have had something to do with it. Even her father had been impressed enough to accord Ryan a certain amount of respect, if not liking.

"You look...incredibly beautiful, Lace."

She had sensed his approach from behind her, but, as always, he warned her in the most wonderful of ways. Perhaps sometime soon she wouldn't need even that, perhaps she would no longer feel that start of fear whenever someone came up behind her unexpectedly.

She leaned back, knowing he would be there; she could feel his heat from where she stood. His arms came around her, and he cradled her shoulders, bare in the off-the-shoulder burgundy silk dress she'd bought for the occasion, against his chest.

She'd certainly gotten over the rest, she thought, flushing at her own thoughts. Ryan had cured her of that in the most wonderful of ways, as well, slowly, gently, at first merely letting her get used to the delightful feeling of being pulled into the curve of his body at night, nested like spoons. She'd been wary the first few times, when he'd quickly become aroused, but he'd sensed her unease immediately and whispered reassurance in her ear.

"I can't help what feeling you against me does to me, Lacey, because you've got the sexiest little backside in the world. But I can help what I do about it. And that will be absolutely nothing, until you tell me otherwise."

For a week, then two, then a month, night after night, whether they'd made love or not, he'd done just that, holding her there, ignoring the erect readiness of his own body as he tenderly cradled hers. Then, slowly, he'd begun to add the slightest of caresses, then more, but always stopping the instant she began to tense up.

And then one night she'd twisted her head around to plant a good-night kiss on his mouth, and, as most of their kisses did, this one sent the swift heat of arousal rocketing through her. And when, in response, Ryan's hands had slipped first to her breasts, his fingers gently tugging her nipples into tight peaks, and then down to delve between her thighs and stroke already slick feminine flesh, she'd found to her amazement that the position could be incredibly erotic. . . with Ryan.

He'd given her every chance to tell him no, to change positions, but she hadn't done it. She'd wanted to get over the fear, and there was no one better to show her it was safe than the man she loved so completely. And when he at last gently raised her leg back over his and slid easily into her, she welcomed him with the joy she always felt at their joining. Even when he shifted their bodies until she was bearing his weight she felt only the barest flicker of the old fear. And felt a luscious thrill when she realized he was deeper inside her than ever before. She'd climaxed with a fierceness that made her sob out his name.

And later, in the soft darkness, she had thanked him for his patience in the best way she could think of, rousing him to a fever pitch with her hands, and then following the trails she'd blazed with her mouth. He'd gone rigidly still when her lips had brushed over his distended flesh. And when she'd taken him in her mouth he'd cried out her name in a voice that made her wish she hadn't waited so long to confront and conquer her old fears. She found a joy she'd never imagined in giving him this pleasure, had found to her surprise it inflamed her nearly as much as it did him, and had felt a sweet, feminine triumph when Ryan had been racked with shudders that seemed to go on and on.

And both of them had known that night was somehow the seal on their relationship. In the morning she'd awakened to find him beside her, holding the otters. She'd read the question in his eyes and had answered it easily.

"They did it. So can we."

And when he'd asked her if that meant she would really marry him again, she'd felt no hesitation in telling him yes.

"Whatever you're thinking," Ryan's voice said now, so close against her ear that she shivered, "Yes. Tonight. If I can wait that long."

She tilted her head back and to one side to look up at him. "I'm thinking that you look rather beautiful yourself," she said.

"I'm happy," he said simply.

Lacey smiled. "So am I." She looked around the room. "It's a lovely party, Ryan. Thank you."

He shrugged. "A new promotion deserves a party. I'm just sorry it's so late."

"It doesn't matter. It was sweet of you to put it together." And amazing that he had, she thought. Arranging a party, especially a formal affair like this one, was hardly Ryan's kind of thing. But he'd done it, even convincing her parents to come.

Across the room she spotted a tall, lean man with patrician features and dark hair silvered at the temples.

"I see that Chief de los Reyes is here. Does that mean you're forgiven?"

Ryan chuckled. "He says I've done my time. Paid my debt, as it were."

"I thought it would be worse."

"So did I. Five days' suspension is a pretty light sentence, considering how mad everybody was. I got off easy."

The chief had actually been angrier that Ryan hadn't reported being hurt than that he'd missed his check-ins. Although when he'd learned that Ryan and Lacey were going to remarry, he gruffly told Ryan he'd taken that out of his final report. Which said a lot for the chief, Lacey thought.

She also knew Ryan wasn't about to complain about his suspension. He'd managed to keep Cruz out of it, keeping his friend's record clean except for a verbal reprimand for not calling in that they were going after Carlos.

As she thought about him, Cruz passed by, looking absurdly pleased about something. He gestured at Ryan with his glass. "Somebody looking for you," he said. He nodded toward someone over Ryan's right shoulder, then grinned at Lacey and kept going.

Lacey turned as Ryan did and saw a couple approaching. The man was, in a different way, nearly as striking as Ryan himself. Although he was two or three inches shorter than Ryan's six-two, she thought his size was deceptive; he had an air of wiry, quick strength. But he was just as beautiful as Ryan, with dark, smoldering good looks, perfect golden brown skin and eyes that made you think of a choirboy gone bad.

The woman was a petite redhead with a wavy mane of hair. And suddenly Lacey knew who they were. Ryan had told her that Quisto Romero had approached him a couple of days ago, when they'd met at the station after Ryan had come back to work. Romero had joined the Trinity West crew, and he'd wanted to thank Ryan for saving Caitlin's life. Ryan had thanked him in turn for not even mentioning him in his report and thus not giving him away to the Trinity West brass when he'd been shot.

"I owed you that for Caitlin," Romero had said. "Even though I didn't know then you were a cop."

And it had been then, Ryan had told her, seeming rather embarrassed, that he had impulsively invited the man to her party.

"Quisto," Ryan acknowledged as the man approached. Then, to the redhead, "Hello, Caitlin."

She smiled, so brightly, so joyously, that Lacey felt a twinge of jealousy. "Hello, Ryan. It's good to see you looking so well."

Ryan shifted uncomfortably. "Congratulations," he said finally, gesturing at the ring on her left hand.

"I wish you could have come," she said. "You would have been welcome, even before I knew who you really were."

And suddenly, with those simple words, Lacey decided that she quite liked Caitlin Romero.

"And you are as lovely as I have heard, *querida,*" Quisto said, bowing over Lacey's hand in a courtly gesture that should have seemed silly but didn't at all, not from this man.

Lacey blushed, stammered out a thank-you and looked at Ryan in time to see him frown. Caitlin laughed, a lighthearted sound of complete understanding, and when Lacey looked at her, the woman with the fiery strawberry blond hair winked.

"We brought you something," Caitlin said, holding out a small box tied with a cheery blue bow.

"You didn't have to do that," Lacey protested. "It isn't that kind of party."

"It's not . . . that kind of a gift," Quisto put in.

Something about the way the man looked from her to Ryan and back made Lacey immensely curious. She untied the bow and opened the lid. And lifted out of a nest of blue tissue paper a small carved wooden owl. An owl that was unmistakably Ryan's work.

Her gaze flicked to Ryan's face.

"You left it behind the night you saved my life," Caitlin said softly.

"You . . . saved it?" Ryan's voice sounded oddly tight.

"It seemed important somehow," the redhead answered. Then she gave Lacey a smile that would have warmed the coldest of hearts. "And now I know why."

"Thank you," Lacey whispered.

And when the couple took their leave, she looked up at Ryan. "I can see why she . . . impressed you so."

Ryan's mouth quirked. "And I can see why he had a reputation as a ladies' man before she reined him in."

Lacey smiled. "He is rather . . . charming, isn't he?"

Ryan sighed. "We'll invite them to the wedding."

She went still.

"Wedding?" she said carefully. This was the first time Ryan had said anything about a wedding, she'd assumed they would simply go to a judge again.

He turned her to face him. "Yes. No impersonal civil ceremony this time, Lacey. A wedding. A real one. With your friends and family... and my friends."

Lacey's breath caught.

He looked at her steadily. "I...asked Cruz. If he'd be my...best man. I know I should have made sure you wanted this first, but I was afraid if I didn't ask him tonight, I never would."

A wedding. With her family and friends, and—miracle of miracles—his own friends. And Cruz as his best man. So that was why Cruz had been looking so pleased.

Emotion welled up inside her, and she wondered if Ryan realized how much this meant to her. She would make sure he did, she resolved. Tonight, when they were alone.

Tonight she would show him her joy.

Her lone wolf was truly a loner no more.

The sound of the pager's beep interrupted the jovial after-dinner conversation around the restaurant table. Cruz grimaced, then reached down to his belt.

"It's dispatch," he said, as he confirmed Ryan's questioning look. Cruz was the on-call detective for the weekend, so there was little doubt what the page was for. "Something's up." He stood, dropping his napkin on the table. He gave Ryan and Lacey a crooked grin. "Maybe it's just as well she stood me up, huh?"

Despite the lightness of his words, there was a shadow in Cruz's eyes, and Lacey wondered suddenly if perhaps all his steady, unfailing cheer was a front, a facade to hide how deeply he'd really been hurt by Samantha's mother.

"Stupid woman," Lacey muttered. She wasn't sure if she meant Ellen or the woman who hadn't shown up tonight. She didn't even know the woman Cruz had invited, but anyone who would do such a thing to a man like Cruz wasn't winning any points in Lacey's book.

She watched as Cruz headed for a phone to call in. She fought a flicker of her old fear, remembering all the times

Ryan had left on a case and she hadn't seen him for days, even weeks.

She felt Ryan's left hand cover hers on the table, and she looked up at him. There was a gentle understanding in his eyes, as if he knew what she was thinking, recognized her fear and its source. Since he'd gone back to work he'd been safely inside, cleaning up the mountain of paperwork the final breakup of the Pack had engendered, but the threat was always there. At any moment he could be called out, as Cruz had just been, to deal with the ugliness the world seemed more prone to every day.

Ryan shifted his fingers until his plain gold wedding band rested over her wedding ring—the unique swirled gold setting cradling a piece of jade, its carved shape suggesting that of a running wolf—that he'd slipped on her finger three months ago tonight. He did this often, touched the two rings together, as if it reassured him that they were indeed together again. It gave Lacey an odd sense of security herself, to feel the two endless circles meet.

They watched as Cruz came back and grabbed his jacket off the back of his chair. Ryan lifted a brow at him.

"Duty calls," he said with a mockingly wry smile.

"Need company?"

Cruz's smile turned genuine. "Not yet. But I'll let you know."

"I'll be there," Ryan promised.

"I know," Cruz said, and this time his smile was for Lacey.

Lacey found herself blinking rapidly against a sudden welling of tears. She wiped at her eyes with her hands as Cruz left them. When her vision cleared, she found Ryan looking at her as if he again knew exactly what she'd been thinking. And his quiet words proved it.

"I know now that running alone was what got me in a lot of trouble. I'll never trust anyone as much as I trust you, Lace, but I know I have to trust other people, too."

Lacey knew he meant it; he'd made great strides since their remarriage. With a silent wish that Cruz would be all right on whatever piece of evil had called him out into the night, Lacey reached for her husband's hand and touched their rings together again.

And later that night she decided it was time. Ryan had started a fire, though it wasn't really chilly enough to need it, but he knew she liked the coziness of it. He had taken his usual spot on the floor in front of the sofa, his back resting against her legs. Then, as Lacey had set the recently returned owl on the table beside her, he had picked up his knife and his latest carving, a sleek, very clever-looking raven.

But this time Lacey didn't settle back to read. This time she leaned forward and gently took the unfinished raven out of his hands.

"You need to start something else," she said.

Ryan gave her a startled, puzzled look over his shoulder. She'd never asked him for a particular work before.

"You need to carve another otter," she said.

"Another? Did they... break?"

He looked concerned, and Lacey hastened to shake her head. The carved pair had become such a symbol to them that she understood his worry; they'd even, to the puzzlement of some and the entertainment of others, put the tiny pair atop their wedding cake.

"No. They're fine. Almost perfect, in fact."

He shifted position then, turning to face her, brows furrowed. "Then why—"

"You need," she said softly, reaching down to cup his face with her hands, "to carve a baby otter."

For a split second his expression didn't change. Then his eyes widened. His knife clattered to the floor, and he scrambled to his knees before her.

"Lacey...?"

She nodded.

"Oh, God."

She'd had the corrective surgery three months ago, but they hadn't thought anything would happen this soon. This time it was she who read all the old fears, all the old terrors, in his face. She saw in his dark eyes the haunting memory of that long-ago night, and she grabbed his hands with hers, threading her fingers through his, ring again touching ring.

"It will be all right this time," she said determinedly.

She saw the effort to believe, to trust, warring with the past in his taut expression.

"It will, Ryan. Everything will." She tightened her grip on his hands. "Neither one of us is ever going to hear that damn wolf again."

"No," he whispered. Then, stronger, "No. Never again."

A smile spread across his face, the smile of a man who'd left his lone-wolf days far behind. And done it with joy and gladness . . . and love.

Lacey's wolf was home for good.

* * * * *